THE SURVIVORS BOOK SEVEN

NEW ALLIANCE

NATHAN HYSTAD

Cover art: Tom Edwards Design

Edited by: Scarlett R Algee

Proofed and Formatted by: BZ Hercules

ISBN-13: 9781094868820

Also By Nathan Hystad

The Survivors Series

The Event

New Threat

New World

The Ancients

The Theos

Old Enemy

New Alliance

The Gatekeepers

New Horizon

The Academy

Old World

ONE

The streets of Haven were packed as beings from around the universe mingled amongst each other. I heard at least a dozen languages chatting around me as I walked down the sidewalk with purpose.

The little homestead village had transformed in the last two years. Haven still held on to the charm of a welcoming colony for those in need of respite, but was also drawing in various groups from around the universe to share the soil, and live in what Leslie and Terrance were dubbing the first real intergalactic melting pot.

I loved what I saw and would have lingered in the crowds listening to people's stories, but I had more pressing matters. The noise was becoming too much for me, and I flipped my earpiece translator off. There'd been plenty of times over the last two years, since the Lom of Pleva incident, that I'd considered the neural implant and voice box modifications that would permit me to speak and hear almost all languages. Now was one of the times I was glad I'd held off.

"Come in, E-Base. Any sign of them?" I tapped my other earpiece, sending the communication.

The base was in orbit above the planet. A reply came quickly. "Roger that. We have a ship of unknown origin, arriving from deep space." A woman's voice carried over the earpiece.

"Keep an eye on them. What's their current trajectory and ETA?" I asked, a nervous bead of sweat dripping over my back.

"Heading straight for us. Two hours at their in-system velocity," the woman advised.

Two hours. Right when I was supposed to be at the ceremony. "I'm rounding up the team. We'll be up there in thirty." I ended the communication and inhaled deeply, smelling various foods simmering at the end of the town square. My stomach growled, but I didn't have time to stop for anything.

My feet picked up speed, and before I knew it, I was jogging. Maybe there was time to detain the incoming vessel's crew and return to the surface.

"Slate, come in," I said, tapping my earpiece.

"Slate here," he said. He was chewing, and I knew where to find him.

I spotted his bulky body at one of the food stands, beside the much shorter Shimmali girl Suma. I passed by a cluster of humans, a few of them wearing familiar faces. Next, I nodded to some Keppe who were drinking deeply from tall cups, laughing and speaking loudly to one another. The entire area held an energy I hadn't seen before on Haven.

The world and its capital city of the same name were thriving now, and the ceremony had been a great excuse to show off how far the colony had come. Sarlun had been hesitant to allow the event to take place here, but with help from Mary and our favorite hybrid couple, we showed him why it was the best idea for everyone involved.

Seeing the different races intermingling in the town square, with the sun high overhead in the cloudless sky, I smiled. We'd come so far.

"Dean?" I heard Suma's voice through the crowd as she spoke to me in English. We'd learned each other's languages while stranded on Sterona over two years ago. So far, I'd had plenty of opportunity to speak the Shimmali squawks and clicks since they'd sent a contingent of colonists to Haven to live and assist in building up the city. I really enjoyed the people from Shimmal. They were hard-working, and brilliant engineers.

As I thought of them, I spotted a few scattered in the crowd of people, eating various foods, gathered for the festivities. I waved to one I knew and brought my attention back to the task at hand.

"Suma, sorry to bother you on your big day, but I need Slate," I said as my old friend turned to me.

His hair was longer than ever, his beard bushy but trimmed. It was still odd for me to see him like this, after years of a crew cut and a closely-shaved face. Once the whole incident with Denise betraying him had happened, he said he needed a change, and so far, he'd embraced it.

"What do you need me for, boss? Mary just asked me to come bring some more chairs to the amphitheater." Slate smiled and popped another piece of meat on a stick in his mouth. "So if this is about the chairs, I'm heading there now." He chewed a few times. "You know, after I eat."

I leaned in, looking around to make sure no one was listening. "Slate, we have an incident. We received a transmission from Volim. It seems our friend Sergo has landed in some hot water, and they warned us he may be heading here. The Inlor are searching for him and are likely following his ship as we speak."

Slate shrugged. "I don't know what the Inlor are."

Suma took over, pushing between us, regarding us with her big black eyes. Her snout twitched up and down. She was wearing tights and a blouse, and I thought it was endearing, seeing her wearing something different from the uniform she tended to sport. "Inlor. Not a social race. They've only had FTL capability for a thousand years, and have primarily kept to themselves. There's no portal stone near them, and they haven't been sighted more than five light years from their home planet, RXM8."

Slate raised an eyebrow, and popped another bite into his mouth. I didn't stop Suma; she was on a roll. "They are slight in appearance: pale, thin, six arms, two with opposable thumbs, four with claws. Two legs and great eyesight, from what we know. To balance that, their sense of smell is on the lower end of the spectrum, and they eat all their food raw; strictly a plant-based diet." Suma stopped speaking and grinned at us.

"Someone studied hard for her entrance exam," I suggested. "Maybe that's why she got the best grade ever posted, according to Sarlun."

Suma beamed at that. "Seriously? I did? He didn't even tell me!"

I cleared my throat, realizing I might have ruined a surprise. "Anyway. Yes, that's the Inlor in a nutshell. It appears there's a unique metal on their world, one that might change the way a weapon holds a charge. Sergo was there stealing from them."

Slate swallowed and threw his plate in a trash can behind him. "I knew that guy was trouble."

Slate hadn't been there with me on Volim. It had only been Magnus, Leslie, and me. He was still mad about it.

I nodded. "He's a gangster, and apparently, he's been

spotted on other worlds doing much the same thing, and I think I know how he's been getting away with it."

Suma interjected: "The Relocator?"

"The Relocator," I affirmed. Kareem had gifted me the device, which allowed you to save a location in it, and from any point out there, you could transport yourself back to that spot. It would work on more than one person if you were touching. I'd bartered it away for the location of the crystal world we'd unleashed the Iskios from, during my search for Mary. Thinking back to that time, and the anger that I'd constantly felt, reminded me how good I had it now.

"What's the plan?" Slate asked, clasping his hands in anticipation. He was always up for a good mission.

"Yeah, what's the plan?" Suma's snout lifted, and I shook my head.

"No way, Suma. Today's your big day. I can't take you out there into danger." I instantly saw her disappointment.

"Isn't that what being a Gatekeeper is all about? Learning about new cultures and worlds is part of it, but protecting our people from danger, helping those in need, that's the true calling of the Gatekeepers," she said, eyes wide.

I couldn't argue with her. "Fine. Your dad's going to kill me. Let's go."

The town square was busier with each passing minute, and the noises were refreshing. Strange music played on every street corner, and I was starting to appreciate the variety. Today, I had one thing on my mind: detaining Sergo and preventing trouble from reaching Haven. We couldn't have these Inlor chasing the Padlog insectoid onto our world, especially when so many visitors were present.

We needed to convey Haven as just that: a haven away from a hectic universe; a safe place for each world to send a selection of colonists, where they could learn from one another, set up trade between systems, and improve the overall serenity of space.

Having a battle arrive during the Gatekeepers' ceremony would destroy everything that we'd built. I picked up the pace, moving quickly through the crowds. Suma was somehow able to keep up, even on her short legs, and I slowed for her as we edged out of the crowds.

The day was shaping up to be a hot one. I wished I was wearing a pair of shorts and a t-shirt rather than my jumpsuit, but it didn't matter. Soon I'd be in a climate-controlled EVA.

"This way." I waved Slate and Suma forward, toward a lander I'd parked on the outskirts of the festivities. I opened the gullwing door and motioned for them to enter first, and scanned back to the crowd, wishing we could stay and enjoy the moment with the gathered beings.

I moved past Slate's big form and settled into the pilot's seat. I'd gotten the hang of flying these things and found myself smiling as I lifted it off the ground, guiding the ship high in the sky, straight up and over the buildings before heading for the landing pad at the west side of Haven.

"What does Mary think about you doing this today, of all days?" Slate asked, reminding me I hadn't even told her about it yet.

"Uhm… let's find out." I tapped the console as I saw the line of vessels on the edge of town.

"Dean, where are you?" Mary asked, her voice calmer than I'd expected.

"I'm in a lander with Slate and Suma, honey."

"Well, you better get over here. The Molariuns are

causing a stink over being placed next to the Padlog, for some reason," Mary said.

"What's with these Padlog?" I muttered.

"What do you mean?" Mary asked.

"You remember Sergo?" I knew she would. I'd told her the entire story in explicit detail while we'd waited to be rescued on the abandoned world.

"Sure. Insectoid. Gangster. Threatened you and Leslie."

"The very same. He's on his way here, and we're going to intercept him before he lands," I said.

Mary was quiet for a moment, and Slate leaned forward, his head over my shoulder. "Mary, don't worry, I'll keep Dean from doing anything stupid."

Mary laughed, and I heard Jules talking beside her. "Just be quick. You only have ninety minutes before it starts. Suma," Mary started.

"I'm here," Suma replied.

"Make sure you're back in time. Your dad has a lot riding on today," Mary said. "We all do."

Suma's voice carried from her seat behind me. "I'll do my best."

"Papa," Jules said over the speaker.

"Hi, Princess. I'll see you soon." Every time she called me that, it melted my heart. We didn't know why she'd started. She called Mary "Mommy."

The call ended at the precise moment the lander touched down, and we rushed out, filing into one of our modified Kraski ships. It was smooth and white, and I ran a hand along its outer surface as the ramp lowered, allowing us entrance.

Terrance met us there. He had a grim look on his face as we entered into the ship's cargo hold. He was suited up already and had three prepped for us. "I wish you'd given me more notice. Sorry, Suma. This suit isn't custom for you." He pushed an EVA toward her, and she shrugged and started to put it on. Minutes later, we were ready to go, and Terrance took the helm at the compact bridge.

I'd spent a lot of time on board these ships, mostly at the beginning when we'd first followed Terrance and Leslie from the New Mexico base, when we thought they were our enemies. So much had changed, and every time I stepped onto one of them, all my past within them came rushing back. I suppressed it now as Terrance lifted us from the landing pad. We all watched out the viewscreen, catching at least a hundred different vessels settled on the ground from races around the galaxy.

"This is amazing, Dean," Terrance said, and I nodded behind him, astonished at the turnout we'd received. "Sarlun said there's never been a gathering like this before."

I cracked my knuckles. I was nervous. With so many unknown races in attendance, there was a wide variety of issues that could arise. Many of them had bad history together: wars, famine, betrayal among the list. I moved around the seats and sat beside Terrance. "E-Base, can you patch the ID through so we have it on the sensors?" I asked the in-orbit base.

The same voice from earlier replied quickly, "You should have it now."

The blinking red icon appeared, moving through the system toward Haven. I let the computer calculate our interception point. "We have thirty-seven minutes. We need a plan," I said.

Slate was the first to speak. "We demand he gives himself up. Do we know what kind of artillery his ship has?"

I was using the ID search on the console. "Looks like

this ID string belongs to a Motrill vessel. How did he acquire one of those? A Skipper, like the one Polvertan had."

Slate tapped the back of my chair with a finger. "Okay, we can use that. They aren't heavily armed. Actually, they can't do much more than blast an invasive asteroid. We lance them with the new beams we got from the Keppe, and fire the ionized particle blaster at them, rendering them dead in space."

"What about their life support?" I asked. I didn't want them dead, only detained.

"You always complicate things, boss," Slate said.

"We'll talk to him first. See what Sergo has to say. He might come along with us." I highly doubted the troublemaker would be so pliable, but it was worth a try.

"I suspect they have suits like we do. They should be able to breathe, should it come to that tactic," Suma said.

"See, she gets me, boss." Slate reached over my left seat arm and tapped the console screen. "Wait, what's that?"

I followed his finger and noticed the other red icon blink onto our radar. There was only one at first, then two, and eventually, we could see five angry red dots following behind Sergo's ship.

"I think the Inlor found him," I said, wondering what we were going to do now.

TWO

"Why don't we just leave them to handle Sergo?" Slate asked.

"This is our system. We can't allow skirmishes to take place so close to Haven, especially not today. We have to prevent them from attacking Sergo," Terrance said.

He was right. "We'll know soon enough. Send a message to the Inlor only," I started, and Suma was beside me, tapping into the console.

"Go ahead, Dean. It'll translate for you," she said, motioning to the screen.

"Honored Inlor, we know you seek retribution on the one we know as Sergo of the Padlog, but we ask that you refrain from harming him at this time," I said, trying to be inoffensive.

The response came within seconds, translating into English. "Stay away from this one, Kraski."

They thought we were Kraski, based on the ship's design. My skin crawled at the idea. "We're not Kraski. We're human and Shimmali, representing the world you're closing in on."

"What world is that? We see no listed occupied planet for this system." The voice spoke in a mumbled tone, deep and sloppy-sounding, before translating for us.

"Haven. Let's detain Sergo, and you can meet with us formally. Perhaps we could even consider an alliance," I said, maybe a little too soon. My voice was also too light, too hopeful.

We were nearing interception, and I knew we'd get to Sergo before they did. We had to make a decision. "How long until we reach his ship?"

Terrance answered, "Four minutes."

The Inlor had taken their time now, but the response arrived. "We will take what is ours, then meet with you."

My EVA felt constricting now, and I wished I'd left it off. "Suma, target Sergo. I have a message for him."

Suma nodded, and I spoke. "Sergo, you've put me in a bind here."

He spoke my language with ease. "Dean Parker, is that you?"

I was surprised he recognized my speech, but he likely didn't know many humans. Terrance knew Sergo too, after the insectoid had spent some time on Haven during its early years, when Kareem had been around. It seemed the gangster often needed somewhere to hide out while his trail cooled off. It made sense that he'd chosen to come to Haven, seeking asylum once more.

"It's me. What did you take from them?" I asked, knowing full well what he'd done. I just wanted to see if he was willing to fess up to his crimes to me or not. My next actions relied on his answer.

"I didn't take much, I swear. They have mountains full of the stuff, I saw them with my own eyes," Sergo said, his voice frantic. I could imagine his antennae flipping around his head in distress.

"Do you still have the Relocator?" I asked, hoping there was a way I could secure it back. It had come in handy so many times, and it was far better suited in my hands than Sergo's.

"A barter, Dean Parker." Our icons were close now,

and I saw his ship approaching in the viewscreen.

Terrance tapped the mute icon. "Weapons charged and ready for action. Be careful, Dean. As much as I like Sergo, he's shifty. You can't trust him."

I tapped the icon again, opening the channel. "Go ahead. What do you have in mind?"

"Help me avoid the Inlor, and you can have it back," Sergo suggested.

I considered his desperate offer, and glanced at Terrance. "I don't know if this device is worth having the Inlor angry with us at this moment. The best course of action is to let them take Sergo." The hybrid was probably right.

"Or we can hold him for them, handing him over when they arrive," Suma said.

"What's it going to be, Parker?" Sergo asked, and I tapped the line open again.

"Come aboard our ship. We'll take care of you," I said, not actually saying just what that would entail.

"I knew you'd come to your senses," Sergo said.

Our two ships neared one another, his a sleek Skipper, like the one we'd first seen underwater when we'd found the young Motrill prince searching Fontem the Terellion's hidden cache of antiquities. I used the tractor lance and it attached to the ship, creating a containment tube between the ships.

"At least we don't have to test the ionized particle blaster," I said, knowing too much could go wrong experimenting with new technology right now.

"I wanted to see her in action," Slate admitted, and I laughed. This was working out smoothly.

"I'll bring Sergo in," I said.

No one argued, and I stood up, stalking to the back of the ship, where I tapped the ramp open to reveal the containment tube between the Skipper and our ship. Space lay beyond the thin layer of energy, and I took the precaution of latching a rope to the inside of the ship. I passed through the ship's field and floated through the tube, where Sergo was coming toward me in his own Padlog armored suit.

I noticed the gun in his hand right away. I'd been so distracted by everything, I hadn't even picked up a weapon on my way to meet the rogue insectoid.

"Sergo, put that down," I ordered.

He kept moving toward me. Soft green pulses shot from his suit's thrusters and he grinned, his lipless mouth forming a strange semi-circle. "Dean Parker, it's been far too long." His slender gun latched to his hip with a click. He was dragging a large crate behind him, and it floated weightlessly.

I relaxed and turned around when he was between me and my own ship. The tube extended forty feet between the two crafts, and we were almost back on board ours when Terrance's voice cut into my earpiece.

"Dean, you'd better come quick. They're arriving," Terrance said, and we hurried, moving into the cargo hold, our feet once again planting on the solid surface. I shut the ramp seconds later. "I've cut the beam. They won't know he's with us yet," he added.

Sergo stared at me through his helmet visor, bulbous black eyes searching for direction.

"Get to the bridge, Sergo." He was playing with the crate now, and I didn't have to ask what was inside. "You brought it with you? Really?" He'd stolen the material from their world and put a target on his back. Now that he was inside my ship with the pilfered materials, I worried we'd made a grave mistake bringing him on board.

"What would you have me do? They'll destroy me,"

he said, and I didn't quite comprehend what he meant until we arrived at the bridge.

"Boss, they're charging weapons," Slate said, sitting beside Terrance. His fingers hovered about our own weapon controls, ready to stand his ground should it come to that.

"Hold your fire, Slate. They wouldn't attack us, not after what we told them," I said, hoping I was right. "You're sure they didn't see the tractor beam connecting us?"

"I don't think they were within reach yet. We should be safe," Terrance said.

Sergo spoke in his accented English. "What does that mean? How do you propose to deal with them? You *are* on my side, right, Parker?"

I turned to him. "Why should I be? You tried screwing us over on Volim, and you threatened Leslie." Terrance looked back, anger in his eyes. Leslie was his wife, but he knew the story already.

"I only suggested I had her captive, but you and I both know I didn't. No harm came to her. We are colorful characters, Parker. We sometimes have to embellish the truth to discover what we need, correct?" Sergo was grinning foolishly.

I stepped in closer, our helmets almost touching. "First, you and I are nothing alike, got that? Second, I may have just 'embellished' the truth to get you on board." I grabbed the gun from his hip so fast, he didn't have a chance to react.

"What trickery is this?" Sergo spat, and I moved a few steps away from him.

"There's no trickery, but we have to see what the Inlor say before we fight to keep you safe. I'm not starting another intergalactic war just because you can't seem to steal anything without being caught," I said.

"But we had a deal! You said we'd barter." Sergo was nervous, but I was okay with that.

"The Inlor are closing in," Terrance said.

"Shields are up?" I asked, and Slate nodded.

Something was off about Sergo, and I needed to know what it was before I talked with the Inlor about him. "You told me you had the Relocator to trade. Where is it?"

He shook his head. "You don't think I'm that stupid, do you? It's in the safe I brought with me, among other things. If you kill me or give me over to them, you'll never get it back."

He thought that was enough of a bargaining chip, but he was dead wrong. "How were you caught?"

"What do you mean?" he asked, shifting from foot to foot.

"If you had the Relocator, why didn't you sneak in, take the goods, then Relocate out? They wouldn't have caught you," I said, seeing if I was barking up the right tree.

"So…" Sergo's head dropped, and his shoulders lost all their posturing toughness. "Fine. You know. It's broken. The stupid thing stopped working right there in the middle of the warehouse outside their mine on RXM8. I was lucky enough to steal a visiting Motrill vessel and stay alive for another day!"

Suma spoke up. "And the haul of stolen goods, of course."

Sergo eyed her suspiciously. "I couldn't go to all that trouble to leave empty-handed, now could I?" His gaze came to meet mine again. "What are you doing associating with a Shimmali?"

I ignored his question. "If the Relocator is broken,

what can you offer me to keep you safe?"

"Riches! This metal is pure, the best there is on the market, straight from the source. It will go for more credits than you've ever dreamed of," he said.

The truth was, I didn't want for anything in my life, and if Sergo really knew me at all, he'd know I didn't care about possessions. But I played along. While I didn't personally require money, the colonies did need more materials than they'd been able to procure.

"You might have said enough to start a conversation. Let's see what the Inlor have to say." Suma opened a line of communication, and I reached out. "Honored ones, we have... What…"

I didn't have a chance to finish my sentence. I was distracted by the incoming ships on the viewscreen. They were lava red, white lights pulsing along the edges of them. They were at least four times the size of our compact Kraski model, and I expected they outgunned us as well, even with our recent modifications.

Proving my assumptions, fire erupted from the front two vessels, blasting into the Skipper with ferocity. The shields held for a few moments, but seconds later, the pulses hit the surface of the ship Sergo had arrived in, and Terrance was moving us farther away from it, trying to avoid the irrevocable damage.

Sergo fell to his knees as he watched through the viewscreen. My heart was beating hard in my chest as we witnessed his Skipper exploding into a million tiny pieces.

"Thank you for detaining the target. We will allow you to escort us to this Haven for further discussion," one of them said, translating through our speakers.

"Mute it," I whispered, and Slate did.

Sergo remained on the floor, for the first time utterly silent.

"That was… unexpected," Terrance said.

"Boss, what do we do?" Slate asked.

"We oblige them with an escort. They came to kill Sergo, apparently, and now they think they have. Let them believe that story. Unmute it." Slate did. "Please follow us. The trip is short."

"Very well." The communication ended, and Terrance turned us around before heading back toward Haven. Sergo glanced up at me, and I helped him to his feet.

"Looks like you got lucky, pal." I passed his gun to Slate, who took it with a smile.

Sergo was visibly shaken, and I didn't blame him. He'd stolen from the Inlor, and they hadn't even tried to procure the goods before attempting to kill him. Instead, they'd sent five vessels to hunt him down and destroy him. I didn't want to get on their bad side, and I knew it was going to be imperative to keep Sergo from interacting with them on Haven.

THREE

We arrived at Haven, and Sergo was pacing a hole in the floor the entire trip.

"You have to hide me. Maybe they know I'm here, Parker. How are you going to keep me alive?" His questions were never-ending, and after trying to placate him for the first few minutes, I gave up and ignored his rambling.

"Geeze, boss, can you make that guy shut up, or do you want me to? I thought he was a tough thug type." Slate looked pleased at Sergo's reaction.

"Listen here, you pale worm! I'm Sergo, one of the most feared…"

Slate cut him off. "Most feared what? Mosquito this side of the Mississippi?" His joke went over the Padlog's head, and they stared at each other, Slate laughing, and Sergo tapping his facemask.

"Enough. Sergo, head into the bedroom, cover yourself up with a sheet, and keep your fly trap shut." My voice was laced with anger. I was supposed to be introducing the members of the festivities in ten minutes, and here I was escorting some angry aliens to the surface, with the source of their wrath hiding on a cot.

Sergo stalked away, out of the bridge and down the hall.

"Dean, are we sure this is a good idea?" Terrance

asked. "What if they catch wind he's still alive?"

"They're not going to, because we're keeping Sergo on board until they leave. Slate, go to the cargo bay and take the portable containment field." I gave the instructions and Slate hopped up, running for the rear of the ship.

"Suma." The Shimmali woman's snout twitched, awaiting orders. "Can you adjust the setting on the field to make sure no one can get in or out? I want Sergo trapped in that room, and I don't want anyone near him. Is that doable?"

"On it." She hesitated, then smiled at me. "...Boss."

I laughed at her using the nickname Slate had given me years ago. Then I plopped into the seat vacated by Slate and leaned back. "Terrance, tell me everything is going to work out today."

Terrance turned and clapped me on the shoulder. "Whatever you say."

I tapped the console and advised E-Base that we were coming with five unexpected dignitaries from RXM8. I added that we might need extra security at the landing pad outside the city of Haven, and they acknowledged the instruction.

"Think that'll be necessary?" Terrance asked as we entered the atmosphere with the slightest of shakes to the ship. Only two of the Inlor ships entered behind us, and on the radar, I noticed the other three turning, moving away from the planet.

"That solves that. Less of them to worry ourselves with," I said.

"Dean, where are you?" Sarlun's voice carried through my earpiece as soon as we were close enough to receive domestic communication.

"Sarlun, we had something come up. Do you remember the Inlor?" I asked.

"I've read of them. We all have at some point, as Gatekeepers. What about them?" he asked, all the patience stripped from his words.

"We have two of their ships coming to the surface with us."

"Wait, what?" he asked.

"It's a long story. We'll be there in ten," I said, knowing that wouldn't go over well.

"Dean, everyone is assembled, what do you want…"

"Juggle for them or something, Sarlun. We'll be right there," I said, and cut the line. "I'm going to hear about that one, aren't I?"

Terrance nodded but laughed.

We'd somehow managed to recruit Sergo, have his attackers think they killed him, and make it back in time for the ceremony. Sometimes, things worked out.

I stood at the front of the stage, wishing I'd had time to comb my hair. I was in my Gatekeeper attire, a crisp white uniform and polished black boots, and I was already sweating as I addressed the entire outdoor amphitheater.

Thousands sat in the chairs, and thousands more crammed in beyond on the grass to get a view of the ceremony. I glanced over to the side of the stage, where Mary held Jules' hand. They both waved at me, and I waved in return, unable to stop from smiling like a buffoon at the two most important people in my life.

Someone cleared their throat behind me, and I glanced over my shoulder to see Sarlun tapping his wrist.

Since Shimmali didn't wear watches, I wondered where he'd gotten the gesture.

I tapped the mic attached to my uniform and turned my attention to the crowd. I'd never had a problem with public speaking, but today, after the last couple of hours, I was out of sorts and felt flustered. Mary mouthed the first line to me, and I nodded to her before I continued.

"Welcome to Haven, everyone." The crowd began cheering. We'd handed out translator earpieces to those who didn't own them, and it was odd to think that, right now, my words were being converted into at least fifty different alien languages. I waited for the noise to dwindle before I spoke again.

The stage was black and shiny, and the sun was high in the sky above, making the entire area a pressure cooker. I took it all in for a moment, while the various hoots and hollers echoed around the event grounds. I recognized some of the people in the crowd, but there were alien races even I'd never seen before. This was a one-of-a-kind occasion and, we hoped, the first of many celebrations for our ever-growing galaxy.

"My name's Dean Parker, and I'm here to introduce the newest members being inducted into the Gatekeepers." More cheering, louder this time. I was always surprised to hear how many of them had heard of me, or knew anything about our history as a people. To them, it all began on the day of the Event, and though we had a long past before that, it was the day we were reborn as a race.

"We couldn't be happier at the turnout, and we know that by working cohesively, we can solidify our newly formed Alliance of Worlds. There won't be a health issue, a logistics problem, or a border dispute that we won't be able to work together amicably on ever again. The Gatekeepers are going to work as explorers, knowledge gatherers, and surveyors of this vast universe, and assist with clashes when necessary.

"Because of this, we've decided to add in new partners to the ancient Guild." I stopped and looked behind me, where a huge group of people in white uniforms began walking toward the front of the stage. I knew many of them and was surprised to hear there were over two hundred members of the Gatekeepers. Their missions often took them months to years to complete, using portal stones to explore distant uncatalogued planets. Even at that moment, there were twenty Keepers absent because they were on endeavors.

Sarlun was at the lead, and I motioned to the group. "I give you the Gatekeepers!" I shouted, and the crowd erupted. Most of them had at least one of their kind in the Guild, and now we were expanding to five more races today. It was an exciting time for everyone, and it would only strengthen the group and increase their reach and resources.

"We're proud to invite the newest member, from our friends the Keppe, forward as we present Rulo Uli." Rulo walked over to me, and I could tell how much she hated wearing sleeves over her thick armored arms. She bared her sharp teeth to me and smiled, pumping a fist for the crowd. The Keppe were a strong force, and I'd asked Lord Crul personally if they would join the Gatekeepers organization. He obliged after a few rounds of his favorite beverage.

"Next, we have Polvertan, prince of the Motrill!" The young Motrill walked forward, far less sure of himself than Rulo had been. His eyes darted around to immense crowd and he lifted an arm rigidly, before following his Keppe cousin into line.

The crowd was into it, and I found myself caught up in the excitement. It was a little more of a show than I thought necessary, but I was only following the playbook the entire group decided on going with. They wanted the people to be thrilled and optimistic about the Gatekeepers and our new foothold into the Alliance of Worlds.

"We also have Dreb from the great and powerful Bhlat joining us!" The huge Bhlat stalked over, and I caught the Empress in the front row, flanked by guards. Her red eyes swirled in joy at seeing one of theirs in our ranks. It was a good thing they were on our side, because most races out there feared them. The amassed throng of creatures gasped as Dreb marched towards me, and I clapped him on his broad shoulder. "With the Bhlat on our side, we have no need to concern ourselves over past events. We can look forward, as partners with the great culture."

It took a moment, but everyone seemed to clue in this meant peace from the dangerous Bhlat. I knew I'd rather be on the same side of the fence as them. The cheer progressed slowly, from the far reaches of the grassy region, and it carried forward, gaining volume until I had the urge to cover my ears, it was so loud. Dreb clapped me on the back in return, nearly sending me sprawling. I glanced over at Mary, who was stifling a laugh.

I watched her, standing in her white uniform, and wished she was beside me. We'd discussed it, and I didn't want a larger target than we had on ourselves. It had taken a lot of convincing Mary to even let me stand before so many strangers.

"Good, we're also thrilled to have the Bhlat on board. Next, we have Rivo Alnod, a Molariun hailing from the one and only Bazarn Five." Rivo walked over to me, her blue skin contrasting the stark white uniform. Her suit was modified to accommodate her extremely short stature. Her four pupil-less eyes stared at me as she smiled. I remembered finding her aboard the robot pirate ship a few years ago, on my search for Mary, and I was so happy to see her healthy and donning the Gatekeeper uniform. Having her and her father's support was important. The crowd knew of Bazarn Five, and I doubted there were many that hadn't heard of her dad, Garo Alnod, one of the universe's wealthiest entrepreneurs.

"Thanks, Dean. I can't wait to get out of this suit and party." She barely said it loud enough for me to hear, and I laughed.

"You just got in it, and already you want out?" I asked.

Sarlun peered at the rear of the stage, where Suma walked over. Relief flooded his face as she neared us, wearing a crisp white Gatekeeper uniform.

"And what great ceremony would be complete without a legacy member joining us? Suma is the daughter of the great Sarlun of Shimmal. She's passed the tests with flying colors, and had the top grades of anyone in the last three centuries. She's also a great friend of mine, and I'm thrilled at her inclusion." I bent over, hugging the girl tightly. "You deserve this, Suma."

She squeezed me in return and smiled as we separated. Her snout wagged in excitement as the assembled stood and cheered in various ways. The reaction to today was fantastic: one for the ages.

"We want to thank you all for representing your people here today and for joining the Alliance of Worlds. Without your support, we couldn't venture into a future that's more promising than any we could have imagined. Remember, this is Haven, and there's room for you to send a colony to grow roots here. Our goal is to have all members of the Alliance represented on Haven within five years. If you haven't decided on participating at this colony yet, please reach out to one of us, and we'll happily discuss the steps necessary to make this a reality."

So far, we had twenty races with members living on Haven, and that number was growing by four or five a year now. We wanted to keep it expanding exponentially.

People started leaving the promenade, music began playing from all corners of town, and drinks were being passed out of various smells, consistencies, and potency.

Sarlun stepped over to me, setting a hand on my shoulder. "You did well, son. I never foresaw the Gatekeepers heading in this direction, but it's time for us to stop hiding in the shadows and playing archeologist on barren worlds. This" – he waved his hand to indicate the mingling white-uniformed Gatekeepers on the stage – "is the future, and it's thanks to you."

I shook my head. "I didn't do much. Happy to help where I can, though."

The crowds stopped moving away momentarily, and shouting carried from the grounds to my ears. I scanned for the source and spotted them.

Suma was at my side, and she whispered, "The Inlor."

We'd left them at the landing pad to be escorted to the ceremony, since we didn't have time to greet them. It seemed they might have taken exception to that, and judging by the expressions on their faces as they neared the stage, they felt slighted. They had dense fur, which was something I hadn't expected based on Suma's explanation. The lead one had two thick brown furry arms at the top of his torso; the other four arms were lower, the middle pair jutting out from his sides, the lower pair from his hips.

I'd been permitted into the Gatekeepers without

needing to study or take an entrance exam, and I realized there was so much I didn't know about the worlds and the people that inhabited them. His head was shaped like a dog's, with a short snout accented by a pink nose. He spoke in growls, and I tapped my earpiece translator on.

"You are the one from the ship above?" he asked, while one of his clawed arms scratched idly on his leather vest. He wore pants as well, hair tufts shooting out on an exposed section between the pants leg and the heavy boot on his foot.

"I'm Dean Parker." I stuck my hand out, as if to shake, and he growled something my translator couldn't pick up. "Extend your hand."

He jabbed a claw out, and I nodded to his hand with a thumb and three other digits. "Use that one. I'll show you how we humans introduce ourselves."

The Inlor listened, head cocked to the side as we shook. He was flanked by several more Inlor on the stage now, and they watched me closely. Two of them were shorter, and even though they weren't any less tough-looking than the one in front of me, I took them for females.

"I am Etar Nine," his name translated, and I wondered if that made him the ninth in his namesake's line, or if it was unrelated.

"Hello, welcome to Haven," Mary said. She was holding Jules in her left arm, and my daughter was trying to squirm free of her grasp. She shook the Inlor's hand as well, and he stared at my little girl for a moment before speaking again.

"Haven. What is this place?" Etar asked.

"How do you mean?" I prodded.

"We Inlor are new to a lot of things. We only recently became a destination for trade, because of…" He stopped, glancing around. "We've become a place of trade. We haven't seen many of the beings you have here."

"They don't live here, not all of them. As you saw, we're working on building an Alliance of Worlds. A treaty to prevent wars, a trade structure to ensure safe bartering and stop theft and piracy." The group of Gatekeepers on the stage were moving off now, leaving Sarlun, Mary, and me alone with the newly entered Inlor. Slate stood at the edge of the stage, pretending to not pay attention to the newcomers, but I knew he was watching us like a hawk.

"We've had issues with all of those factors. We found metal that can be manufactured into wire coil that allows large fleet weapons to hold charges and increase energy outbursts. This has drawn a lot of attention to our world. Perhaps we can discuss things while we're here." The openness Etar relayed was surprising, but I was relieved.

"We'd love to talk about you entering the Alliance of Worlds. Come by the town square tomorrow morning, and we'll explain how everything works," I said, passing him a tiny chip with details embedded in it.

"The Inlor would also like to speak about joining this Gatekeeper club," Etar said, and I grinned at him.

"We'll discuss that tomorrow as well. Perhaps Slate and Suma can show you around the festivities?" I motioned for Slate to come over, and he jogged, hand ready to grab his pulse pistol. I shook my head.

"Come with me," Suma said in her native language, and Slate followed along, leading the Inlor away.

When I was alone with my family and Sarlun, I blew out a deep breath. The stage was empty save us, and the seats held only a few beings, chatting amongst each other in the sunny afternoon.

"How did you think that went?" I asked Mary and

Sarlun. Jules had found her way out of Mary's arms, and she was dragging her stuffed rabbit around the stage nearby.

Sarlun shrugged. "I've never met an Inlor before, but talk of their metal is widespread. I think it'll be a huge success to bring them in so soon. How did you manage to smuggle them here?"

I told Mary and Sarlun about Sergo, and how they'd destroyed his ship without so much as blinking.

"They barely mentioned it after, like nothing happened," I said, while keeping an eye on my daughter. She was so mischievous, always exploring and pushing the boundaries we set in place for her. Mary claimed it was all my influence, but I had to admit we were both to blame.

"We'll have to keep an eye on them, won't we, Dean?" Sarlun suggested, and he let out a squawk. "I can't believe my little Suma is fully grown and one of the Gatekeepers now. I always planned on keeping her in a classroom, studying theoretical sciences, but ever since that day you and Slate stumbled upon her on Sterona, she's had it in her head that she needs to be like you. All of you." He pointed at Mary to make sure my wife knew she was also culpable.

Mary laughed, a light comforting sound I'd never grow tired of. "She's headstrong and brilliant. If we're pointing fingers at anyone, it's you, Sarlun."

He nodded. "Maybe you're right. We made the correct call, didn't we?"

"Letting Suma in?" I asked, trying to pinpoint the direction he was going.

"All of it. The Alliance, the open invitation to participate in the colony here on Haven, the expansion of the Gatekeepers." Sarlun stared into the distance, watching the thousands of people mix together in the town square.

"We did the right thing. This is all the start of something special, you'll see." I wrapped an arm around Mary's shoulder, feeling her head lean into me.

"I hope so. I really do," Sarlun whispered.

I noticed someone standing at the edge of the stage, and I instantly recognized the long white hair on the tall man. "Mary, do you mind if I catch up later? I want to talk to Karo for a minute."

She picked up Jules as our daughter played with her toy, and shook her head. "I don't mind at all. Don't be late for dinner. And whatever you do, don't go running off on another crazy mission." Mary got closer, out of earshot of Sarlun, and said quietly, "And remember we have somewhere to be after it's all over tonight."

"How could I forget? Nothing will stop us. We need the night off." I kissed her, feeling the press of her lips against mine, and Jules leaned in, kissing my forehead at the same time.

"Bye, Papa," Jules said.

"Bye, Princess."

When I was alone, I went to the edge of the stage, seeking out Karo, but he was gone.

FOUR

The day had been too long; the entire week and month leading up to the big event had been even longer. Mary and I walked home, exhausted. Jules was there already, being babysat by a local human girl who lived next door to us. We had homes on New Spero, Earth, and Haven, and while we separated ourselves on those other two planets by living far away from civilization, we'd decided to stay right in the heart of things on Haven.

The planet had changed tremendously since the days when Kareem had lived here; nothing but a few wooden buildings stood erect back then, and there was no real industry or any plan to develop. Now, tens of thousands were living on the world – most of them at the capital city, but there were at least five separate villages popping up in the most fertile sections of the world.

Mary had been there with me when we'd first landed on Haven so long ago, searching for Terrance and Leslie. I'd almost died from a creature trying to drown me, and Mae had saved me. Like most worlds I frequented now, I had a long list of memories. Far too many of them involved me nearly dying.

Now, walking the sidewalks leading out of the town square, heading for our penthouse apartment in a twelve-story building, it felt like a safe place, with nothing to worry about but when to go to bed and what time breakfast was being cooked.

A few beings walked the streets, and I spotted two short blue Molariuns nearby, as well as a hybrid leading three Bhlat through the street, animated banter among them.

"It's good to see, isn't it?" Mary asked.

"It sure is." We arrived at our building: the exterior bore a slate-gray façade, and an immense glass door led us into the grand foyer. Minutes later, we were up the elevator and inside our penthouse. Even though we'd spent a lot of time here in the last year and a half since the construction had ended, it never felt like home. There was only one place that truly did.

Bernadette, the babysitter, was in the living room, the dim lights of her holotablet glowing against her youthful face.

"Jules behave?" Mary asked, and the girl's head snapped up, as if she'd only just realized we were in the room with her.

"Like an angel," she answered, getting up and heading for the elevator doors.

My little Jules was a lot of things, but being on her best behavior wasn't usually one of them. She was too feisty for most older sitters, but this girl had bonded with her easily.

I headed for the bedroom, past the modern kitchen, and poked my head into Jules' room. It was late, hours after her bedtime, and she was sleeping soundly. I almost regretted having to move her. Seconds later, she was in my arms, her little head limp against my cheek. Together, we went into the master suite, where Mary was pulling a device from a safe built into the wall.

She set the half of the portal device into the bedroom doorway, and the web spread out inside the frame, creating a gateway to the other side. I nodded to her to go first, and Mary stepped through, disappearing. I grabbed a bag with my left hand and walked into the portal, appearing in our farmhouse on New Spero.

After spending a month straight on Haven, the silence of the country was off-putting. "Do you hear that?" Mary asked.

"What?" I looked around, ready to fend off an intruder.

"Dean, always so quick to expect nefarious attackers. I only meant the lack of noise. It's quiet," she said.

"You don't think I have a right to be prepared? I think the Boy Scouts were onto something with that motto of theirs," I said with a laugh. Jules was coming to, and I took her down the hall, settling her into her bed in the end room. I flipped a switch, and a soft orange light displayed butterflies on her wall. She briefly met my gaze as I pulled her covers up to her chin, tucking her in. Her eyes were bright green, almost fluorescent.

We still didn't know what effects she'd have after growing inside Mary while she was possessed by the Iskios, but we could only love her and treat her like any normal little girl. Her eyes were beautiful, and that was what we told her every day. Already, other children acted like she was different, and all we wanted was for her to grow up happy and healthy, like any parents would.

I loved having the portable gateway device I'd found in Fontem's collection. It had proved invaluable in my plot to isolate Lom of Pleva, and now I could use it to escape other things, like obligations, to whisk my family away to our home base. Jules closed her eyes, and I kissed her forehead gently before returning to the living room.

Mary's shoes were off, and I joined her, happy for the relief. She was in a dress, and I was in a formal Gatekeeper uniform. I plopped beside her, and she loosened my collar. I glanced to the coffee table to see two wine glasses full of what could only be a robust Shimmali red.

"What's the occasion?" I asked, picked up the glasses and passing one to her.

"Did you see what we pulled off today? We're making a safer unified galaxy out there. We need to celebrate the successes, Dean." Mary was close to me, and I could smell her perfume. She was gorgeous tonight, and I took a sip, instantly feeling the wine calm me. All the work and efforts over the last month washed away as I leaned into the couch, putting my feet up on the table.

"What if it doesn't work? People better than me have tried this before. Do you remember Earth? Someone always screws it up," I said.

"If that happens, then we'll deal with it when we have to." Mary had a good outlook, and somehow worried less than I did about the future.

We clinked our glasses together, and my eyelids closed slightly as I let myself relax. We chatted for a while about commonplace things: work we needed to do in the garden at our house on Earth, updates on the new Terran sites being built here on New Spero, and eventually, we settled into a silence where we just sat there, enjoying sitting still beside each other.

I woke hours later to the sound of my communicator notification going off. The only one who had access to this particular device's other end was Magnus, and he was off on the tail end of his three-year stint running an exploratory Keppe vessel. When Mary, Slate, Suma, and I were stranded on Sterona while Mary was pregnant with Jules, Magnus had bartered his services away for their assistance to retrieve us. Now they were coming close to the end of those three years, and we were excited at the prospect of welcoming our friends home.

We spoke once every few weeks on the communicators, but hadn't in some time. I blamed it on the fact that we were both busy, but we should have made time for our talks.

I shook the cobwebs from my brain as I eased off the couch where Mary slept, and I crept across the room to the communicator. The sun was starting to peek over the horizon, sending a light red color across our sky. With the tap of an icon on the palm-sized device, I heard Magnus' frantic voice as I stood on our front porch, breathing in cool morning air.

"Dean! You have to help..."

That was all that came through, and I tapped it again, seeing the connection was still active. "Magnus, what is it?" I shouted.

No sound emerged; then a crackle, and his voice again. "We're stuck..."

Then nothing further. The communication was over.

Mary's silhouette was in the doorway, and she kept her voice quiet, but her question was laced with concern. "What's happened to Magnus and Natalia?"

"I don't know, but I think they need our help."

Two days passed, and we couldn't reach anyone on Keppe about Magnus. Lord Crul was apparently indisposed, and Admiral Yope was away on a mission. I'd had enough of everyone's avoidance and decided I had to make a trip to the Keppe home world of Oliter.

Our gang was inside our home on New Spero, and I glanced around, grateful they'd all come on such short notice. Sarlun was on Shimmal, overseeing the training of the new Gatekeepers. We were in the process of building an intergalactic academy on Haven where the classes would eventually be held, but for the time being, Sarlun was using their own facilities.

Suma was here, nervously sitting at the table, eating some nuts Mary had placed out. Slate was pacing around the room angrily, and Karo sat solemnly on the couch, not saying much. I was worried about my Theos friend. He didn't seem the same lately, and even the offer of pizza didn't sway his mood.

Leslie sat still, a constant reminder of Mae and Janine, since she was a clone of the same person as they were. Her better half, Terrance, was on Haven making sure the last of the dignitaries launched home without complication.

Jules sat at the table with us, coloring a piece of paper. She'd drawn a space ship, and a fuzzy alien with six arms was on the page beside it, looking much like a child's version of the Inlor we saw on the stage.

Rulo, the Keppe warrior, was the exception. She should have been with Sarlun on Shimmal, with Suma, but the girl had escorted her to our house through the portal stone earlier in the day.

"I told you, I don't know how to reach them," Rulo said, her words translating for me. She stared at me with her snake-slit eyes, thick armored skin bulging through her white uniform. "If I did, I wouldn't keep it from you."

"Then you have to come with me to Oliter. Magnus is in danger, and I'm worried we don't have much time," I said, unable to hide the tremor from my voice. Magnus had been there for me without question, and it appeared it was my turn to return the favor.

Suma chewed a nut and tapped her finger on the table. "'We're stuck.' What do you think it means?"

"I'm not sure it's worth speculating over. We have to find out where they were, and if your people were tracking their movements," Mary told Rulo.

A scar on Rulo's face was a reminder from the day when I first met her, when we'd rescued Slate from the underground monsters, and she grimaced, running a hand over her bald head. "We have tracking, but they aren't always foolproof. Our exploratory vessels have been pushing the borders of the known universe, and often the readouts don't transfer back to their server until the ship is close enough."

"But you'll come with us to Oliter to find out?" I asked, and she nodded.

"I will. Magnus is a friend to my people. If trouble has befallen his ship and crew, then it affects the Keppe as well as you. Admiral Yope will also want to know." Rulo stood behind Jules, watching her make even strokes with a blue crayon. Something was bothering Rulo more than she was letting on.

"What is it?" I pressed her.

"Kaspin, someone close to me, is on *Fortune*. I'm worried about him." I hadn't known that Rulo had a significant other. Three years was a long commitment to be separated.

"Then we go in the morning. First thing," I said.

Mary locked eyes with me. "Dean, can I speak to you in the other room for a moment?"

I noticed how everyone else avoided looking at us as she led me to the porch, and shut the door before speaking. "We have so much going on, and we have Jules now. I know you have this insatiable urge to help everyone and go on adventures, but do you remember what happens when you go out *there*?" She pointed to the sky, indicating space beyond.

"I know." I ran a hand through my hair and leaned against the wooden siding of the house. Maggie was at my feet, and I petted the cuddly cocker spaniel, who was sitting on the steps with Mary. "I told you I was done with that stuff, but this is Magnus. You didn't hear his voice. He sounded petrified. He was really scared. Natalia's there with him, and the kids, Dean and Patty. Not to mention the dogs, Charlie and Carey." I'd been surprised to hear my old cocker friend was still kicking; even up in the Keppe ship, he seemed to have a lot of spunk left in his aging body.

Mary sighed and nodded, looking away from me. "Then you have to go. I'll stay here with Jules." I knew she wanted to come with me, and I wanted my family by my side, but it was too dangerous to be traipsing around the galaxy with the whole family.

"Maybe we won't have to go anywhere. Maybe the Keppe know where they are and are already on it," I said, failing to believe my own hopes.

"Go to Oliter tomorrow and find out what you can. Take the other end of the movable portal with you, just in case. That way, you can get home to visit us," Mary said.

"I don't know if I should bring it. What if something happens to me? What if someone steals it? They'd have direct access to you and Jules. I'm not sure I can risk that." I loved her idea, because I'd be able to come home and see them anytime.

"Oh, Dean, why can't we hide away from everything, and grow old taking care of our daughter?" Mary asked, leaning into me.

The door opened, and Karo popped his head out. "Dean and Mary, may I speak with you candidly?"

"Of course. Come and join us," Mary said. Karo was seven feet tall, and he still looked odd wearing jeans and a t-shirt. I wasn't sure I'd ever get used to it. His white hair was pulled into a ponytail, and his eyes bore into mine.

"I'd like to join you, Dean."

"Are you sure?" I asked, not wanting to burden the Theos with dangerous adventures.

"I'm bored here, and on Haven. I don't fit in, and few people want to talk to the lone gray alien. I'd prefer to be in your small company, doing something for once," Karo said, and I felt terrible for him. Here he was, the last of his kind, knowing that all other remaining Theos were trapped inside the portal stones we used to transport from world to world. It was a sad tale, and his request was one I was only too happy to accept.

"Come with me. I'd love that, Karo. We have no idea what to expect here." I glanced to Mary. "We might be gone a while."

"That suits me just fine. Mary, thank you for all your hospitality. I'm going to miss having dinner with you and little Jules a few times a week, but it will do my mental health wonders to be out there instead of wallowing in my own loneliness," Karo said, and while we'd talked a lot about him being the last Theos, he'd never spoken quite so openly of his feelings about it.

"Welcome to the team," I said, starting up the stairs. Maggie hopped to her feet when I did, and shook her little body before sticking her nose on the door. She was ready to go in to see if Suma had dropped any food on the floor.

Mary gripped my arm, holding me back as Karo reentered the house. "Come back to us with Magnus and Natalia, okay? I know I've given you a hard time about staying safe with us around, but I know part of you needs this."

I was about to deny it, but she lightly placed a finger on my lips, preventing me from arguing the fact.

FIVE

We were in the portal room outside Terran Five on New Spero when I remembered the "guest" we'd left aboard the ship on the landing pad near the capital city on Haven. Leonard stayed at my house with Mary and Jules, and before I left, he whispered that he would protect them with his life. I wasn't sure that was necessary, but I didn't tell him that. The truth was, I was happy for Mary to have someone there for company, even though she was more than equipped to protect herself. Part of me wished Slate could stay with my family, but he'd never let me go without him.

W, the android we'd found on Larsk Two, was with us, along with Slate, Suma, Karo, and Rulo, and I'd nearly pressed the icon on the portal table for Oliter when I recalled Sergo's insectoid face. "Damn it. We have to make a quick detour," I said, and no one argued as I brought us to Haven instead.

I led our group out of the portal room on Haven, through the tunnels, and out to the surface, where a guard waved us through. He pointed to an idle lander and motioned for me to take it. Sometime later, our assorted group arrived outside the city of Haven. I'd told Terrance a few times that we needed to change the name of either the capital or the planet, because it was confusing to have them both named the same thing. He disagreed, so I'd digressed and hadn't brought it up since.

We almost all wore our Gatekeeper uniforms, and I thought it was a little funny to have a crew in matching outfits. Our EVA suits were waiting for us to don them before heading to Oliter. We looked like a real team, comprised of two humans, a Shimmali, a Keppe warrior, and the last Theos in existence. Karo and W were the only ones not part of the Gatekeepers. The Theos man wore a black jumpsuit instead, causing him to stick out like a sore thumb. W was an android and didn't wear clothing at all. Where his gray exterior was once scuffed and dirty, he was smooth and polished after a little maintenance on New Spero.

He piloted the lander to a pad that was only a quarter full now: a vast difference from the other day, when the ceremony was taking place and there were hundreds of various vessels from around the galaxy parked for the event.

I spotted the ship we'd used to intercept Sergo, and boarded it while the others waited outside, W staying inside the lander.

"Sergo! Look, I'm sorry. We got tied up," I lied. I couldn't believe we'd actually forgotten the guy trapped in a bedroom on the ship.

I approached and saw his form lying on the bunk in the corner of the room. I pulled a gun from my hip as a precautionary measure and held it behind me as I called out to him again. He wasn't moving.

"Sergo?" I asked. Still nothing. Seconds later, I had the force field deactivated, and I crossed the compact room and rolled him onto his back. Black eyes stared up at the ceiling. I was sure he was dead.

He licked his thin lips, and his head snapped toward me. "Parker! What do you think you're doing leaving me here like that? I could have died! Good thing we Padlog can slow our metabolism and go into a deep sleep."

I breathed a sigh of relief. I couldn't say that I liked the guy, but I didn't want to be the one to kill him either. Unless he deserved it. "I said I was sorry. Come on, let's get you out of here," I said.

"Where are you taking me?" he asked.

I hadn't given it much thought. I'd call Terrance and get him to do something with the Padlog gangster.

"Weren't you coming to Haven for a reason? Well, here you are. Have fun," I said as we walked by the safe he'd brought aboard with him. I pointed to the container. "Wait. You owe me something."

His gaze darted from the safe to me and back. "Fine. A deal's a deal, but like I said, it's busted." Sergo tapped in a series of codes onto a screen, and the trunk-like black case hissed apart. A cold mist poured from the edges before he hinged the lid open, revealing dark blue metallic rectangles cut and shaped like gold bars.

"That's…"

"That's what nearly got me killed. Inlorian bars." Sergo was staring at them with greed in his buggy eyes.

"That's what they called them? Not very original. How much is this worth?" I asked him.

"I'm not really sure. The stuff's going for about five hundred per bar," he said.

"Five hundred?" That wasn't much. There were hundreds of different currencies out there, but the universal credit was growing as a trade tool.

"Thousand." His gaze flicked to me, and his tongue ran over his mouth again. If I didn't know better, he was drooling. "Five hundred thousand a bar."

"That's a lot of credits. What were you thinking, stumbling in there and trying to steal it?" I grabbed the

Relocator and fiddled with it, finding the power didn't come on. I hoped Suma would be able to tinker and get it up and running.

"What happened with the Inlor?" he asked.

"They came to the Gatekeeper ceremony we were hosting, and after a few hours of discussion with us, have agreed to join our coalition. Now that they're part of the Alliance, we'll be returning their merchandise to them." I kicked the crate lightly, and Sergo's eyes got even wider, his antennae flicking back and forth quickly.

"You can't!" he shouted.

"And why's that?"

"Because they'll figure out I'm alive," Sergo said.

It finally clicked. "If they know we have the bars, then they know we took them off the ship before they destroyed it. Gotcha." My brain wasn't operating at full capacity. I was too worried about finding Magnus and bringing them home safely, and returning to my own family as soon as possible. I wasn't sure I was cut out for dealing with issues like this one any longer.

"Does that mean I can keep it?" he asked.

I shook my head. "No. Terrance is on his way here, and he'll deal with you." I didn't really care what happened to the stolen goods, as long as I didn't have to decide. Terrance and Leslie were in charge; they could take care of the problem better than I could.

"Where are you off to?" Sergo asked, as if the thought of adventure spelled out financial opportunity.

"None of your business. The Supreme is asking what happened to you, and we've had to tell him the Inlor destroyed your ship to keep up appearances. You might want to lie low here for a while," I suggested as Terrance entered the ship.

"Parker, we'll meet again. Of this I'm sure." Sergo

remained staring at the container of stolen materials longingly. "I guess I owe you one, don't I?"

"I suppose you do. I'll bank it for now," I said.

I got Terrance up to speed, and when we were all done, I pocketed the damaged Relocator. When Sergo wasn't looking, I grabbed ten of the Inlorian bars and met our group near the lander. The bars were lighter than I expected.

"Everything good, boss?" Slate inquired.

"Perfect. I don't think we'll be seeing Sergo anytime soon." I headed inside the transport ship, and the rest followed.

On the way, I scanned the landscape below, smiling as we flew over a modest village. Drones and robots were assembling the base of a residential facility, and already there were tiny ant-like forms moving along the ground.

A few minutes later, we were at the portal's landing pad, ready to get to the Keppe world and find out what we could about Magnus' venture and where his ship, *Fortune,* was last seen.

"Was this delay really necessary?" Karo asked me, nodding to my pocket, where the Relocator sat tucked away. I'd told them about the bargain, and Suma was anxious to look at the damaged device.

"Let's hope so." I set foot on the ground and listened to the rustling of the nearby leaves in the wind. It was calming, and I closed my eyes, stepping away from the group. I was going to be holed up with our team in rooms, on ships, and God knew where else for the next foreseeable while, so I soaked it all in. My helmet was off, and I let the wind brush against my freshly-shaven face. I breathed in the air, and felt the sun warm against my cheeks.

I stood like that for at least three minutes while the

others chattered among themselves, probably thinking I was going nuts. I didn't care. The next few weeks were going to be intense and unpredictable. I needed the recharge, and it worked. I instantly felt better, rejuvenated. Sometimes it paid to stop and smell the roses.

When I turned around, the others were already walking toward the portal cave, and I followed, slipping my helmet on. By the time I made it into the room, the portal stone was glowing, the hieroglyphs in the shapes of icons for each distant world the stones linked to were pulsing, and I stepped into the circle, ready to go to Oliter.

No one spoke as Suma tapped the table's icon for the world, and the room was bathed in white light before dimming, eventually settling in pitch black.

"What's wrong with the portal room?" Rulo asked, her words translating for me in my earpiece.

"I don't know." It shouldn't have been dark. The Keppe portal was directly beneath their leader Lord Crul's base, and it should have been well lit, the room immaculate and architecturally designed, unlike some of the unkempt caves we visited on most worlds. The Keppe took pride in theirs, and guarded and maintained the space with the utmost care.

A light flashed on: Slate had activated his suit's beams. We all did the same, and soon we had a better image of where we'd ended up.

"This isn't Oliter," Suma whispered, and Rulo rolled her eyes.

"Of course this isn't, child. Do you think my people would leave a resource like the portal stone in such disarray?" Rulo barked. She was normally so affable that her outburst caught me off-guard.

Suma stood her ground. "I'm not a child, and we know what the Keppe portal looks like. Most of us have traveled through it."

I hated to second-guess my friend, but she might have made a mistake. I cleared my throat. "Suma, is there a chance you chose the wrong icon? They can be hard to get right, and you've been studying so many things. Maybe you picked a similar symbol?"

Suma glared at me, her snout snapping upwards. "I didn't screw up. Slate, tell him. You saw me."

Slate nodded. "I did, boss. She chose the right one, I'm sure of it."

Karo was standing away from us, facing a doorway. I watched him stare at the wooden slab without moving. He was acting even stranger than normal lately. It was something else for me to have to watch out for.

"W, what kind of readouts are you getting?" I asked our robot friend.

"Captain, the air is within reasonable parameters for each of your races' capacities," W responded.

"Good. I think we should try again, see if we can get to Oliter." My hands were already moving across the crystal-clear table, swiping over the dozens of symbols on each page. We'd recently opened up the blocked icons on all of the stones, allowing the hidden symbols from the Theos Collective to be visible to all Gatekeepers. Sarlun had fought it at first, but when he saw the advantage of finding more worlds to explore, making more connections out there, he'd agreed with me.

I found the icon and looked around, seeing if everyone was close enough to travel with the press of the image. The stone pulsed and glowed, but before I pushed on the symbol, Karo's voice carried over to me. "Dean, do not press that."

His words caught me off-guard, and I stopped short. "Why not?"

Karo turned, his white hair faintly glowing in the dim corner of the room. "Something's wrong with the stone," he said, stalking across the room. He was tall, and between his voice and his imposing statuesque figure coming at me, I stumbled away from the table.

Suma stood there, not flinching away from the last remaining Theos. "What's wrong with it? How do you know?" she asked.

"It's not that I know what's wrong, but I can feel it. The Theos themselves power these stones. They needed to sacrifice their physical forms in order to retain the universe's Balance when their fight with the Iskios transpired so long ago. Their essence is inside the stone. You saw what happened when you tried to travel through a portal stone while Leonard had an Iskios possessing him. The two energies collided and negated one another." Karo was staring at the table and at the stone below.

"Do you think someone here is carrying an Iskios?" Slate asked, causing me to glance around at my companions.

"No, nothing like that. I can sense the Theos inside. There are a few of them," he said as he knelt on the dusty stone floor. I moved around the table and crouched beside him.

"Are they aware?" Suma asked.

Karo shook his head. "I don't think so. We might be able to pull some patterns from them if we had the tools, but they're only an energy source at this time. There's a chance that they're drying up, dying off inside the stones."

I cringed at this theory. "That would mean the stones could eventually fail."

"That's correct." Karo placed a palm on the stone, which was growing brighter, hotter; I could feel the heat emanate off the surface, but Karo didn't even seem to notice. "They could fail, but for now, they might act like they've crossed wires, sending users to the wrong place."

"If the wires are crossed between the symbol selection and the actual destination stone, then the Gatekeepers will be sent to random places," Suma said softly.

"That's also correct," Karo agreed. "Or it could be isolated to the stone at Haven, or perhaps even the stone leading to Oliter. We must cogitate on this before attempting a return."

"We don't have time for this. Maybe you should all leave the room, and I'll go through alone, testing it to see if I can get to Oliter. Magnus needs my help," I said, unable to keep the tension from my voice.

Slate set a hand on my chest. "Magnus needs *our* help, not just yours. Did you bring this team so you could abandon us at the first opportunity?"

Slate was still upset about me leaving them behind after the attack at Bazarn Five, when I went looking for Mary. I didn't think I'd ever live that one down; plus, he was right. Magnus and Nat needed all of us around to help get them back. I wasn't equipped to do it alone. "I'm sorry I even suggested it. Let's take a look at what this world has to offer while we're here and see if we can figure out where we landed. It's a good thing Suma's spent the last five months studying six hours a day, right?"

Suma smiled and took the lead, heading for the doorway. I knew she wanted nothing more than to go recover our missing friends, but I could also tell she was excited to explore a different world. This was her first real mission as a Gatekeeper, even though she'd already been on countless assignments with us.

"Ready or not, here we come," Slate said, stepping in front of Suma. His pulse rifle was raised, and he opened the wooden door slab, ready for anything.

It creaked as he pushed it, and we saw more of the same. Stone floor, dirt walls, but a crack of light cast at the end of a slowly escalating corridor floor, promising an outside. Slate led us through, our suits' lights showcasing nothing of interest, and three minutes later, we stood at another wooden door. It had a metal ring handle, but no visible locks.

"Let's see what we're working with," I said, pushing the door open.

SIX

Slate grabbed, pulling me from the ledge. I was leaning over a sharp descent that was hundreds of feet above the surface below. The walls shimmered, and gone was the rocky disposition, replaced with translucent glass barriers. I lost my breath, and I struggled to find it as I stared at the entrance where the tall wooden door had existed moments earlier.

"What happened?" Rulo asked from behind me. Slate pulled me away, waiting until I had a secure foothold on the floor before releasing me again.

"I don't know, but this was all a show." I walked the perimeter of the room, trying to understand what I was looking at. The walls were clear, the symbols lit up in a soft blue glow, but they were moving around the surface of the glass in fluid motions. The portal table appeared as it had before.

I glanced toward the surface far beneath, and a wave of vertigo swept over me. The floors were clear glass too, and I noticed blinking lights far underneath the tower we were stranded in.

"Look up," Suma said, and I did, witnessing a dark, cloud-covered sky above. I couldn't see a moon or any stars through the blanket over the heavens. Beyond the glass, we pointed out what was an elaborate and complex hive of buildings connected by enclosed pedways.

"W, what are you picking up now? Are we in the same place?" I asked, worried we'd been sent somewhere else by an erratic portal stone. If the stones began transporting us on their own, we were in even bigger trouble, unless we found a way out of this room. The exit was a thousand-foot dive through the air.

"We are on the same world upon which we arrived. Readouts show the same results." W didn't have to use a tablet or arm console like we would; his sensors were internal.

"Any ideas?" I asked. Karo was wandering the far side of the room, looking through the glass toward the ground.

"I think the portal room is floating," Suma said.

"Floating? There has to be a stand somewhere, doesn't there?" Slate asked, ducking by the other end, looking into the bottom corner.

"Not necessarily," W offered. "Judging by the slight variance in altitude every few seconds, the room could either be using thrusters to hold itself in the air or a powerful magnetic force. Since I am not affected by the energy a magnet of that strength would require, I think thrusters are the answer."

"Karo, do you think this room could be the cause of the disturbance on the portal stone?" I asked the Theos. His gaze met mine with a vacant stare. He was really out of it, and I needed to find a way to get him back to normal.

He shook his head. "While this is an odd location for us to end up, I don't think the correlation is so simple. From what I can assume, my people are dying inside the portal stones, and our arrival here is happenstance of that fact."

"Okay," I started, "what do we know?" I flipped a

finger in the air. “One. The portals brought us here instead of to Oliter, the Keppe world.” Rulo grunted, her minigun in her hand, but it dangled toward the floor. “Two. We’re in a clear glass portal room, hovering nearly a mile from the surface.”

Suma took over. “Three. We didn’t bring much in the way of supplies.”

She was right. We’d been expecting to arrive right on our ally’s planet, under Lord Crul’s palace. This wasn’t good.

I liked talking it out. This group was resourceful, and I had confidence we’d figure this out like we always did. We just needed to put our heads together. “What are the options?”

Slate went first. “We pick another symbol and see where the portal takes us.”

“That’s not a terrible idea. At least that might give us a chance to arrive somewhere a little more hospitable,” Rulo suggested.

“I don’t think there are other options, at least not any that make sense. We can’t wait. We don’t have much food and water.” Each of us had a small pack, but the combined sustenance would only be enough for a day, two days max.

Karo was back in the middle of the room. “I don’t like to use it again so soon. It’s like I can feel them inside the stone, fading away.”

“Then it’s better if we go sooner rather than later,” Slate said, urgency thick in his voice.

I agreed, though I hated going into the portal again with so many unknowns. “This is so frustrating.” I stared out the glass toward the intricate pattern of structures beyond. I didn’t see anything moving, but still… there were a lot of blinking lights, and that told me someone had to be in the city around us.

"There's always a third option," Suma said.

"What's that?" I walked over to her side, my gaze catching what she was seeing.

She pointed to a distant dot that was getting larger with each breath. "We wait for the welcoming party to arrive."

Slate and Rulo had their weapons raised in a flash, and they came to stand between the rest of us and the doorway, which was wide open. There was nowhere to hide, and I was considering using the portal to make a quick exit, but Karo's worries over its functionality made me hesitate.

"What is it?" Slate asked.

We stood in a line between the entrance and the table hovering over the crystal. The glow was absent from both the portal stone and the walls, and all the symbols were gone, leaving the room feeling empty.

A cube approached us, glowing thrusters urging it up and forward to meet with our room, which shook slightly at the gentle impact. A sound indicated the cube had locked in place with the portal room, and my back tensed as we waited for a door to open from the newly arrived hosts.

We didn't have to wait long. One second, a barrier was there; the next, it had vanished, revealing a dark box beyond.

"What do we do, boss?" Slate didn't turn around to ask. Instead, he took a single step forward before stopping.

"There's something inside," I whispered after hearing a noise emanate from beyond our doorway. "W, any life signs?"

"Not on my sensors, no, Captain," W said, far too

loudly. The robot needed some programming in tact.

Rulo's imposing minigun was raised as she walked stealthily toward the cube. She turned her suit's lights on, casting beams into the dark space. Seconds later, she turned around, facing us, and shrugged her broad shoulders. "Looks empty," she said, and I saw it then.

"Rulo, behind you!" I shouted, but it was too late. The mechanical being moved with a speed I'd never seen before. Her gun was on the ground, and a lance of energy tethered to the weapon's grip, casting it to the side.

Rulo stumbled, unsure what to make of the intruder. It clearly wasn't organic, nor did it look humanoid. It walked on four legs, a thin torso rising from the center of them, and dozens of protrusions shot out from all angles of the body. Lights blinked and pulsed as the functional arms moved around slowly, cautiously.

"What is it?" Slate asked, likely not expecting an answer.

"It is a robot, is that not obvious?" W said, stepping around us and toward the newcomer.

"Be careful, W. We don't know how dangerous it is," Suma said, but W didn't seem to care.

"If we want to leave this world, we will need the locals' help." W stood five feet away from the other robot, and they couldn't have been more different. Humans and other humanoid creatures built robots in their own likenesses, mostly so they'd feel comfortable around them. I always thought it was a little bit of a god complex mixed in there as well, and if there was one thing sentient beings were full of, it was ego.

"This is the local?" I asked.

"Since we're getting no life signs within this region of the world, I have to assume the ones who constructed the city are like the one before us," W said.

Suma moved over beside W, and I watched the alien robot closely, trying to stay alert for any signs of danger. "Could this place be like Sterona, where the inhabitants vanished, leaving things like drones behind?" she asked.

W stood silently for a moment, pondering the Shimmali's question. "It is doubtful, Suma. The patterns of the city around us are too mathematical, too precise. I understand the structure of them on a basic level built into my positronic brain. This robot is made for optimized function, hence the multi-tooled design. I suspect it is able to do the work of dozens of drones on New Spero. There seem to be no limits…"

W's speech was clipped as it ended. His eyes glowed bright red, and his arms shot straight out, rigid and tense.

Suma jumped, and I caught her. Slate was still holding a pulse rifle up, and I motioned for him to lower it.

"W, what's happening to you?" I asked, worried about our companion. I glanced back and saw Karo standing at the stone, his hand resting on the smooth surface, a distant look in his eyes. I'd have to deal with that later.

"It is speaking to me." W's voice was strained, more robotic than normal. Gone were his programming's pretenses of trying to sound human in tone.

"What does it want?" Suma asked, ever curious.

"Can you understand it?" I inquired, since the robot hadn't made a single sound since entering our space.

"Yes. It's pushing the communication directly into my core." W's eyes were bright and red, causing concern. I hoped that whatever the other robot was doing wasn't risking harm to our team member.

"What's it saying?" I asked, reiterating Suma's question.

"The information is streaming into me in a version of

binary code. It's taking my processors… there it is. We are the first beings they have seen here in centuries, if I perceive the timeline properly. The last carbon-based being that entered through the room had feigned being an ally, but eventually turned on them." W's eyes were returning to normal, the red lessening with each sentence.

The robot hadn't moved in several minutes, and my gaze lingered on it, catching a blinking light on its midsection. I had a bad feeling.

One of its many arms shot out, a beam pushing toward Slate, the only one still holding a gun in his hands. Slate fell to the ground, and I started to rush toward him when W stopped me.

"Captain, refrain from moving. I'm speaking with it, assuring it we mean no harm." W's hands were raised, showing he wasn't a threat. Slate was breathing, and I took solace in that fact.

W and the robot were only a foot apart now, and I wished I could hear the silent communication passing between them. Suma was tense beside me and she grabbed my arm, holding it tightly. She was looking at Slate, who was slumped along the wall, gun displaced to the clear floor next to him.

"It is willing to discuss our freedom," W finally said, after at least two silent minutes.

Rulo shifted on her feet and grunted. It was almost as if I could read her mind. She thought we should blast our way out of here, heading for the portal again. There were too many variables with the afflicted stone. Karo was right to be concerned. We had no idea where we might end up if we traveled through it right now.

"What does it need?" I asked, knowing there was always a trade involved. That much was universal, whether we were flesh and blood or wires and metal.

"This city was once a wonderment of robotics. From what I understand, someone was here long ago, leaving behind an advanced AI prototype. Perhaps they tried to hide it somewhere isolated, to protect their own interests. They don't know. From there, that single robot expanded, using pieces of a crashed ship to make small drones. It expanded continuously, growing, utilizing the planet's metals, geothermal energy, and various other sources." W paused, as if getting further transmissions. Suma and I leaned in, both caught up in the tale.

"You're telling us that everything we see around us was created from that first robot?" I asked quietly.

W nodded. "That is what this one tells me. They call it Origin. Origin is powerful beyond our understanding. It created a matrix of such complexity that even this one can only briefly communicate what Origin's capabilities are."

My gut tensed at the implications. "You didn't answer my question. What does it need from us?"

W turned to look at everyone, finally breaking his lock with the four-legged host. "The city goes on for most of the planet, but there is a section of the world where they cannot survive because of the magnetic poles. The beings that came hundreds of years ago seized Origin from here and took it to the northern pole, rendering much of their world useless.

"The cities used to be alive with drones, robots like this one, and countless other forms, all interconnected like a hivemind. Now the ones with enough energy stored roam aimlessly. Only a few still have purpose, like J-NAK."

"Who's J-NAK?" I asked as I glanced over to Slate, who was coming to.

"This is J-NAK. That is the character equivalent of

his binary ID. He seems to like the name," W said, though I hadn't seen J-NAK react in the slightest.

"Can he speak?" I asked, and W turned to the robot, silently asking the question.

"He can if he has the proper translation tools. I can pass those to him if you like, Captain," W said, and I nodded.

"It'll make this easier." I watched as W pulled a datastick from a cubby inside his chest cavity and passed it to one of J-NAK's thin, outstretched black metal arms. Another arm took the portable datastick and scanned it, covering it with a yellow glow before two more skinny arms began working.

Suma stepped closer as it cut into its own metal torso before five or six arms worked, soldering and adjusting pieces from around its own body.

"It's making a receptor for the datastick. It doesn't have a slot that size, so it's constructing one. Fascinating," Suma said, and I had to agree. It was amazing and scary at the same time.

The whole process took only minutes, arms flashing so quickly, we could hardly follow. Soon it was pressing the stick inside the newly formed port, and seconds later, a sound carried from a speaker in its chest.

"Greetings, visitors. As our mutual acquaintance has advised you, you may call me J-NAK." The voice was robotic, reminding me of the old phone voices you'd dial to get the local weather or time.

"I'm Dean. This is Suma; Rulo; W, or Dubs as we call him; Karo is back there; and that" – I pointed to the ground, where Slate was blinking his eyes open and reaching for his gun again – "is Zeke, but you can call him Slate." I shook my head at my friend, and Slate left his hand off the weapon.

"That was uncalled for," Slate said, and I moved over to him, helping him to his feet.

"We do not want to be threatened. We will not tolerate further destruction," J-NAK said plainly.

"Good to know." Slate rubbed his head. "Don't worry about me," he said with some attitude. "I'm fine."

"Can you help us get home?" I asked, nodding to the stone Karo was kneeling beside.

"We do not travel through the portal. It takes an organic to activate." J-NAK moved toward it, his four legs moving methodically.

A disturbing vision crept into my inner mind's eye: robots like the one in front of us spread across New Spero, thousands of them building a hive like the city around us, stifling our human life in favor of their own AI needs. We couldn't let them or this Origin travel through the portals with us. They had to remain here. It also begged the question of why they hadn't created space travel yet, or maybe I was being short-sighted and they had. It wasn't a question I was willing to broach with the robot quite yet.

W cut in. "I did mention the portal's erratic behavior, referring to the potential crossed wires between the locations and the symbols."

I silently wished he hadn't talked about the portals with this robot at all, but since he already had, I decided to press it. "How did it respond?"

"It thinks it could work out a program mapping the issues, if given time," W said.

I sensed some logical bait being placed. "What should we do in the meantime?"

Karo got up and blinked at J-NAK, as if it was the first time he'd looked at the robot who'd been in the room with us for the last ten minutes. "Isn't that clear?"

he asked. "This J-NAK would like us to go to the pole, retrieve Origin, and bring their leader and founder back safely. Then they'll trade us safe passage to wherever we choose on the portal table."

For a guy who hadn't seemed to be paying attention, he'd hit the nail on the head.

"This one is accurate in his understanding of the situation. If it pleases you to begin your quest now, that would be ideal," J-NAK said through a speaker. He didn't have a head or face, so I stared toward the center of the torso, where the couple of dozen arms moved slowly.

"Can we have a moment?" I asked it, and when I didn't receive a reply, I motioned everyone to come with me to the far corner of the clear-walled room.

"We don't have time for this," I muttered, angry with our predicament. "Why can't a rescue mission in space ever be simple?" The question almost made me laugh.

Rulo was the first to speak. "We either risk another portal trip or we do what they ask. W, do you believe they'll find a way to get us to Oliter?"

W paused before speaking. "I do. They appear to be quite high-level. When this model communicated wirelessly with me, I could sense others pressing in to join its conversation. As it said, many are aimless in their intelligence now, because the core of their hive is Origin. If this creature came and took Origin to the magnetic polar fields, where Origin can no longer function, then they do need it returned. We would be doing a great favor to these robots."

"I want to get Magnus home, not save a bunch of robots from wandering through the streets of their constructed city," I said, and regretted the words as W averted his gaze. "Dubs, I didn't mean it like that. I only want to help our friends."

"Boss, this might be the one way we can do that. How hard can it be?" Slate asked.

Now I did laugh. It was an asinine quest. We had no idea what we were up against out there at the poles. "I guess we have no choice. Are we all in agreement?" I had a bad feeling about it all. What was to stop these robots from all becoming activated, then forcing us to help them through the portal to devour and expand to other worlds? Unfortunately, we were out of options.

One by one, they nodded. First Rulo, then Suma, her snout waving lightly side to side. Slate was next, a determined look across his face. Karo met my gaze and nodded softly.

"Then it's settled. J-NAK, tell us everything you can about this being that took Origin."

SEVEN

We were ushered into the dark cube, and we each set our lights on as we entered. The walls were black, no light emerging from the outside. The door shut, and I couldn't discern if we were moving or staying still. J-NAK was silent as we waited, and a few minutes later, I felt the cube settle onto something solid.

"I guess we were moving," Slate whispered to me. We were in our full EVA suits, and I felt claustrophobic in mine. W claimed the air was breathable, and I expected to take the helmet off as soon as possible. It was kind of ironic to find a world that would suit our needs for air, but to find it inhabited by robotic beings.

We were led by the six-foot-tall multi-armed robot out onto the ground, which was a strange sight in its own right. The entire pathway was smooth light-gray metal, not a bump or ridge to be found.

A drone whirred by above us, and now that we were on the surface, I noticed different devices roaming without purpose. There were a couple of models much like J-NAK; some had more legs, or fewer arms, but that was where the differences ended.

"Come with me. We will supply everything you need for your journey," J-NAK said, and a hovering platform approached us. White light emanated from beneath, and a glowing barrier like a fence surrounded the trolley. It was meant to carry us to a destination.

"Everyone on board," I said, taking the lead up two steps. Once we were all on, feet planted firmly, it began moving slowly. We all watched with interest as the city moved by us. There were buildings, but I had no clue what sort of function they had. When I asked J-NAK about it, he said they were integral to the Panel. W tried to translate this, claiming the city was like an electronic panel. The buildings and pedways were bridges, connectors, and conductors.

Suma nodded along, but this was all well beyond my comprehension. Slate rolled his eyes and laughed. It was good that he could still be in high spirits after today's events. He'd even been shot with a pulse from J-NAK, which he claimed hadn't hurt. It had only incapacitated him in an instant.

"You're saying this entire city is some sort of computer board?" Rulo asked.

"In a simplified sense, yes," W said.

Rulo reached for our android with a powerful hand, and I stepped between them. "What else can you tell us?"

J-NAK's toneless voice told us we would receive a map, and asked W for vehicle blueprints that would suit our needs.

The hovering transportation platform came to a stop, and I peered up, seeing the sky for the first time. The clouds were dissipating, and the sun was up now, low in the horizon. It was yellow, and across the sky, I noticed a full moon contrasting the star. "This world seems like a good one for a colony," I suggested.

Suma agreed. "If you don't mind sharing it with sentient robots," she said quietly.

"I might mind that," I replied. "W, what does it want with vehicle blueprints?"

W asked it silently and quickly responded, "The location of the poles is not nearby. They wish to manufacture a vessel to take us there, and they figured one to our specifications would be ideal."

"Wait, you're telling me they'll make us any kind of ship we ask for?" Slate asked, eyes going wide. "Boss, let's get a killer copter."

"This isn't a game," I said, "but that's a cool idea. If Mary or Magnus were here, that might be a good option, but I don't think any of us should be learning to fly a helicopter on this alien world." I turned to W. "Do you have the prints of our basic ten-person landers?"

"I do, Captain," W said.

"Everyone good with that?" I asked, and when no one complained, W sent the details on another datastick.

"We will comply," J-NAK said.

"How long?" I asked the robot, wanting nothing more than to get this task over with. I expected to hear the answer in days, but its response startled us all.

"Two of your hours." It didn't wait for further discussion; instead, it walked off, quickly moving into a walled-off facility that seemed every bit like a robotic manufacturing plant, even from the street. Its walls were at least a hundred feet high, white-paneled, and two hundred feet long.

"Two hours." I mouthed the words in surprise, and we settled on the street, leaning against the building's exterior walls.

"Can you believe this place?" Slate asked as he took his helmet off. Like every time one of us took our EVA helmet off on a foreign world, I held my breath, waiting for Slate's reaction to the air. He grinned at me and inhaled.

"Either they're producing oxygen or not everything

on this world is metal and robotic. There has to be some greenspace somewhere," Suma suggested, pulling her own helmet off. We all followed suit and began going over the small amount of rations we had. Once all our bags and pockets were emptied, we took inventory.

"Four water bottles and seven protein bars. Not a lot to go on," I said, reviewing the meager pile along the edge of the manufacturing warehouse.

"Good news, one of us is a robot, so W doesn't need food," Slate said. He eyed Karo suspiciously. "Are you sure you're not hiding any pizza under there?"

Karo's face broke into the first smile I'd seen on him for a while. "I did, but I already ate it."

"We can joke all we want, but we might be in some trouble. I expect these robots don't have much need for water." Slate reached for a bottle, and I cringed.

"W, how far is the northern pole?" I walked over to W as he pulled a screen from one of his multiple compartments. He activated it and showed me the display with a satellite image, presumably of the planet we were on.

"It looks to be twenty-five hundred and eleven kilometers to the center of the pole," he said. I scanned the image, which showed most of the terrain covered in streets and buildings, like the city we were inside. The picture showed light clusters spread around the continent, and my gaze drifted to a body of water stretching a couple hundred kilometers south of our current position in Origin's first settlement.

"How will we find Origin when we get there?" Suma asked, using English to make it easier to talk among the group.

"J-NAK said Origin has a unique identifier. They cannot track it from the pole, but they know for a fact that Origin did enter the pole when it was taken," W replied.

"What kind of alien arrived back then, and who would risk plucking the main power of an entire world's robotic hive?" I scratched my chin, wondering if W was given this information.

"That I do not know, Captain. It didn't have that information either. They don't appear to capture video feeds of anything going on here. They don't get a lot of visitors, and they are all interconnected, so having cameras is an unnecessary use of energy." W's gaze turned toward a doorway, but it remained closed. "It is strange here. I feel multiple *voices* pressing into my mind, some focused communication, some random strings of binary. It is very unsettling."

"Are you able to block it at all?" I asked, really having no understanding of how the robots could speak and pass information between each other.

He shook his head and glanced toward the doorway again. "No."

"What are you looking at?" Suma asked Dubs, as she glanced toward the door as well.

"I hear them in there. At least twenty drones, working as a strong unit to build our lander." W stood, while the rest of us sat leaning against the wall as we waited for J-NAK to come back with an update.

We spent the next two hours discussing where Magnus could have gone, Rulo adding insights to how life was on a Keppe exploratory vessel. I'd made a habit of talking to Magnus with our communicator over the duration of his three-year stint, but he rarely gave his location. Instead, we opted to discuss his mental state, my pressures running between Earth's new colony cities, New Spero's ever-expanding Terran sites, and Haven bringing in the

Alliance of Worlds members.

We frequently discussed our children, Magnus telling me about little Dean, whom he and Nat had named after me when they thought Mary and I had died on our trek chasing the hybrids across the galaxy. He was seven years old now, doing well in a Keppe school. Baby Patty wasn't a baby any longer. She was around a year older than Jules, and we liked to predict how Patty and Jules were going to become fast friends when they returned home.

I'd tell Magnus about my smart and willful little daughter, sometimes confiding that I was afraid she'd been affected by her time in the womb while Mary had been possessed by the Iskios. Her bright green eyes were only part of the reason I thought she might be special. Only time would tell exactly what that meant.

Mary didn't want to talk about the possibility of Jules being different based on her pregnancy's circumstances. She rarely spoke about the time under the ancient race's control. Not that I blamed her, but there were nights when she tossed and turned in bed, waking up in a sweat, and I knew it was because of her nightmares of the Iskios. She'd seen herself wielding immense power, destroying moons and planets with no regard for life. I knew I had hybrid blood inside me, and that brought a sort of deeper kinship between me and my daughter.

Mary admitted it wasn't her, none of it was actually under her control, but the effects of being used as such a destructive puppet were enough to scar anyone. I loved my wife ferociously, and now my daughter, and I needed to protect them so something like that never happened again. I looked around the strange city as we sat there, chatting amongst ourselves, and I wished I was home.

I should have brought the portal. What had I been thinking? We could have climbed through to my house on New Spero. At the same time, I'd been right to worry about carrying it on a journey with me. I was always getting into danger out here, and the last thing I needed was an enemy getting hold of the portal device and walking straight into my house, where Mary and Jules resided.

"Dean, are you all right?" Suma's voice broke me from my reverie.

"Sure. I was thinking about Magnus, and our kids. Suma, how's the academy coming along?" I asked, wanting to talk about something else.

"They broke ground on it around a month ago on Haven. Can you believe there's going to be a Gatekeepers' Academy? I'd hate to be a teacher there. Young ones from dozens of races from around the galaxy, all under one roof."

"Isn't that part of the point? Getting everyone together to work toward a common goal?" It had been Slate's idea, and after some serious deliberation, our makeshift Alliance of Worlds council had approved it.

"You don't throw a bunch of kids together and expect them to forget thousands of years of prejudice and issues passed down from generation to generation," Suma said, sounding older than her twenty-plus years.

"You're right there, but what if this new alliance sets everyone toward a new path? One that makes them not forget the old ways, but look toward the future, standing side by side with their neighboring systems instead of against them?" I said.

"Always the idealist, aren't you, Dean? Not everything can be solved by waving a treaty around. But I do think it was a good idea, even if Slate thought of it," she said with a smile.

"I heard my name," Slate said from a few yards away. "What did I do now?"

The door opened at the side of the building, and J-NAK emerged. "You may see your vessel. It is ready."

We all got up off the ground and gathered our supplies before heading to the entrance of the manufacturing building. I was excited to see inside. A place where a full ten-person lander could be built in two hours had to be interesting.

There were soft lights cascading from the ceiling, and I wondered if they were for our benefit or the robots'. Did robots need light? I'd have to ask W later. He was beside me, head tilting from side to side as he took in the sight of the space.

The ceiling opened, sections folding in smooth patterns until we could see the sky above. That was handy. My gaze dropped to the middle of the warehouse floor. The surface was the same metals as the streets had been: their version of concrete. A lander exactly like the ones we'd used at home was sitting there.

"It appears to be missing a few details," Suma said, and I noticed the dull exterior. The materials were different from ours; instead of a smooth, polished gray exterior, this was leaning toward a matte black, with no lines painted on or numbers designating the vehicle ID.

"As long as it does the job, I'm happy," I said, running a gloved hand along the surface of the lander. The door opened as I tapped the icon beside it, and I let out a low whistle. The seats were metal grates, definitely made for function, not comfort.

"Let's make this trip short. I don't know how long I can sit on something like that," Slate said, and Rulo grunted beside him.

"Humans. Always complaining." Rulo stepped in first, stacking our EVA helmets and packs in a rear storage compartment.

"Not all of us have armor on our butts," Slate retorted, getting a shove for his efforts from the large Keppe woman. At least she was smiling now. I'd never seen her so cranky before. I think she'd been excited to go searching for the missing Keppe exploration ship and hated the delay as much as I did.

"J-NAK, you didn't do this by yourself, did you?" I asked the lone robot in the warehouse.

"No. I had help." As soon as he said this, a red light flashed from the center of his body, and the floor spread open twenty yards past the ship. Out came dozens of mechanical arms and hovering drones. "They did most of the work. I oversaw the project."

Suma walked toward the collection of robots and turned to us. "Dean, we need to get these guys into our Alliance. Imagine the things we could do with just-in-time manufacturing like this. It's like our 3D printers, but far more advanced. It takes weeks for us to put together a vessel like this, and far more resources."

I wanted to tell her to be careful what she asked for. I wasn't sure we wanted a city of AI robots building anything on our worlds. Maybe we could offer a trade for their assistance, but I was already skeptical of a robot takeover, even if J-NAK seemed like a fair partner. Part of me knew it was being so accommodating because it needed our help.

"We'll talk about it later," I said.

"You have the location of the northern pole. You have the frequency Origin will be emitting. These functions are built into the lander as well. Should you encounter any resistance, there is weaponry attached to the vessel." J-NAK went inside and showed Rulo how to use it. The fact that the robots took our concept and blueprints, and automatically added weapons, concerned me again.

A few minutes later, the four-legged robot crawled out of the tight-fitting lander, and Rulo nodded to me, confident she could use the weapons with ease.

"Bring back Origin. Without Origin, this entire complex system will fail within three hundred years," J-NAK said. That sounded like a long time to me, but I suspected they'd been here for a lot longer than that.

"J-NAK, you're going to work on getting a patch for the portal stone while we're gone?" I asked.

"Yes. I will have your patch completed."

"Dean, I'm going to stay with J-NAK. I'd prefer to be near the stone and the Theos within while the robot works," Karo told me.

I was worried about our Theos friend, but didn't want to argue with him in this case. It might be better to have one of us behind, making sure J-NAK met his end of the bargain.

I waited as the others got on the lander, before turning to the robot and asking one more question privately. "What if we can't find Origin?" The words came out in a whisper, hardly loud enough for J-NAK to hear them.

"Then I am afraid you will not be leaving." The robot turned and walked away, leaving me with cold blood running through my veins.

I shut the door once inside the lander and gave Suma a smile as Rulo lifted the ship up and out of the manufacturing warehouse. The whole time, J-NAK's last words echoed in my mind.

You will not be leaving.

EIGHT

*T*he landscape didn't change much for most of the trip toward the pole. Robot cities stretched out before us, lights blinking below, the whole thing feeling empty and alone. If what J-NAK had told us was true, there weren't many intelligent robots thinking for themselves any longer. They'd reverted to a hive mind or autopilot, as it seemed. When Origin was in charge, controlling the world, would there have been thousands of robots on the streets and in the skies?

"Look ahead. We've found the border," Slate said from his perch beside Rulo at the front of the lander.

We neared the edge of the robot world and came into something completely foreign-looking on this planet. Greenspace.

"How is their pole so lush?" I asked. I'd visited a lot of planets, and not all of them had ice caps at the poles like Earth. But this was the greenest I'd ever seen.

"There could be a variety of reasons," Suma was quick to answer.

Slate cut her off. "Let's save the science for another time."

"Any sign of Origin?" I asked, doubtful we'd pick up a reading the second we entered the pole vicinity.

"Not yet," Slate said, and Rulo lowered the lander, getting our altitude closer to ground level. The landscape was beautiful: thick brushes of trees, all blue and deep green in color. Every now and then, they'd spread apart, unveiling a lake, various minerals giving the water colors I'd never dreamt of seeing.

Something beeped from the pilot's console, and I leaned over Rulo's shoulder to see a faint signal blinking for a second before disappearing.

"Looks like we have something," Rulo said, changing the lander's trajectory toward the icon, which for the time being had vanished from the console screen.

I was nervous and excited to get to Origin, and wondered if it really could be this easy. These robots had accomplished so much, but for some reason, they couldn't function at the poles. It was strange, because our ship was working just fine. It had something to do with their positronic brains and interconnected system.

"W, you holding up okay?" I asked, and the android nodded from behind me.

"I am well, Captain."

That was good to see. Why hadn't the robots created an android like W to complete this mission? I felt like there were a few missing pieces to the puzzle as we lowered toward the location where Origin had shown up on our sensors minutes earlier.

"Still nothing?" I asked, seeing no blinking light on the screen.

"Nothing. It was in this region, though," Slate said as Rulo found an opening in the trees and landed the ship on the surface. "Walk from here?" he asked.

"Yes. W, you have the sensors on your internal system, right? You'll know if we're near Origin?" I asked.

"Yes, Captain. I will know," he replied.

That was good enough for me. I'd really been hoping we'd see Origin on the sensors quickly, and pick it up within minutes of landing. It seemed nothing was ever as simply done as the best-case scenario.

We funneled out of the lander, leaving our helmets behind. Slate was the last one out, and he passed us weapons before closing the lander doors.

I took a deep breath inside the blue-leaved forest, finding it oddly comforting. The ground was hard here, thin blue grass rose a few inches off the surface, and I noticed a lake between the tall tree trunks to my left.

Slate's gaze darted about the copse. "There's no way the alien who took Origin would still be around, right?"

"We can't tell. There was nothing unusual from above, but the tree cover's pretty dense here," I said, looking toward the lake.

"Should we split up, cover more terrain?" Slate asked.

I contemplated this but settled on staying together. "Less to go wrong by sticking as a group. Dubs, what are you picking up?" I asked the robot.

"Nothing yet, but I think it's ahead." Dubs started forward, walking toward the water that had to be close to a kilometer away. Slate shrugged and went after the android. I grabbed Rulo's arm and leaned in.

"We have no idea how hostile these beings will be. They may not want to part with Origin. I have to make sure we're ready for anything," I said.

Rulo grinned, lifting her minigun. "I'll be ready, Dean. Don't worry about that."

"Good." Suma was ahead of us, and I hung back, walking with Rulo near the rear of our convoy. Tiny bugs hovered around me, attracted to my scent or blood. The others were waving arms around, trying to fend off the insects as well.

"Did you bring the bug repellant, boss?" Slate laughed from the lead position. I didn't think he'd be chuckling for long if they became worse.

We arrived at the lakeside a few minutes later, and I bent down, touching the water with a bare hand, letting my fingers submerge in the cool liquid. It was musty, swampy, and I jumped back, recalling the variety of water creatures that could possibly live beneath the red algae-covered surface.

"Why do you always do that?" Suma asked me.

"It's something I've always done, ever since I was a little boy. The first time I saw the ocean, I opened the car door before my dad was parked and ran to the water, feeling the urge to touch it. Ever since then, it's become a habit of mine. Don't you guys have a few behaviors you always do?" I asked. It was good to talk, to chat about ourselves to pass the time as we wound our way beyond the lake. I was hoping Dubs wouldn't find a source of Origin's signal in the water, and there was no indication that the robot overlord was anywhere underneath.

"I guess I twitch my snout when I'm nervous or excited… sometimes," Suma said.

"Sometimes?" Slate said from ahead. "Suma, you're either nervous or excited most of the time. I mean… I do find it endearing."

Suma laughed, and I watched as she attempted to keep her snout from wiggling.

"How about you, Rulo?" I asked the Keppe woman.

"I don't want to say," she said, too quietly for the others to hear.

"Come on. It can't be that bad," I told her.

"I have to clean my weapon four times after each use," Rulo admitted.

"See, that's pretty normal." I glanced at her, seeing there was more to it.

"I sing a song from my childhood while I do it. My

father taught it to me when I first got a gun, and he used to use the timing to show me how to remove and replace all the components. I still do it. I don't have to, but I choose to. It reminds me of him," she said, showing a softer side.

"You've never spoken of your parents before," Suma said.

"That's not common practice in my culture. Once a loved one is gone, you hold their memory inside you. If you speak of them, their essence leaks away, and you have a little less remaining of them," Rulo explained.

"That's strange," Slate called back.

"I think it's nice," Suma said. "You must hold their essences closely, Rulo."

The Keppe warrior smiled and nodded, but didn't add any further details.

"Doesn't anyone want to hear my thing?" Slate shouted down the line.

I took the lead on this one. "You work out when you're feeling caged? You like to eat fried food? You make bad jokes?"

He paused. "I do those things? I was going to say I have a habit of looking handsome."

We all laughed, but Dubs froze in his footsteps.

His eyes were red, and his voice wasn't his own. "*Behold the Origin. I see you. Find me on the platform.*"

"Well, that was unexpected," Slate said, tapping W on the chest.

Dubs' eyes returned to normal. "What did I miss?" he asked.

"Do you have a pin on Origin's location now, Dubs?" I asked the android.

"It appears I do. Another two point three kilometers. We're on the right track," he said. "Why are you all looking at me like that?"

"Origin spoke through you," I told him.

"That makes sense. It explains my missing thirteen seconds," Dubs said.

The lake ended, this end covered by large rocks and boulders. The water was even deeper red in tone here, and more of the small bugs droned around my ears as we passed through the treed region into an open field. Once clear of the forest, we spotted the ruins.

The grass was tall and turquoise, flowing like waves in the gentle breeze. The sun above was lowering beyond the horizon, and I assumed we'd be walking in the dark within the hour. From here, the distant structures were obviously worn down, almost like a crumbling pyramid. They had to be tall for us to see them from this far away.

My arms tingled as I imagined plucking Origin from this platform it mentioned and rushing back to the ship. I wanted nothing more than to be on our merry way. Oliter awaited, if J-NAK was able to accomplish the portal patch like he'd suggested he could.

"I have a feeling whoever stole Origin isn't around any longer," Suma said as she pointed across the fields.

"I think you're right, Suma. But that doesn't mean we shouldn't be prepared for the unexpected." Slate led us through the grass. There were fewer bugs hovering around us now that we'd moved beyond the lake's edge, and I was grateful for it. I glanced at my hands, seeing a few angry red welts rising from their incessant bites.

The grass was waist-high on Suma, and she struggled through it, where on Rulo, it only came above her knees, allowing her ease of passage. I was somewhere in the middle, but eventually, we all emerged from the field just as the sunset cast a red glow over the ruins. There were multiple smaller stone buildings, each with steps around them leading onto flat roofs. The entire village reminded me of a visit to Mexico in my early twenties.

But these rocks seemed shaped with a precision the ancient Mayans had lacked. "They appear to have been cut with lasers," Suma said, reading my mind. She was standing beside the first building, running a hand over the exterior.

Slate held his pulse rifle at ready; Rulo, at the opposite end of the group, held her minigun toward the structures. Paths joined the buildings, but weeds and grass grew through the stone walkways, telling me no one had been here to do maintenance in some time.

"Where's the platform? Dubs, what are you picking up on your sensors?" I asked.

W pointed to the epicenter of the ruins. "There."

I followed his finger, which aimed at the largest edifice in the area. Smooth steps were carved into the side. "Let's go." I ran forward, the others close behind.

There were no signs of the race that stole Origin, at least not of their physical bodies. There was ample evidence they had lived and even thrived here, with all the work they'd put into their village. I wanted to know what had happened to them and hoped we could solve the mystery before returning Origin to J-NAK at the robot city.

I paused at the bottom of the stairs and glanced up. There had to be at least forty stone steps, and I let Slate take the front position before hopping up after him. As expected, there was a platform on the top: a perfect square area with a stone ledge three feet tall. I placed a hand on Slate's arm to hold him back. In the middle of the platform was a box made of stone.

"That has to be him!" Suma exclaimed, and started for it.

The platform vibrated as she neared the container, and the second she touched it, I knew we'd been had.

NINE

The force field lifted up from the ledge around the dais, covering us in a red energy barrier. The instant it closed, W fell hard to the ground, like a puppet whose strings had been cut.

I rolled him onto his back, but blank dead eyes stared up at the sky. "Dubs! Are you there?"

He didn't reply.

"I'm sorry, Dean. I thought…" Suma started, but stopped when I shook my head.

"Any of us would have set it off. It's a trap," I told them.

"There has to be a way to get you guys out," Rulo said, and for the first time, I noticed she was still on the stairs. She hadn't entered the platform like we had.

"Thank God one of us had the common sense to be cautious," I said.

"Or slow," Slate mumbled from beside me.

"What kind of trap is this?" Suma asked, looking at the red barrier surrounding us.

"If I had to guess, this was set by the creatures who took Origin." I walked over to the middle of the roof and set a hand on the stone box. "Slate, help me with this," I said, and soon we slid the top slab off, revealing nothing but empty air.

"So they left this in case the robots found a way to

the pole, and this field deactivates all robots?" Suma asked.

"Slate, check your pulse rifle." I nodded to the gun.

"Dead." He tapped his earpiece. "Testing. You guys getting this?"

"Nothing. They've killed all our electronics inside the force field." I kicked the stone case, instantly regretting it. I sat down on the ledge of the container and ran hands through my hair. "There has to be a way to shut it down," I said, glancing at Rulo.

Suma took over. "If I was going to guess, whatever's powering this field would be inside the building we're standing on. Rulo, can you go inside and see if there's any power source down there?"

Rulo nodded firmly. "I'm on it," she said, running down the steps.

I looked over to W, who was in a heap of metal, and I hoped we'd be able to find a way to shut this down: not just so we could escape, but so he could be initiated again. He was a robot, but still an integral part of our team.

"I'm going to test the barrier." Slate walked over to the side of the platform and started to reach his finger toward the buzzing red wall.

"Stop!" Suma yelled. "Don't touch it, you big dummy. Take something and throw it."

Slate appeared to consider this, and he pulled a water bottle from his pack. It was almost empty, and he drained the last bit before pulling his arm away and throwing the steel bottle at the barrier. It bounced back with excessive force, the force field sparking brightly at the contact.

Slate held his hand up, staring at his fingers. "Good call, Suma."

I stayed seated, hoping Rulo would be able to shut the barrier's power source down sooner rather than later.

My eyes snapped open at the sound of Rulo's voice. "You guys have no idea how much fun that was." Her voice dripped with malice.

The barrier was gone, but Dubs was still deactivated, and my gun was dead as well. I stretched and woke the others. "How long have you been gone?" It was pitch black out; a few stars lit the sky, but they were few and far between, as clouds had rolled in.

"I don't know. Five hours or so?" Rulo said, staying back on the stairs.

"Did you do it?" Suma asked groggily.

I had the urge to run from the platform in case the field sprouted again, and I got as far as W's limp form before I stopped. "Slate, give me a hand."

He wiped sleep from his eyes and ran over, helping me slide the robot to the ledge.

Rulo didn't have to be asked to help, and together, the three of us hefted the robot onto the steps. "What do we do now? We can't lug him around all day," she said.

"Show me what you saw down there. There has to be a hint to Origin's real location," I said, and we left W lying on the top step, away from the ledge.

"I'll stay with W… you know… in case he starts again," Suma said, and Slate passed her his pulse rifle.

"If he activates, the gun might work. Otherwise, if anyone comes near you, hit them with it." Slate feigned swinging a bat, and Suma nodded.

I didn't love leaving Suma alone up there, but it might be safer. We hadn't seen anyone around, and the force field appeared to have been set up a long time ago.

"What's so bad down there?" I asked Rulo.

"It's not that it's bad, just tight. There are a lot of components inside too, most of which I have no clue about. Maybe we should have brought Suma," Rulo answered.

We were down the stairs in a few breaths, and the Keppe woman led us around the side of the structure, merging into an entranceway. There was no door to cover it, and the frame was arched smoothly. Inside, we were met with a hallway, and now I understood what had Rulo irritated. The corridor was narrow, and only about five feet high. Whatever race had built this place was small in stature.

"I think I should wait with Suma, boss," Slate said, starting to turn around. I grabbed him and pushed him forward.

"I don't think so. You're with us. If Rulo can fit, then you definitely can," I told him, and he grunted as he turned sideways to allow the walls to accommodate his proportions, which was hard when he was ducking low to avoid hitting his head.

Rulo laughed as Slate did just that, and I cringed at the solid thump noise his forehead made against a cross beam on the ceiling. I narrowly avoided hitting it too, and that made Rulo laugh again.

"It's so funny, isn't it?" Slate asked, rubbing his head.

"It would be funnier if I hadn't hit my own head about five times," she admitted. "This won't take so long now that I know where I'm going." The hall ended, and we had to choose left, right, or straight. I noticed a scratch in the stone wall. "I marked them. That's what took me so long. The entire inside of this pyramid is a maze, a labyrinth of tiny halls. Whoever made this place was demented, or they had a really sick sense of humor."

I noticed now that the pitch of the floor was rising and falling, meaning there were probably corridors above and below us, making for a convoluted 3D maze within the ruins. We followed Rulo's markings, and it still took us almost an hour to navigate into the central room where she'd turned off the barrier.

We entered the open space, Slate pouring into it and stretching his arms out. We all did, my spine cracking as I stood up straight. The walls were lined with technology, electronics softly beeping, and dim lights triggered as we entered.

"Pretty fancy for a place that looks straight out of an ancient civilizations textbook," Slate said, and I agreed with him.

"Why build rock buildings when you have this?" Rulo asked.

"Maybe they did this with the help of Origin?" I offered.

Slate tapped his chin like a professor contemplating a serious problem. "Almost makes sense. Couple holes in the theory, though. Why would Origin help them if they stole it? And why would Origin help set a trap?"

"I don't know. Maybe the secrets lie inside this building." I noticed the frayed wires in the center of the room; the computer screen was flashing. "Your work, Rulo?"

She smiled. "I didn't have any other way to shut it down. Kind of the only option."

Origin had to be nearby. W had interpreted a reading from this area, unless that was part of the trap. I began sorting through cabinets, and Slate attempted to access the computer files. He keyed something into the console, tapped a screen, then proceeded to get an energy burst attacking him from the wall of computers. Slate fell to the floor, his hair standing on edge.

"Oh, and don't touch the computers," Rulo said, receiving a glare from me. "What? It's only a little buzz."

I helped my friend up, and he dusted his pants off. "I'm fine, boss. It more surprised me than anything. Thanks for the heads up, Rulo. It seems whoever left this doesn't want anyone messing with it."

I took a moment and scanned the room, trying to decipher the puzzle. If Origin was inside this room, where could he be? "The power source. Origin has to be powering this place. Do any of these consoles have wiring?" We started searching for hardwired components, and just when I'd begun to assume the entire place was wireless, we found a line running from the left corner of the room into the center console that Rulo had destroyed.

"It's in here. It has to be," I said, stepping to the square system. It was the size of a fridge, and the one screen Rulo had damaged sat at chest level. I crouched behind it and noticed a seam. "Rulo, can I have your knife?"

It flashed out, and the hilt stretched out for me to grab a second later. I used the sharp edge to pry the metal backing off the unit, and there it was: a sphere the size of a volleyball. It hummed as tiny pinprick lights flickered on the exterior.

"Origin," I said, and I swore the lights flashed faster in response.

"You did it, boss. Let's get out of here. If we have to carry Dubs back, this is going to be a long enough night," Slate said, and headed for the exit.

We spent the next hour crammed into the narrow corridors, but eventually broke free and outside the structure. The world felt so open as we walked into the night air, and I took a deep breath, feeling like it was my first inhale in ages.

I clutched Origin in my hands, and so far, it hadn't done anything but hum with energy. The lights had dimmed, possibly conserving its energy. We ran to the stairs, and Suma met us halfway, immediately glancing to Origin in the dark night.

"You found it!" she shouted as she ran down the rest of the stairs to get a closer look. "This is what started the entire robot community? How is that possible? It's so… small and round."

Origin lifted from my grip and rose into the air, tiny thrusters sending it upwards. It hovered toward the top of the stairs, and we chased after it. Origin was our ticket out of here and through the portal. Without it, we were stranded, and I didn't want to have to find another way to get J-NAK to help us.

It stopped above the deactivated form of W, our pilot android, and a glow emerged from underneath Origin, shooting into Dubs. He sat up straight, his eyes red once again. "Greetings. I am Origin," W said in an unfamiliar voice. "Who are you?"

The others paused, each looking to me to answer the spherical robot speaking through our pilot. "I'm Dean Parker, and we're here to take you back to your city." I didn't want to elaborate until the robot replied.

"I've been helpless here for far too long. You've freed me," it said through W.

"You were stuck in that box?" Slate asked.

"I have been forced to power this temple's system for centuries."

"Who stole you?"

"They were a stocky carbon-based creature. Good with their hands, but not so great with their minds. They seized me to power their planned colony, but they couldn't survive here. They died out after a few generations," Origin told us. "They created a barrier at the pole, one that wouldn't allow my creations to cross the threshold. I suspect the blockade is no longer functioning."

That would explain how we were able to get through it with our ship, and why W didn't falter upon our arrival at the pole. There had to be more to the story, but at that point, I really didn't care. I only wanted to get back to J-NAK with their leader in hand. "Will you return with us?" I asked.

"Let us proceed," Origin said through W, and our android began to walk down the steps, his eyes still red, implying he was under the small hovering sphere's control. Origin floated above him, and soon we were all walking back toward our ship, a few kilometers away.

"You have done well." J-NAK reached for Origin, lights blinking quickly across its body as it picked up the smaller spherical robot. We'd made the lengthy trek to the lander in the dark. It was twelve hours after we'd first left J-NAK's city with the lander, and we were all tired, each of us grouchy and short-tempered.

Origin wasn't much to look at, yet it had arrived on this world and created everything we saw. Thousands of miles of robot cityscape, all started by the round energy-drained robot cradled in J-NAK's grip.

"You've found a way for us to leave safely?" I asked it, and J-NAK began to walk away from us. I chased after it and jumped in front of the robot, happy to see it actually stopped instead of bowling me over.

"I have. Proceed to the box we arrived in. It will lift you back." J-NAK opened a compartment on its side and pulled a device out. It was crudely finished and consisted of a panel, clear wiring soldered between conductors. On one side, there was a smooth, clear screen. I had no idea what I was looking at.

"What do we do with this?" I asked.

"Trigger it, set it on the table controlling your portal, and choose the symbol on this screen, not on the portal's. It will relay the correct information, and you will get to your destination safely. It is a Portal Modifier." J-NAK stepped around me and carried itself forward on its four legs, faster than I'd seen it move yet.

"Thank you for your assistance, Dean Parker… and others," Origin said from Dubs' speakers. The same light lifted from our robot, entering the sphere again. W continued to stand, though his eyes faded back to green.

"W, that you?" I asked the android, and his head turned to meet my gaze.

"It is I, Captain."

"Are you okay? Functional?" Suma asked him.

"I am operational," W said, not expanding on it.

Dozens of robots emerged from the shadows, and before I knew it, hundreds of hovering drones, scuttling dog-sized robots, and countless other mechanical shapes were following J-NAK as it transported Origin somewhere.

I didn't intend to stick around to find out what happened next.

"You got that, Suma?" I asked my Shimmali friend, and she grabbed the panel.

"Got it," she said, heading to Slate's side.

We made the quick trek to the elevator box, and W stopped short, turning back towards the manufacturing plant.

"What is it?" I asked him.

"Nothing. I only wonder what it's like to be part of a collective rather than being a solitary programmed positronic brain. I had a taste of it for the last few hours, and it was intriguing. Do you ever wonder the same thing?" Dubs' voice carried a wistful tone that caught me off-guard.

The entire idea of being connected to thousands of other minds horrified me, but I did understand where W was coming from. Here he saw interconnected robots, each operating solo, but also part of something larger. I hated the idea, but I thought it should be offered. "W, would you like to stay here?"

He stared off into the distance as the others entered the dark cube, waiting for us quietly. They were all exhausted, and I didn't blame them for shutting down right now. We were almost at our end on this world, hopefully.

"No, Captain. I have work to do. We must rescue Magnus and Natalia, as well as the children and the Keppe crew. It would be remiss of me to consider staying," W said.

"If you're sure. I'm happy to have you with us, W. You're part of our collective," I said, and he turned to me, giving me a slight nod before stepping past me and into the cube.

"J-NAK gave me the symbol for their world. I could always return, if someone brought me. Would you bring me if I later decide to be part of all this?" W asked.

"It would be my pleasure," I answered.

"Can we leave now?" Rulo growled.

"Yes." I rejoined them, and the cube once again moved without sensation. It wasn't long before the door opened to reveal the portal room high above the city.

Suma was the first out, and almost ran to the portal table. "Karo!" she exclaimed, waking the dozing Theos.

He rubbed his eyes and stood, towering over Suma.

"Hello, Suma. I take it you accomplished your task?" he asked.

"Did you ever doubt us?" Slate asked with a grin on his face.

"No, Slate, I did not." He clapped Slate on the shoulder, and I watched the Theos closely, noticing he seemed relaxed and happier.

"Everything go okay up here?" I asked him, and he nodded.

"These robots know their way around… everything, it seems." Karo turned to the table, and watched as Suma set down the Modifier J-NAK had given us.

"What's going on outside, boss?" Slate pressed against the far wall, staring toward the city below. Lights began turning on all around the region; buildings moved, as if extensions of a larger robot. Hundreds of drones took to the sky, buzzing past our portal room.

"I think Origin has been initiated. We better leave, Suma. Can you get this working?" I was nervous, and I didn't know why. It was almost as if an energy was cascading in waves through the city, the continent now, and I didn't want to be here when it coalesced.

"I'm on it." Suma pressed the panel device, and the stone powered up, glowing brightly along with the symbols on the clear walls. They burned bright blue, moving around like a screensaver on my old work computer, long before the Event.

"I'll choose the symbol for Oliter, and…" Suma started, and I peeked over her shoulder, making sure it was the right one. She didn't even question the double check, and when I gave her a nod, she readied herself. "Everyone good?"

"We're good," Rulo said, and the others stood in a

circle around the portal stone. The device was meant to correct any "crossed wires" the stones were sending between the portal stone's destination and the symbol for that world. We could only hope J-NAK knew what he was doing, but we had no choice. Even if we asked them to build us a vessel to fly out of here, we didn't know where we were or how long it would take to go home. This was our only shot.

"Please work," I whispered as Suma tapped the icon and everything went white.

TEN

We arrived inside the Keppe portal room, my heart pounding so quickly, I had to lean against the table. I'd half expected to wake in space, being sent into the expanse by the erratic stones.

Rulo grinned, obviously thrilled to be on her home planet. "What are you waiting for? I need something to eat," she said, and Slate ran after her.

"Come on, Karo. It's been a long day. Let's see what we can find out about Magnus and get some rest," I said, patting the big Theos on the back. Suma rushed ahead, and soon we were walking up white marble stairs into the main level of Lord Crul's mansion.

It looked much the same as it had when we'd arrived from our time on Sterona. Keppe people walked by us in their bland robes, a few greeting Rulo. She looked so different from them, wearing a white Gatekeeper suit and a broad smile. I could see why Magnus had been looking forward to three years among the Keppe crew. They could be fun to be around, and were a strong, loyal race.

A thin, bent-over Keppe man approached and whispered something to Rulo, too quiet for any of us to hear. He glanced at our group, disdain evident on his wrinkled face.

"Lord Crul wants to see us. Now." Rulo's posture stiffened, and she took the lead, walking with purpose and pride toward her leader's quarters. Instead of the study where I'd spoken to Crul in the middle of the night so long ago, we went to a larger space, more suitable for our entire group. Inside were refreshments, many familiar from our stint aboard *Starbound*. I saw a pink beverage on the table; Mary's favorite, and it made me miss her.

I had to get it together. It had only been a day, and who knew how long we were going to be gone? At the rate this mission had started, it was anyone's guess.

A chair swivelled to reveal a dark gray Keppe: Lord Eran Crul. His eyes danced as he met my gaze, and he motioned for us to sit. "Have a seat." His words translated, and we each relaxed on the soft seats. It was an informal room, a few pieces of muted art on the walls, all enhanced by soft yellow lighting. Slate moved a pillow from behind him and held it in his lap, hugging it close until he noticed me watching him. He set the cushion to one side and cleared his throat.

"Lord Crul," I said, breaking the silence, "thank you for meeting with us. What can you tell us about Magnus' disappearance?"

Crul drank from his cup and frowned. "First off, five hundred of my good people are missing alongside your friend and his family. This is not just a rescue mission of Magnus and Natalia. You'll do well to remember that." He flicked his stare to Rulo, who nodded and lowered her eyes.

I noticed W loitering at the doorway, and I waved him over to stand next to my chair. I wanted him to be watching and remembering every detail.

"We know that, Lord Crul. We'll hopefully be returning with the crew and ship intact, if at all possible. What can you tell us?" I asked again, noticing how zero details had emerged so far.

The door opened to reveal a familiar face. She walked by me and lightly clapped my arm with her hand.

"Kimtra, it's nice to see you again," I told the Keppe woman. She'd been an integral part of finding Polvertan and getting to Fontem's collection. She still had screens and electronics strapped to her arms.

"I wish it were under better circumstances. We can all catch up once our people are found. Here's what we know." She clicked a hand-held device, and an image appeared on the white wall. It showed Magnus' ship. "This is *Fortune*, the exploratory vessel Magnus is captaining." The 3D image rotated, showing a long, bulbous ship shaped like a peanut. "It holds over a thousand at max occupancy, but for the sake of the exploration mission, we didn't need a full militia crew."

"That may have been short-sighted on our behalf. It is standard procedure, but given the extreme nature of their mission, we should have sent him more prepared." Lord Crul tapped the arm of his chair as he spoke, a clear sign he was agitated.

"What the hell do you mean, 'extreme nature'?" My own agitation was increasing with each passing second.

Crul looked over to Kimtra, who answered for her leader. "They were heading to an unknown part of the galaxy. Uncharted, if you will."

"What did you hope to find?" I asked, trying to keep my anger in check. It wasn't going to do any good to be hot-headed. I needed to be on the same page as the Keppe to get Magnus and Nat back in one piece.

"Dean, we're tired of war, as I know you are. You're building something new with your Alliance…"

I cut Crul off. "Our Alliance. Remember, the Keppe were there on the ground level by our side."

Crul kept going. "As were the Shimmal" – he glanced

at Suma – "and the Bhlat." He almost spat out their name. "We want to discover new worlds beyond our previous reach, don't you understand that?"

I did and told him as much. "That's why we have the Gatekeepers, Lord Crul. Rulo is part of us, and we can explore as much as we need to…"

"Only with the help of the portal stones, which, from what I've been told, aren't going to be around forever," Lord Crul said, and I noticed his gaze darting to where Karo sat, before coming to focus on me.

Crul was informed; I had to give the old Keppe that. I felt like everything was being delayed, and I wanted to go over to Crul and squeeze the details from his mind. "Continue, please," I said through clenched teeth.

He motioned to Kimtra, who tapped her device again, and the image changed to a star map. "Magnus' crew sent us daily updates. Once they were past what we'd call 'charted space,' the messages came more infrequently, and we weren't sure our communication was even getting relayed to them. It didn't surprise us at all, seeing how we'd never been there, and they were reporting irregularities."

"What type of irregularities?" Suma interjected.

"A few minor things, but enough that they were adding up." Kimtra sped along the line of *Fortune*'s trajectory, and eventually, it stopped moving; a red light blinked near a planet. "This is where our mapping ended, but we did receive a few more sporadic transmissions, spread out until almost a month ago."

A month. That was about the right timing as when I'd last spoken to Magnus. He hadn't mentioned anything out of the ordinary.

"And what did you learn from those transmissions?" Karo asked, finally engaged in the conversation. He was leaning forward, his white hair contrasting against his black uniform.

Kimtra stared at the Theos for a moment, probably unsure what he was, and answered him. "They found a system without a star. Four planets were orbiting something, but the star that had to have been there was…"

"Vanished?" I said out loud, even though I hadn't meant to.

"That's right. We didn't hear from them again," Crul said. "We don't have the exact location of this system, because the map ends here." He motioned to the planet where the red light blinked on the 3D map.

"Why have you waited to do anything about it?" I asked.

"Look, Parker, we have a lot going on. Billions of people, colonies, at least a dozen exploration vessels scouring the universe in search of answers and undiscovered life. We hoped they would resurface and everyone would go on, happy and healthy."

"But they haven't." I put my hands behind my head and flopped on the chair, letting out stale air from my lungs.

"But they haven't," Crul reiterated.

"How quickly can we make it there?" I asked point-blank.

"They took a roundabout way to arrive at that point." Kimtra showed us on the map. "If you cut this way, avoiding system 8X36, you can get there in twelve months."

I stood up. A cushion flew to the side, knocking my drink over. "Twelve months! We can't wait twelve months. There has to be another way!" My head was reeling, thinking of a way, a portal, a wormhole, anything that would allow us fast access to Magnus' last known location.

Suma raised her hand, her snout flipping back and forth. "Dean. I know of a portal closer to there, but the people are… a little odd. At least, that's what my research tells me."

I didn't like the sounds of that. "How close?" I asked, knowing she'd understand what I meant.

"Two months with our standard hyperdrive. The world is the farthest portal world on record in that vicinity. It's listed as the edge of the universe in the study material," Suma said.

"The edge of the universe." Karo's eyes were alive as he spoke. "Dean, what other choice do we have?"

"None, it appears. Tell us what you know about these people on the other end of the portal," I urged Suma, not excited to again venture through the stones so quickly after they'd failed us. I only hoped the device J-NAK gave us would continue to work.

Suma stood and began telling the room everything she knew about the race nicknamed the Traders.

Someone knocked on my door, and even though I was running on fumes, I wasn't sleeping quite yet. My thoughts were drifting over the day's events and where tomorrow would take us. At least we were one step closer to discovering where Magnus and Natalia were, and that kept me going.

I was in the same room Mary and I had shared with our newborn Jules a couple of years ago while we waited to go home through the Keppe portal back to New Spero, and the late-night knock was oddly familiar.

Last time, it was Rulo, and as I opened the door after

covering up with one of the beige robes everyone seemed to be wearing, I was startled to find Kimtra waiting there for me to answer.

"Kimtra, what is it?" I asked. One of the devices strapped to her arms translated quietly, and she pointed inside my room. After peeking my head out the doorway and scanning the residential halls to find them empty, I waved her in and turned on the light to a comfortable level.

She closed the door behind her, and I could instantly tell she was nervous, not her normal cool, calculated self.

"Dean, I'm worried about a few things," she said, and I motioned for her to have a seat. The room was like a suite you'd find in an expensive hotel. The bed was in a separate room, then a comfortable living area with space to hold half a dozen guests. She perched on a couch, and I sat opposite her on a hard chair, leaning toward her instinctively.

"Tell me," I urged her, anxious for what she had to divulge. I still hadn't slept, and knew we were getting an early start tomorrow, but I'd rather have all the details I could than jump into something missing some pertinent facts.

"The portals are failing, as you've indicated. Perhaps *Fortune*'s disappearance is linked in some way?" She said it like a question, but I didn't see how that was possible, and told her as much. "I'm not sure. If something that ancient isn't functioning any longer, then what else out there could falter?"

She was the scientific and mathematical one, so her random speculation caught me off-guard. "Kimtra, you understand this stuff far better than I do. The stones are failing because of the Theos. From what we know about them, the Theos are inside, powering them. When they banished and destroyed the Iskios, isolating them on the crystal world, the Theos thought they were doing the universe a great favor.

"When the Iskios were gone, suddenly, there wasn't room for the other end of the spectrum. Black holes and other dangerous phenomenon were popping up, and the only way to regain Balance was to make this ultimate sacrifice."

"They put themselves into the stones, thus regaining the Balance again. Yes, Dean, we know this, but why are they leaving now?" Kimtra asked.

I'd thought a lot about this, and had lengthy discussions with Karo about the subject. "Karo thinks that because the Iskios are gone for good, thrown into another time and place by the Shifter, the Theos, even dead, need to disappear forever to restore universal Balance. They aren't alive as you or I are, but they do possess an energy."

"This must be hard on Karo," she said, and I nodded. Few knew that he was the last remaining Theos alive, but a limited amount of Keppe had been told in secrecy.

"What else? There has to be more for you to look so worried," I told Kimtra.

She ran a hand over her smooth dark head, her teal snake eyes staring at me. "There have been a few reports from other races over the last decade about the area Magnus went into."

That had my interest piqued, and I cracked my fingers nervously. "What do you mean?"

"We aren't the first vessel to attempt an exploratory mission into that galaxy. Actually, we're the fifth in our records," she said quietly.

My heart raced as I considered her statement. "So why is that important?"

"Only one of the other race's vessels ever made it home."

No wonder she was so worked up. I had a bad feeling they hadn't told Magnus about this risk. "What, so you decided to use the human captain to do your dirty work, because who cares if Magnus and his wonderful family die in the name of science?" I was standing up, shouting the last bit.

Kimtra looked abashed and cowered in her seat. The Keppe were such a strong and proud race that the action was unexpected. "Dean, you have every right to be angry. I was fuming when I found out Crul changed their mission plan. I wanted to reach out to them, and even tried a month ago, right when the transmissions began failing," she said.

"Convenient timing." I believed her, but wanted to take my anger out on someone, and she was the only other person in the room. "What's wrong with the system? Why's everyone going missing?"

Kimtra met my gaze, her unblinking eyes staring hard into mine. "We don't know. The ship that left claimed an energy abnormality, and they hightailed it away."

"What about the story of the missing star? Do you buy it?" I asked.

"If a star went supernova, the planets wouldn't have much chance of survival. Either way, the supernova went. But from what little we've pieced together, these worlds still exist. It doesn't add up," Kimtra said.

"But they don't have any life on them, correct?" I asked, doubtful a planet with no star would survive very long.

"We can't be certain. If a star vanishes, perhaps a world can survive for a brief time, depending on how advanced they are. We can only speculate."

"And if you were to make a hypothesis?" I asked.

Kimtra shook her head. "I'd have to say that nothing lives in that solar system any longer."

These details were only enough for me to know this much: Magnus had unknowingly traveled into a dangerous region, one that the Keppe knew to be risky. It was shaping up to be the Bermuda Triangle out in space, and I was going to be chasing him down and endangering my team at the same time.

I didn't have a choice. We were going to find out what happened to Magnus and *Fortune*.

But I still sensed more. "What else?"

"The Traders. They're unique. Be wary of them, Dean. Don't make any deals you can't accept, because even though they appear simple, they have more technology than any other race, including the rich and powerful Garo Alnod, and even the Bhlat. Do not underestimate the Traders," she warned.

The cautioning words set off alarm bells. "What's with everyone's bargains? Magnus needed help to find Mary and me, and the Keppe made Magnus trade three years, and now he's missing with his family. I land on a damned robot-run world and have to trade the return of their founder in order to leave. Whatever happened to good old-fashioned helping out a neighbor?" It used to be the same way on Earth, and I supposed it was going to be the same throughout this universe. Nothing came without a price, a cost, a deal.

"That's the way of things, Dean. Don't be naïve," Kimtra said. I knew I'd come a long way since the Kraski cubes had lifted everyone away from Earth years ago. But deep down, I was still the same good old American boy who loved baseball and running his own accounting business.

Kimtra stood up, and I walked her out. "Thanks for telling me. I appreciate it."

She turned and smiled. "Find them, but watch yourself. There's something in that system that won't want you to leave, whether it's sentient or not."

She started to walk away, and I had to ask, "What happened with you and Admiral Yope?"

"Too many secrets, Dean. Too many secrets," she said, and kept walking.

ELEVEN

"How'd everyone sleep?" I asked as we got together in a common room, cordoned off for our use.

Slate was the first to answer, in the midst of doing a set of push-ups. The guy was always working out and making me think I should be too. "Like a baby, after a day playing with blocks and bouncing in one of those chair thingies."

"I think you spent too much time babysitting Jules, buddy." I was glad to see my friend cracking jokes. I needed him to be focused and diligent as always, and he performed best when he was happy.

"Karo?" I asked the tall gray-skinned Theos.

"I slept a little, Dean. How about you? You look like you've been up all night," Karo said, and he was right.

"I got a couple of hours," I lied. After Kimtra left, I'd typed a note to Mary that went on for longer than I'd anticipated, filling her in on every detail I had. I used a code that only she had the key for, so no one would be able to intercept and decipher the message. Mary was going to be angry with the Keppe too, but I'd asked her to keep it in her pocket for the time being.

Then I'd used the Keppe relay system to send the message to her. It would take a day or so to arrive on New Spero, where she was with Jules and Maggie. By then, I hoped to be on a ship heading away from the

Traders' world.

"Sure. Suma?" Karo asked the young Shimmali woman. She appeared animated, and I noticed a pot of Keppe-style coffee.

"I've been up for an hour, and I've been drinking this… stuff. Dean, you want a cup?" she asked, and I nodded, happy for something to stimulate my brain and make my body feel energetic, even if it was a mask.

W stood at a console, typing away, and I didn't bother asking what he was doing. Rulo wasn't there, and she was the last of our group to arrive. The portal stone was beneath the building, and we all wanted to get suited up and transport to our next stop, before starting the real search for *Fortune*.

The hot drink was slightly bitter, but strong on the tongue, and I sipped at it while eating some Keppe fruit. The world was beyond hot, like Arizona in the middle of summer, all the time. The food they grew outside was hearty and resilient. Everything had a thick protective peel or casing on it, but once you got to the sweet meat within, it was delectable.

I hadn't told the others the news Kimtra had dropped on me a few hours ago, and wouldn't until we were at least gone from Oliter. There were too many hotheads here, and I didn't want this mission blowing up before it began. I already felt like the entire trip was taking far too long, and we were only beginning.

Rulo came from the far end of the hall, with three Keppe trailing behind her. She looked every bit the warrior she was at that moment: armored suit over her large build, her black skin gleaming, her eyes colorful and attentive. For someone so bulky, she moved with a grace that betrayed her size, and I was glad to have her on our team as well as part of our recently expanded Gatekeepers.

The Keppe behind her dropped three packs to the floor with a clunk, and I recalled how much gear Hectal had brought to the tropical island where we found Polvertan. If there was one thing about the Keppe, they were always prepared for whatever came their way. That was why it was a little disconcerting to know they'd purposely sent Magnus and the others head-first into danger.

I peered over to Slate, who rolled his eyes. "Maybe we should find Hectal. I don't want to carry all of that."

"We'll assist you, Slate," Karo said.

W walked over to Rulo's side and reached for a pack handle, easily lifting it in the air. "Captain, I am able to carry these if you so please."

I grinned at Slate, and he laughed in return. "Good call on bringing the robot, boss. Finally, I can save myself some pain."

Rulo glanced over at me, holding my gaze for a second before gesturing to the rest of the group. "The portals await us. Let's get on with this," she said, and we followed her through the white marble halls, down the stairs, past the guards, and into the portal room.

Suma held up the device J-NAK had created for us. "Are we going to use this?"

Karo knelt at the glowing stone, and when he touched it, the crystal dimmed and pulsed faintly. "I suggest we do. I'm not sure how long they'll be around." Karo didn't have to tell us who *they* were.

Suma lowered the panel, activated the table and screen, and together we searched for the icon Suma knew to belong to the Traders world. They were actually named something else, but from what Suma understood, everyone called them some version of the word, and never their race's real name. It was simple enough for me.

Their symbol found, we switched to the Modifier, matching the icon.

Our mixed group stood around the portal stone and table, wearing our EVA suits, weapons quickly in hand, with enough supplies for three months. I really hoped it would be less time, but one thing I'd learned was that things rarely worked out like you wanted them to.

Suma waited for me to do the honors, and I tapped the icon, silently urging the stone to bring us where we needed to go. When the light lowered again, dozens of creatures hurried into the strange new portal room.

I jumped away, and so did Suma, leaving Rulo and Slate to step forward, each of them raising their guns. "Stop where you are!" Slate shouted, and we didn't know if the locals understood him or not. They held firm, and I got a good look at them.

Junk was everywhere. Metal bits stuck to their clothing; the walls of the room were covered in welded cast-off material, forming into the symbols and hieroglyphs like every other portal room. They were oddly humanoid: short, stocky, and pale with bulbous noses, like gnomes who had a penchant for too much ale. Every one of them wore outfits comprised of miscellaneous garbage, but when I looked closer, I saw steel in their gazes. These weren't seven simple little dwarfs, they were hard negotiating Traders, and each of them also had an assortment of jumbled weaponry on their bodies.

"What do we have here?" one of them asked, a woman if I was judging her right. Her hair stuck out of her makeshift helmet, dirty blonde like a scarecrow made of hay after a windstorm.

"You speak English?" I asked, taking the lead.

"We're Traders, human. Do you think we wouldn't have the language modifications imbedded into us?" she asked, her voice as gnarled as an old tree root. She let out a series of other words, some I recognized as Mandarin and Spanish. Those modifiers were quite impressive.

"That makes sense," I said, somewhat startled that this rag-tag group of beings would have the finances to configure the modifications. I'd investigated the surgery, and it didn't come cheap. It was usually left for the patrons of places like Bazarn Five, the wealthiest of the universe. Perhaps these Traders, despite appearances, were among them. "We've come to ask for your help. May we speak with someone in charge?"

The woman was obviously annoyed. "What makes you think I'm not in charge, human?" The Traders around her chuckled, their metal jangling around as their chests heaved. Their laughter was not appealing.

"If you are, then I'd like to speak to you," I suggested. Suma was close beside me, watching them all with interest. We formed a line now on one side of the portal table, the Traders on the other. Rulo and Slate flanked our group, and their weapons were raised. None of the Traders had reached for guns, but I knew better. They had some defense mechanisms on their side; otherwise, they wouldn't be so calm and casual with our arrival. "Guys, let's lower our weapons." I said the order from the corner of my mouth, and Slate did as I asked, followed by Rulo a good two seconds later.

"I guess I know which one of you is in charge. What an interesting group to be traveling together." The woman stepped closer and gazed down the line, from Slate, to Dubs the android, to Suma, whose snout was raised behind her helmet's shield. She skipped over me and stopped on Karo. "Now what in the wise universe is this beautiful creature?"

I quickly responded before anyone else could. "He's

Tralfamadorian from far away. You wouldn't know them," I said, using the alien name from Vonnegut's most famous book.

She must have believed me because she didn't question it. "And a Keppe warrior, complete with a scar on her face. How original," the Trader said with amusement. I'd been there the day Rulo got the injury while we were rescuing Slate on Sterona. None of us would ever forget that time, especially Rulo, who was reminded each time she saw her reflection. She claimed it did nothing to hinder her beauty, and I suspected few would argue the point.

"Come. If you seek help, you must have great items for trade." She waved us forward, and Slate tugged my arm, taking the lead. The other Traders formed two lines, creating a walkway to the exit of the room. They jumped frantically, junk clattering on their bodies as they did what could only be described as a jig. It was an unsettling bunch. I'd been around a lot of menacing aliens, but seeing a group of gnomes with garbage strapped to their backs had to win the prize for most unique.

Once through the doorway, I found myself in a tunnel. Lights sat in random spots on the floor, and on the walls of garbage. It was literally a corridor built out of discarded trash, mostly mechanical pieces from God knows what. It was like the world's worst hoarder's house, and we were walking through the only open spot to exit outside. The ceiling was short, since the Traders didn't reach over five feet. One of them had a hat with six propelling fan blades on it, and the odd time, one of the blades struck a jutting piece of debris.

"This is terrible," Slate said to me as he ducked low to avoid hitting his head. He was about a foot and a half too big for the corridor. I felt even sorrier for Karo and Rulo, who were bent so far over, I could almost feel their discomfort. The tunnels had multiple openings. Every now and then, we'd veer off the main direction and enter a separate corridor, each as claustrophobic as the previous.

"Hurry," the woman Trader said, leading us through the maze and, finally, past a doorway and into an open space.

"I never thought I'd see the sky again," Slate said, loudly enough for everyone to hear.

"It's been ten minutes," Suma rebuked.

"Easy for you to say. You're as short as the tinheads here," Slate said, and I cuffed him on the arm in warning.

"Don't insult them. We need their help," I whispered, and he shrugged in apology.

We were in a courtyard of some sort, hills of garbage piled high around us. It was as if the entire world was a dump. I was grateful for the EVA suit and the fact that I could breathe recycled air instead of the waste around us. A dark red star beat toward us, large in the sky, and my suit beeped as it accommodated the heat with some cool air.

"Can we talk now?" I asked the Trader. She was alone in the courtyard, but as I looked toward her, I saw the minute robotic sentries placed around the yard. Red lights blinked from all around us, and I expected there were at least two dozen weapons aimed directly at us, some of the others likely oblivious to the threat. I could tell Slate and Rulo weren't among those as their heads surveyed the hills, and they gripped weapons of their own at their sides.

"We don't talk here. Don't you know anything of us, human?" she asked, again laughing, metal flaps on her pants clinking like air vents on the fritz.

"Then…" I didn't have a chance to finish my question as a ship lowered from out of nowhere to land on the compact dirt ground. It was the polar opposite of everything else we'd seen in our short tenure on the planet. Where the locals were short and cluttered, this ship was smooth, elongated, and pristine. It didn't fit.

"Welcome to the Marketplace. You may call me Broker," she said as a ramp lowered to the ground with a soft touch. Lights lined the incline, guiding us into the sleek ship. It was about forty feet long, half the length of the courtyard.

"We need to procure one of these," Suma said to me as we entered the vessel. It was state-of-the-art. Even the flooring seemed expensive, and inside Broker's vessel, there was none of the garbage we'd seen all around us out there.

"You can have it," Broker said. "It would only cost you around a million credits."

Slate coughed at the amount, and I didn't blame him. We were getting three hover trains on New Spero for less.

We followed Broker past various other Traders, these ones wearing the same clothing as she, and she led us to a passenger seating area on the vessel. I stood at the window, staring out at miles and miles of debris. It seemed I wasn't far off my assumption that the planet was a dump.

"Relax here. We'll be at our destination soon," the gnarled voice said, and she turned to walk away.

"Broker, we don't have a lot of time. We'd like to start talking now," I called to her.

She didn't stop walking. "In due time." The door shut behind her, and I assumed it locked simultaneously.

"This was unexpected." I really hadn't known what we'd find on their world, nor had Suma's brief studying of them told us enough.

"They're going to be tough negotiators, Dean. Stand

your ground. Don't give away anything you can't afford to lose," Suma cautioned.

"Boss, what do we even have to trade?" Slate looked at the bags W let settle to the ship's floor.

"Captain, I haven't checked inside yet. Would you like me to catalog the supplies for you?" Dubs asked.

"Sure, let's have a peek," I said.

Rulo sat, setting her minigun across her lap, and she watched as we opened the first pack the Keppe had provided us. It was stuffed full of food packets, some dehydrated, others fresh. Cases of water lined the bottom.

"Anyone mind if I grab that brown package there?" Slate asked, and I quickly shut the pack before he could snatch it.

I tapped my face shield and laughed at him. "You do remember this is on, right?"

"Of course. I was going to save it for later, that's all. What else do we have?" He changed the subject.

Suma opened the next pack. "This one's nothing but weapons. W, you might want to be careful with it."

There was a blue energy field around the various guns and ammunition inside the pack. "Good thing it has a built-in shield. Rulo, can you warn us next time that we're hauling around enough punch to destroy a small city?"

She leaned forward. "You have enough ammunition to decimate a small planet in there."

Slate was reaching toward it, and once again, he was cut off by Suma's quick reflexes. "You guys are no fun," he said, moving for the third bag. Survival gear packed the bag to the brim: tents, fire-starting supplies, spare oxygen tanks, face masks, first aid, and anything else we could possibly need, except something to trade for a ship.

"Why hadn't I thought of this?" I asked, cradling my helmet between my gloved hands.

Rulo spoke, her words translating for me. "Because you don't need to. That's what being a part of a team is." She pulled a datastick from a tight pocket on her armored suit.

"What's that?" Suma asked.

"Something they're going to want," Rulo said.

"Information?" Karo asked.

"If there's one thing they desire, it's more stuff. One of our vessels stumbled across a special location on a mission. It appears there was a massive battle there, and they found over two hundred derelict ships in the system. Some were partially intact, but the exploration ship didn't have the means to salvage anything. Plus, that's not really our way. We saved it for just such an occasion," Rulo answered.

I was genuinely astonished. "That's perfect. What if they need proof it's there?"

"Footage included. Broker will be drooling by the time you show her this. Don't get settled in. We won't be here long," Rulo said.

TWELVE

I paced around the circular room, walking the perimeter for the tenth time. Floor-to-ceiling windows stretched around the entire floor, giving me a view of their planet below. It was strange seeing it from this vantage point. I stared to the ground a couple hundred yards beneath us, where the garbage stopped in a perfectly straight line. Beyond it was fresh green grass, and an enormous body of water. I spotted at least a hundred of the Traders walking amidst the field, some playing at the beach.

They didn't appear to be wearing metal suits made of refuse there, and I wondered what they thought of their neighbors over the fence. Maybe the junk-covered clothing was only their work uniform, and the others were spending time with their families after hours. Judging by how our negotiation was going, Broker wasn't going to fill me in on the details.

Rulo was playing the hard-nosed one, while Suma was hinting at the great power of the Gatekeepers becoming allies of the Traders. Evidently, they'd already been tipped off about the location of the long-ago battle and were heading there as we spoke.

I wasn't buying it. The datastick was in Rulo's pocket, and I'd noticed Broker's gaze wandering to it at least half a dozen times in the last three hours. She wanted that information, but they were proving to have more guile than I anticipated.

"It isn't going to work." Broker was at one end of a long table, Rulo and Suma at the other. It was another tactic. Broker's side stood two feet taller, and she had to look down on them, like a judge in court. It was all over the top, and I was getting tired of the charade.

I crossed the room and stood beside the table. Slate and Karo watched with interest from their seats overlooking the sea below.

"We need a ship. A fast one. According to you, you have dozens of such ships for sale. Make an offer. If you really don't want this datastick, tell us what you want. We can deliver it for you. I'll sign a contract. I'll get the Empress of the Bhlat to hand deliver it to you, if that's what it takes!" I shouted, banging my hand on the tabletop.

Broker's pale gray eyes widened, and she forced a smile, showing crooked yellow teeth. "That won't be necessary. I'd bargain, only you don't have anything I need."

I sighed out, and it hit me. I did have something: the Inlorian bars that Sergo had stolen. In all the action of the past few days, they had totally slipped my mind. I had ten of them in the rear compartment of the EVA I was wearing.

I closed my eyes for a second, opening them before raising a hand to silence Broker's rambling. "What do you know of the Inlor?" I asked, and she instantly stopped speaking.

"Very little. There isn't much to know." Broker was leaning toward me, and I could almost see the drool forming in the corners of her mouth.

"Interesting. I'm friends with them now. They're joining our Alliance of Worlds. Signed up a few days ago." I turned, glancing at Suma, who was looking at me inquisitively.

"Is that so?" Broker asked. "What of it?"

"Have you heard of an Inlorian bar? It's a dark blue metallic block being processed on their home world. They stumbled on it, and apparently, it's become quite the hot commodity." I left the bait and spun slowly back to her.

"What are you saying, human? You know where to find one of these?" Broker asked.

"I heard they're going for… what… five hundred a pop?"

She appeared visibly shaken at the number, her greed nearly oozing from her pale skin. "I doubt they would go for any more than two hundred," she said, trying to deflate the value in case I actually did hold on to one of them. It was a solid effort on her part. Negotiating was second nature to her, but I thought myself well-trained over the last few years.

"Whatever you say, Broker. You'd know better than me. What if I told you I had one on me right now?" I asked her.

"I'd say you were a liar." The answer came out quickly, and with a sharp tongue.

I leaned in to Suma and asked her to open my pocket and pull one out. We were far enough away that Broker could do nothing but lean toward us, trying to hear the faint words. Suma did so quickly, her own black eyes wide as she passed it to me, doing up the pocket where Broker would have seen another nine lined up.

I held it in my palm. The dark blue bar didn't look like a lot, and it was lightweight in my hand. The Trader was pressed so far forward, I thought she might topple over the table.

"It has to be a fake," she said.

"Why? You know nothing of us, yet here I am with an Inlorian bar, ready to bargain with you. Now, how about we see the hangar with our options?" I watched her face change from anger to excitement, and then to resignation. I instantly knew she was going to make the deal, even if she didn't want to cave on value. She didn't own any of the metal being sought after for weapons charges, and I expected she'd be able to procure even more than the going market value to a desperate buyer, if she didn't keep it for herself.

"Fine. This way," she said. With a wave of her hand, a yellow-framed doorway appeared a short distance from our group. I could see space ships on the other side of the door when I peered through the energy border.

"What is that?" I asked. It was obviously some portal or gateway, but it was unlike any I'd ever seen.

"Trader secret. Come on. I have other deals to make after this one," she said stubbornly. She walked through the glowing opening, and Slate, Karo, and Dubs trailed behind. Rulo went next, and Suma set a hand on my arm.

"Dean, I think we need to see what else they have to offer. I expect them to have a lot of… interesting tools to trade," she said, looking at the doorway that had appeared in the air from nothing more than a wave of a hand.

"You're right, Suma. If there's one thing I learned from my dad while car shopping, it's that you negotiate each deal separately. Let's get the ship first, then see what's next." I let Suma take the lead and followed her out of the meeting room into a huge hangar. There were around twenty vessels in the large open-air room, in varying sizes and shapes.

"That's a Padlog ship." Slate pointed to a bug-shaped vessel.

A shiver trickled up my spine, ending at my neck as I saw the ship beside it. It was a white Kraski vessel. Slate must have seen it at the same moment, because his rifle aimed toward the ship in a flash.

"Don't worry yourselves. There are no Kraski here. All of these ships belong to us, and they've been thoroughly scanned and sterilized," Broker said. The way she said "sterilized" made me imagine they'd found a few unsavory things on board over the years.

The sky had a greenish tinge, and dark gray clouds rolled above, promising rain. The instinct to jump into a ship and race out toward Magnus' last known location overcame me, and I didn't want to see the rest of the vessels, even though Rulo was walking the line, knocking her knuckles against some of the hulls.

"We'll take this one." I pointed to the Kraski ship, mostly because we knew how to fly them, since all our own fleet was structured after the model.

"Are you sure, Dean? Maybe there's something a little… more stylish?" Slate recommended.

"We know this one inside and out. Now's not the time to be experimenting. Even at full speed, we're going to be aboard for two months." My team was huddled around me while Broker stood a ways away, pretending to not hear our private discussion.

"We'll need more supplies," Karo said. "I didn't see any pizza inside the Keppe food pack."

I couldn't tell if he was kidding or not. "Broker, what's the price?"

"You will give me the Inlorian bar, and I'll take the datastick off your hands, even though we don't need it," she said, eying Rulo's pocket.

I wasn't going to call her on it. "Deal." I passed the bar over to her and nodded to Rulo, who gave the gnome-like Trader the stick.

"Okay, next… We're going to need a few things. Food, water, and," I lowered my voice, "I want to see the hidden room where all the gadgets are held."

Broker hefted the light bar in her palm, her smile oddly terrifying. "I may have some items of interest. Come."

Twenty minutes later, and a quick trip through two more energy doorways, Suma and I entered a private chamber. Once again, I was amazed at how different it was from the rest of the trash-covered world. What we found was a collection that would make Sarlun jealous. On Shimmal, Mary and I had the pleasure of seeing his antiquities from around the universe. Items that had belonged to long-dead races lined his shelves, and that was where we'd first encountered the shadow that we were tricked to think was a Theos. Were we ever wrong.

"Dean?" Suma got my attention. I'd been staring toward the edge of the room with a blank look over my face.

"Yes. What do we have here, Broker?" Rulo had expressed concern in not bringing either her or Slate along for this final bargain, but I didn't think it was necessary. These Traders were strange, but I didn't particularly think Broker was dangerous. If she was, and she suspected I had more Inlorian bars on me, we'd probably all be dead already. It wasn't a good way to keep up a reputation with future business partners.

"We have things from your wildest imagination. I don't let just anyone in here, I'll have you know," she said, and I'd bet she was telling the truth. Broker grasped the blue metal bar, and her gaze kept drifting to it.

The walls were covered in hooks; devices of all sizes and natures hung behind energy barriers. They were all labeled in a language I couldn't read. Suma was already walking along the perimeter of the room, stopping every now and then to take a closer look at something before moving on.

In the middle of the floor, five floating tables held more product under containment fields. This was the real showcase. I walked over to it, seeing a bunch of unfamiliar contraptions. "What do they do?" I asked.

"What do you need?" Broker countered, and she had a good point. I wasn't exactly sure what I was looking for, but it would help to consider what we might end up needing.

Thinking of Fontem's time-travel apparatus, I decided to ask, "Time travel?"

She looked me in the eyes and let out a shrill laugh. "If I knew I was dealing with a crazy person, I would have asked more for the ship. There are a lot of things in existence, but time travel is not one of them. Unless it's naturally occurring in space, which we have no way of harnessing at this point."

"How about cloaking?" Clare had made some serious contributions to hiding our ships and people, but some of the material was quite cumbersome.

"That we have." Broker led us to the far corner and pointed at the shelf. "These are cloaking devices. The large one can be adapted onto your ship, but will only work for a limited time before needing to be charged. The same goes for the hand-held." There were four of the more compact ones.

"How long to fit the ship with it?" I asked.

"Not long," she answered.

"Get started," I said, taking a leader's tone. I was a wealthy tycoon on a shopping spree, and I wanted her to feel the pressure.

She hesitated before waving a yellow energy doorway open. Two male Traders entered, listening to her whispered orders, and they left moments later with the cloaking drive in hand. "It will be done." Broker tapped some notes on a tablet, and I pointed to the portable cloaking units.

"Let's take two of those too," I added, and soon we had a small pile of tools in a hovering cart.

Broker was about to leave the room when I pointed to the doorway she'd created. "I want one of those too. The gateway magic."

"You don't have enough credits." She was quick to assume.

"Source me one of those, show us how it works, and I'll pay," I said with an arrogant tone. She needed to think she was dealing with someone who wasn't a pushover.

"It'll be another two Inlorian bars." I saw a sparkle in her rheumy eyes.

"For all of this," I motioned to the cart, "the food, and the gateway maker, you'll get three bars." I stuck my hand out, and she eyed it suspiciously.

She shook my hand, setting the tablet down. "Deal."

THIRTEEN

Two months. It was going to be another two months before we even made it to the system where Magnus had been lost. W was piloting the Kraski ship, and we'd been gone from the Traders' world for half a day.

Rulo, Slate, and Suma were sleeping, and I found Karo in the kitchen. It was far different from the ones we'd modified in our new ship designs; these weren't made to suit human needs. They didn't suit Theos needs either, apparently, because Karo was struggling inside it.

"Nothing makes sense in here, Dean," he said as he rummaged through the cupboards.

I sat in a chair by the table, staying out of his way. "What are you trying to make?"

His hair was pulled into a ponytail, like he always did when he was cooking food. On New Spero, Karo would cook Mary and me dinner once or twice a week, and we later learned he'd been taking cooking lessons from a celebrity chef from before the Event. The man had run a food empire, and it was humbling to know he now took time to teach an obviously alien man to prepare delectable meals.

"Not pizza, if that's what you're thinking." Karo laughed, but I saw dough on the counter in front of him.

"I'll have a slice of that not-pizza when it's done," I said, and he laughed again. "It's good to see you like this.

I know you've been having a hard time looking for your place in this new universe, Karo. You know we're all here for you."

"I know, Dean. Somehow being on board a ship, heading on a rescue mission, my own self-pity feels far down the list of real problems. *Fortune* has over five hundred souls on it that need help. Magnus and Natalia are also some of my closest friends." Karo had spent a long time living with them.

"You miss them, don't you?"

"I do. Three years is a long time, even though I haven't known everyone long. Those children were little miracles. I wished I could have seen them grow up." Karo was kneading the dough and staring at the wall.

"We're going to find them, Karo. We never leave anyone behind." I meant every word of it.

"I know. I'm grateful to be part of your team, Dean. We've come a long way, haven't we?" he asked, his smile returning.

"We have. I don't know what the future holds, but I see happy times ahead, contradictory to what we've been feeling about losing Magnus," I said. I still hadn't told the others about Kimtra's warning, but I would, soon. They deserved the truth.

"I hope you're right, friend. I truly do." Karo kept kneading his dough, and we chatted for another hour while the food cooked in the complicated oven.

By the time it was all done, the others were up, rested after a busy couple of days, and we shared a meal together around the table. It was the best way we could kick off the two-month journey through space.

We were in our plain gray jumpsuits, and Slate's already had a big red stain on it, which he tried to wipe clean. "Karo, I know you have a pizza obsession, but I'm not sure the supplies we got from the Traders were quite on par. Just what was that tomato substitute? It tasted like dirt."

Rulo threw another napkin at Slate. "Don't ask what kind of animal the cheese came from."

This got a laugh from Karo and me, and a grimace from Slate, who pushed his plate away with half a slice sitting on it. "I won't, thanks."

It was time to fill them all in while they were rested and fed. My hand shook slightly as I built up my nerve. "Guys, I have to tell you something."

"What is it, Dean?" Suma asked. She was sitting across from me, and I could tell she was picking up my uneasiness.

"Kimtra gave me some news. Information the Keppe didn't want to share with us, for some reason." Rulo stared at me as I spoke. As much as she was part of our team, I was apprehensive to make her choose between us and her people.

"What is it?" Slate asked.

"This system Magnus and Nat disappeared in… a few other races have found the same place and never made it home," I said.

"What does that mean? Why wouldn't they tell us that?" Suma was looking at Rulo.

Rulo lifted her hands in supplication. "Don't ask me. I'm a warrior. No one tells me their plans."

Karo was in the midst of eating, and he finished chewing before speaking. "I don't think it's as big a deal as we're making this out to be. So what if others have gone missing before Magnus? Does it change anything?"

I pondered this as Slate answered, "I guess not. Even if they'd told us, we'd be going to save Magnus regardless, right?"

"You're right. I keep thinking there was a reason Crul wanted to keep this from us, but I can't put my finger on it. Time will tell." I peeked over at Rulo, who was avoiding my attention.

"Suma, what else have you found out about a system with no star, but orbiting worlds?" Karo asked her.

Suma shrugged. "Not a lot. It's happened before, far away. Not a sun, but a whole planet disappeared. One day it was there, the next it was gone. No one knows why."

"When was this?" I asked.

"Nearly a millennium ago, I think. If you search hard enough, almost everything has occurred in nature," she said.

A planet disappearing had me wondering something. "What do we know that could move a planet?"

Suma sat up straight in her chair. "Dean, what about the Shifter?"

"Yes. The Shifter could do it. Remember what Garo Alnod said? It was supposed to be a tool that could potentially move an entire planet into another dimension. Let's say a star was going to die, or go supernova. The Shifter could transport an entire race somewhere safer," I said in a rush.

"*Potentially* safer. That was the problem with the Shifter, right? You didn't control what the alternate dimension contained. You could end up anywhere… or any time." Slate had the gist of it.

"Dean, there's something else that can cause a world to vanish." Karo's voice was quiet, ominous.

"The Iskios," I whispered, recalling only too clearly the bright green vortex used to suck entire moons, planets, and stars into its singularity, Mary's body a puppet to the ancient evil bastards.

"Do you think…" Suma started, but I shook my

head.

"No. I really don't see how they could be back. If there was a thousand-kilometer-wide vortex eating up solar systems again, we'd hear about it. Garo claimed there had only been one Shifter, the one Lom of Pleva started a war for on Bazarn Five. If it was worth that much to one man, I imagine someone could have built another like it," I said.

"Who created it?" Suma asked the question I wished I'd asked of Garo when I had the chance.

"I don't know. But Lom's gone, and Garo wanted nothing to do with another Shifter, so we're at square one." It felt great talking this through with the team. It was like old times. Four different races, sitting around eating a food resembling pizza, and trying to determine what could possibly cause a star to be wiped out without collateral damage to the immediate region of space.

"Any other theories?" Karo asked.

Suma tapped her chin. Slate was once again pecking away at the pizza he'd discarded only a few minutes ago. "Maybe it's not so bad. If you're hungry enough," he told Karo, who clapped him on the shoulder for the semi-compliment.

"The good news is, we have two months to think about it." I got up and headed for the kitchen door. "If anyone needs me, I'll be sleeping. So please… don't need me."

"Goodnight, Dean," they chorused, bringing a smile to my face. I plodded down the hall toward the room with two bunks and took the unused one. I could hear the others gabbing from here, and I contemplated closing the door before deciding to let their happy conversation lull me to sleep.

I pictured Jules, her green eyes watching me with interest, her curly chestnut hair falling in her face as she played with Maggie. I missed my family, and it had only been a few days. We'd become such a close-knit group that it was hard being separated from them. Two more months, and then what? How long before we could all go home again? I hated doing this to Mary, and lying in the bed, staring at the plain white ceiling and walls, I silently swore to my wife that I would never do something like this again.

If only I could believe my own promise.

"Captain, would you mind coming to the bridge when you have a free moment?" W called through the ship's speakers.

I was with Slate in the cargo hold, working out like the old days. If there was one thing being on a long cruise was good for, it was having time to exercise. The cardio and fighting training took all our minds off the otherwise boring and monotonous trip. The daily routine was uninspired. Suma read a lot, researching anything that might help. I was learning about Keppe exploration ships from Rulo, who had been on four two-year ventures in her life, and Slate was teaching Karo how to fight.

"Dean, I don't want to hurt you," Karo said, looming over me. His seven-foot-tall frame and broad shoulders made him an imposing opponent, but there were a few tricks I'd learned over the years that gave me the upper hand, or at least I hoped that was the case.

"Go!" Slate said, commanding us to start.

Karo stepped to the side, which caught me off-guard, since I'd been expecting him to lunge forward in a quick attack. That was what he'd been doing in his practice with Slate, so he was already using his intuition to best me. He was strong; the Theos weren't built to be weak creatures. His arms were twice the size of mine, his legs powerful, but I didn't care. I had the experience, and hundreds of hours of training with Mary, Natalia, Magnus, and Slate, all of whom could kick my butt at one point. I wasn't ashamed to admit that.

As his right foot set to the floor, I darted in, ducking under a swinging punch. I rammed into his hard chest with my shoulder and pushed him backwards, but not off-balance like I'd hoped. His other hand caught my ribs with an uppercut, and I was thankful for the padding we wore. It felt like a boulder dropping onto my chest.

He tried again, but I rolled away, kicking out to catch in front of his leg. He was already moving toward me, and this time, he couldn't stop his momentum. As he stumbled forward, I pushed him to the floor, only he didn't land on his front like I expected. He quickly rotated, landing on his shoulders, and as I sprang at him, his fist caught me in the jaw, sending me sprawling overtop of him.

Karo was trying to get to his knees to come after me when Dubs' voice carried over the speakers again. "Captain, please come to the bridge. This is urgent." The android wouldn't say that if it wasn't important, and I was happy for the interruption. Karo was looming over me, his fist cocked back, and my arms were in front of my face in a defensive posture.

"Saved by the bell," I said.

"Don't think I didn't hear you bet Rulo you would best me, Dean." Karo stuck a hand out and helped me to my feet.

"Jeeze. Did you have to hit me so hard?" I asked,

rubbing my ribs. They'd be okay; maybe a little bruised.

"Slate thought it would be good to teach you a lesson," Karo said with a laugh.

I glared at Slate. "Is that so, Zeke Campbell?" I used his full name in a tone only Mary could usually pull off.

"Yeah, boss. I had to remind you that I'm the best fight instructor ever. I taught a newbie to beat you in a week. Admit it."

I laughed too, wincing at the effect on my chest. "Fine. But face it, Karo is twice my size."

Rulo was beside me, holding her hand out. "A bet's a bet," she said.

"I'm good for it," I said. "Send the bill to New Spero."

I undid the straps on the padding and threw the top to Slate, who caught it deftly. I had to see what W was all worked up about. I jogged to the bridge, passing Suma in the kitchen, where she leaned over a tablet, scrolling through data.

"What is it, Dubs?" I asked, coming to stand behind his pilot's seat.

"I've picked up an odd reading on the sensors and would like to investigate it," he said.

I looked out the viewscreen at the wide-open space beyond. Countless stars twinkled in the distance, light years away. If we were near the edge of the known universe, why could we still see so much out here? It was unnerving.

"What kind of reading?" I sat on the seat beside his and tapped the console to life, zooming in on the radar image. Nothing showed abnormal to me.

"It was faint, but definitely there a few minutes ago. I locked the coordinates, and we could be there in two hours." W was still looking straight forward at his controls, but my screen zoomed on a location not far from what could only be a cluster of asteroids.

"I'm not sure I love the idea of heading into an asteroid field," I told him. "Are you sure the sensors weren't picking up trace amounts of a metal used in interstellar space ships? Asteroids have been mined for materials for thousands of years, according to Suma."

"You could be right." The console blinked, and a familiar chime rang out. "We've received a transmission."

"From who?" There was no one nearby: no ships, no worlds, nothing but the asteroid field.

"That is unclear." He opened it, but instead of a verbal message, confusing images scrolled across the viewscreen. They appeared mathematical in nature; formulas, maybe.

"Suma!" I shouted behind me before tapping into the ship's speaker system. "Everyone to the bridge. We've encountered someone."

The last thing I wanted was to be venturing off on side missions on our trip to find Magnus, but we were so close. Only two hours. What if they needed our help? The chances of another vessel traveling through this system on this course soon were slim to none. We were the only ones that could help them.

Suma was the first one on the bridge, and my chair shifted as she gripped the top of it. "What am I looking at?"

The others piled behind us, crowding the compact space. "Dubs, any chance you can read this?" I asked.

"I think I might be able to. I have deactivated some of my programming in order to be more efficient. I am, after all, a few thousand years old." He said it without self-pity. We'd found him in the closet of a derelict ship of some alien relic hunters who'd ended up stuck on

Larsk, until his battery drained and they'd all died.

"Would you be able to activate it again?" I asked, continuing to focus on the scrolling equations on the viewscreen.

"With Suma's assistance, I think we could have it operational in an hour's time," W said.

An hour. Just enough time to figure out what we were flying into before we arrived at the asteroids. "Suma, can you help W?"

"Of course. Come on, Dubs." Suma led our android friend away from the bridge, and Slate took over the pilot's seat.

"Dean, you sure we should be doing this?" Slate glanced at me. The fact that he used my real name told me he was apprehensive of the detour.

"No, I'm not, but we're Gatekeepers, and we will assist those in need." Slate nodded along and stuck his fist out for me to bump.

"That's what we all love about you," he said, and we sat silently, watching our radar image of the asteroid field.

Almost an hour later, we could make out the shapes and patterns of the rocks. Some were the size of our ship; others were variations of protoplanets, dispersed seemingly randomly in a cluster. The larger would be orbiting the system's distant star, the smaller tugged along.

"Where's the message coming from?" Slate asked, and I keyed in the last transmission. It was sending out nearly four times an hour, and we were due for another ping. A short time later, our ship received the message, and I had a lock on the source location.

We were quite a ways out, but at least now we had a slightly better lay of the land. The message was coming from the second largest hunk of rock, and the computer estimated it at a diameter of four hundred kilometers.

"That's big. What the hell could be living on an asteroid like that?" Slate asked.

"I have no clue, but I guess we're going to find out." I zoomed in as much as possible on the viewscreen, and finally, we were able to see the outlines of our target.

"I think I'll let Dubs pilot us through the thousands of small dangerous clusters, if that's okay with you," Slate suggested.

"That's probably a good idea, even though asteroid fields are mostly open space. Not that I don't trust your skills as a pilot," I added, getting a grin from him.

He was about to comment when Suma announced their arrival. W was close behind her, and they were moving quickly.

"The message is old, judging by the program used to issue it, though it's hard to tell with so many varying races of beings, each in different stages of development. It might be new for the senders, if that makes sense," Dubs said.

"Sure, makes sense. Can you decipher the data?" I asked. His torso cavity was flipped open, a few wires were wire-nutted together, and Suma was trying to fiddle with them, cleaning up the mess.

"Dubs wouldn't let me finish before darting towards the hall," she said.

"I can read the message. It has two parts. One is a greeting from a friendly race. They call themselves the Yuver. They hail from far away; the star map is not familiar to my system," W said, standing in the bridge's entrance.

"I've never heard of them, Dean. I don't think the Gatekeepers know of these Yuver. Dubs, tell them the rest of it." Suma was excited, maybe nervous. The two were hard to differentiate with her at times.

"The main message was basically a greeting, an introduction stating their intentions of meeting new races and learning from them. They have samples of their art and music, not unlike what you tell me humans once pushed out from Earth," W said.

I sensed there was more, and Suma's pacing only fueled the assumption.

"There was something stitched onto the original communication. It was scattered, maybe rushed," W said.

"What did they say?" Rulo asked, emerging from the hallway behind Dubs. She was dressed in her workout gear and wiped sweat from her head with a towel. Karo was with her, and he listened with interest.

"It was a warning. A call for help, perhaps, but a cautionary one." W walked behind me and pointed to the console's radar. "They said they were caught, trapped on this asteroid. Something was holding them there, but it's unclear whether that meant a naturally-existing phenomenon or a physical being."

"And there's no way to timestamp this message or the original?" I asked.

"No, Captain. We have no idea how long ago the transmission was created. We only know it's programmed on a loop to consistently send out to anyone close enough to receive it," W said.

"I have to think there have been others passing through this system," Slate said.

"Maybe, but not everyone will stop to assist a mayday call." I watched the asteroids quickly growing in our viewscreen and tried to determine the right course of action.

"And fewer would have the ability to decode the message in the first place," Karo added.

"Magnus didn't come this way. I'd think they would

have found the message intriguing enough to stop." I tapped the arm of the chair, wishing the answer was simpler. It should be. Magnus needed us, but so could this race confined on an asteroid.

"Have you considered this could be a trap?" Rulo was behind Slate now, staring at the viewscreen with the rest of us.

"That's what I like about you, Rulo. Always playing devil's advocate," Slate said, getting a smile from the Keppe woman.

"Someone has to. If I left you all to your own devices, we'd never stop assisting everyone blindly. I'm happy to be the cautionary voice," Rulo said.

"You have a good point. W, what do you think?" I asked the robot.

"Captain, I don't know how to sense pretense in their mathematical transmission. I do not believe we are being deceived, but that does not mean we aren't. It could be a trap," the robot said.

"Slate, Suma, Karo, what are your thoughts?" I wanted the entire team to weigh in before I made my final decision.

Suma went first, standing beside my chair. "Impossible to tell. I don't think we're being tricked. The last piece of the message seems too frantic, really worried."

Slate nodded, silently agreeing with her. "Let's move closer and take a look. If anything's sending us the wrong vibe, we hightail out of there and keep going on our regularly scheduled mission."

"I concur, Dean," came Karo's response.

I loved having the team sound off on the plan, and they'd basically suggested the exact course of action I was going ahead with; only now it was their idea, and I didn't have to do anything. "Good plan, team. W, do you mind getting back in control of the ship?"

Slate moved away, and Dubs took his spot, directing us toward the asteroids. The second-largest one was our target, and it glowed green on our radar.

"No more details than some ominous message about being trapped?" I asked.

"There was one thing, but I'm not sure what it meant." Dubs' hands moved quickly on the console as he charted a path for our ship. We were getting close to the outer edge of the field, and already we could see big chunks of floating rock along our trajectory.

"What was it?" I asked, holding my breath for the answer.

"The last phrase said something about the ceiling. The context is unclear," he said.

I shook my head slowly from side to side, trying to understand the meaning behind the warning.

FOURTEEN

The next forty or so minutes were tense, becoming more stressful the farther into the asteroid field we got. At the start, the rocky debris was far enough apart that we didn't need to concern ourselves with moving away from one piece and having to avoid another. As we neared our target, the clusters of rocks grew closer together, and W had us on the edge of our seats as we zigged and zagged around them.

"Shields at ninety percent," Slate said, having taken over the co-pilot's seat. Two more rocks struck our side, and he amended his comment. "Eighty-five percent."

However, we were almost there, and I could live with those numbers. We'd elected to not bother with a covert mission. While using the new cloaking device, we weren't able to use the shields, so the choice had been a simple one.

The entire region was teeming with debris, but W managed to navigate us through relatively unscathed, and we lowered toward the round asteroid. In the viewscreen, it looked a lot like a roughly-shaped moon, slightly concave on the top, but mostly spherical. From this viewpoint, I counted three wide craters but couldn't gauge how large they were.

Suma pointed to the largest of the three craters. "The transmission came from the center one."

"It came from there?" I asked, and she shook her head.

"Now that we're closer, I can see it originated from under the surface," she said.

Since there was nothing above the slate-gray surface, that wasn't a surprise. I wasn't sure what wonders the underground of this asteroid held for us, but we were about to find out.

"Taking us down." W directed our ship to face the asteroid, its broad image filling the entire viewscreen.

It was only a matter of minutes before we were lowering into the widest crater – which, it turned out, was over three kilometers wide, and at its lowest, four hundred meters below the rest of the rock's exterior.

The ship settled to the ground on its landing gear, right next to a fault line, a crack in the crater rock.

"There is a minute amount of gravitational pull, but I'll set the anchors into place, Captain," W said as his metal hands sped across the console, giving it commands too fast for me to follow.

This was it. "Who's coming below with me?"

Slate set a hand on my chest, stopping me from exiting the bridge. "Boss, maybe you should sit this one out. You and W can stay on board and be here for backup."

I tried to stifle the laugh but wasn't able to. "You have to be kidding me, Slate. Since when do I hang back on the ship while you all stick your necks out? If anyone should be staying, it's Suma."

"Why me?" she asked defiantly.

"Because your dad will kill me if anything happens to you. And Karo, you're the last of your kind. I'd suggest you stay here with W and Suma," I said firmly.

Karo seemed ready to argue with me, but he sat beside W instead. "Suma, let them have this one. You and I can continue with our plans for the rescue," he said, and the Shimmali girl glared at me before nodding.

"Fine. This time. Keep in contact with us while you're there, though," she snipped.

"Let's suit up." I let Rulo lead the way through the hall to the cargo bay, where we slipped into our gear. Rulo's was by far the largest, and her body armor EVA was impressive.

"I want to get one of those, boss." Slate tapped it with his knuckles, earning him a glare from the Keppe warrior.

"I'll see what I can do. You might fit one of our *smaller* molds." Rulo smiled widely, and Slate took the intended insult with grace.

We each double-checked our suit's sensors, ensuring we were properly sealed, and I made sure Slate's and my video feeds were activated. It was something new we'd added so those aboard could watch with us and hopefully help if they spotted anything of use.

Minutes later, we were ready to exit the ship, but not before I did one last thing. I unlocked the crate that held the items from the Trader world. The portal Broker used had turned out to be less magical than I'd initially thought; she only waved her hand for the theatrics. I recorded my location into the device, and now we'd be able to return here with ease, should we encounter any trouble.

It was almost like having a functional Relocator, in some respects. This was more like the portal gate I had from Fontem's collection, only a little less secretive. It only worked between close locations, usually on the same planet, so they were handy, yet extremely limited.

"All set?" I asked, and when Slate tapped his helmet and Rulo grabbed her minigun, I knew we were ready to go. We had an assortment of climbing gear and supplies with us, since we didn't know what to expect.

The energy barrier turned on, and I lowered the Kraski ship's ramp, where it settled on the dark, dusty ground with a floating cloud of dirt.

Suma watched us leave, and I gave her a confident wave, which she returned after a hesitant delay. I'd put her through enough, and if anything happened to us, I was certain her clever mind was going to be pivotal in tracking Magnus and Natalia down.

We'd landed the ship a few hundred meters from the crack in the crater, just in case the added weight caused a collapse. W was adamant that on an asteroid with next to no gravity, this wouldn't be much of an issue, but I preferred to err on the side of caution.

Rulo took the ramp first, keeping her feet planted on the ground as she stepped off our ship. Our boots had an artificial mass dial on them, and we'd turned them to ninety percent before exiting our ship.

She waited for the two of us, and as I stood on the surface of the asteroid, I tried not to look up or anywhere but at my feet. Walking on a floating rock in the center of nowhere wasn't my idea of a good time. Slate didn't seem to care, and he marched quickly after Rulo. With a quick breath, I hurried after them. The only thing worse than hiking on an asteroid was doing it alone.

"Dean, it appears as though the crevasse leading into the asteroid is wider than initially expected. We could have fit the ship in if we were careful," Suma said into my earpiece.

"I think it's best we leave the ship where it is," I replied.

"The drop isn't far. We should be able to lock ourselves on here and make the jump," Slate said, simultaneously grabbing a tool from a kit strapped to his suit. With it, he clamped a wide eye-hook into the stone, testing the tensile strength before clipping three ropes onto it. We each attached one to our own suit's waist, and I peered over the edge of the opening.

It was pitch black inside. "I can't believe we're doing this, Slate. Didn't we make a pact to stop going underground together?" I laughed nervously.

"That was on planets. We never specified asteroids," Slate said, readying himself.

"You both talk too much," Rulo said. She flipped on her armored suit's built-in lighting system, directing the beams ahead, and stepped over the edge.

"Boss, you going to let her…" Slate started, but I didn't make out the rest of his words as I walked over the ledge, falling inside the asteroid slowly. My momentum and the artificial mass generator carried me to the ground, and my lights caught movement below me. I swung my rifle around, only to find Rulo jumping out of the way so I didn't land on her.

She pointed to my gun. "Watch where you're waving that thing."

"Wooohoooo!" Slate was shouting as he landed between us. "That was the coolest cave dive I've ever done."

I tried finding my bearings. "Suma, you were right. This place is large enough for a ship." I released a palm-sized light-drone, another item I'd obtained from the Traders. My heart raced as it found the abnormality in the cavern and stopped above it. I left the other two bragging to each other, and crossed the cavern. It was at least a kilometer deep, and the uncharacteristic ship sat halfway between us and the far edge.

"Is that what I think it is?" Suma asked from the ship.

She was watching our feed from the bridge.

"I think we found the source of the transmission." I turned to the others, who only now noticed that we weren't alone. The light-drone stayed where it was, drawing the three of us like moths to a flame.

"This is amazing," Rulo said. Her rowdy attitude was replaced with one of wonder.

"Do you recognize it?" I asked them, including the ones watching from my suit's video feed.

"Nothing I have on file, Captain," Dubs' monotone voice said.

"I don't recall seeing one of those in the Gatekeepers' study material," Suma said into my earpiece.

We got closer, and I saw the shape now. It was round, domed at the top, and had bumps along the outer edge. The light from above cast lengthy shadows below it, making it look like it had long spiderlike legs. It was larger than our Kraski ship, but only by a small percentage. We arrived near it and stopped, waiting for a reaction from within the vessel.

"Whatever was inside has to be long gone, Dean," Rulo said. "You heard W's opinion on the age of the message. They must have come here and gotten stuck. Or they were damaged, looking for a place to land and repair."

"We owe it to them to investigate who these Yuver are," I said.

"Or *were*," Slate chimed in.

Now that we were closer, it instantly made me picture an old UFO. It was shaped like the ones you'd see in countless television shows, hovering over crops, lights beaming cows up from the fields. The similarity caused the hairs on my arms to rise inside my suit.

"Does this remind you of something?" Slate asked

me, and I nodded.

"Growing up in farm country, we had a few sightings while I was a kid. Old Bill Binders claimed he was abducted not once, but five times by a ship like this one. You don't really think…" I cut myself off, giving my head a shake. I'd seen too much out there, been around too many aliens to think that the Yuver had been the ones stalking humans and probing them for an anatomy lesson.

"Probably not. But I'll be ready for them either way." Slate's rifle came up, and we stalked around the round ship, looking for an entrance.

"What are you two going on about?" Rulo asked.

"Nothing. Just something from Earth folklore… or maybe reality. Suma, you see anything that might help?" I asked the girl watching the feed.

"There may have been a discoloration under the dome side. Check there," she said, and I heeded her advice, heading under the ship. It had tall landing gear, allowing us to walk directly under it without hitting our heads on the underbelly.

I saw what she was talking about, and lifted a hand to the rough exterior of the alien vessel. When I didn't feel anything, I sighed in frustration.

"Dean, don't move. We'll zoom in, capture an image, and do an analysis." I did as Suma suggested, and she told me when they had a good enough shot.

"They're going to find access from on our ship's bridge? I don't think…" Rulo was saying when Suma's voice returned.

"We lightened and darkened the image, finding a straight line heading from the center," Suma said, and I pointed, touching the exterior until she told me I was there.

I pressed up, and something clicked, releasing the

door. It flung open, and I had to jump out of the way to avoid impact with the heavy, clunky slab of metal.

"The door's probably controlled by the ship, and since it's powerless, it's become dead weight. Be careful, Dean," Suma said, and I got up, dusting my suit off.

"Who's first?" I asked.

Rulo didn't pause. She leapt up, grabbing the inside of the opening into the ship, pulling herself up with ease. Seconds later, her armored glove stuck toward me, ready to pull us up. I went first, being easily lifted with the almost non-existent gravity.

We emerged in the middle of the round ship. The dome surrounded us, and we found ourselves in a wide-open space. There were two seats at the edge of the room, facing the lower half of the dome. That would be the viewscreen and the pilot's chair, and potentially weapons control. Even though the ship was larger than ours, once inside, the living area was far smaller.

Everything was dead. I couldn't see one active light anywhere, and I walked around the outer edge, seeing unfamiliar computers, mostly unwieldy in appearance. The place was clean, nothing out of place even now.

"How long have they been here?" I whispered.

"I don't know, but… I don't see any sign of *them* on board." Slate was right.

"This isn't a wall here," Rulo shouted from across the room. "I thought it was, but when I took a closer look, it was only stacked containers. It's as if they were…" She was hefting them away, and Slate and I assisted, moving the clunky boxes from the side of the ship's interior.

"It was as if they were hiding… something," I said as we spotted the last container. This one did have soft yellow lights glowing on a console near its bottom.

"Someone, boss. Some*one*, not some*thing*," Slate said,

wiping the top of it with his arm. A thin layer of dust was brushed away, revealing a body inside.

"What is that, Dean? We can't see!" Suma's excited voice echoed in my earpiece. I tried to give them a better vantage shot, but it was dark, and our flashlights reflected more light off the glass than penetrated. I wasn't sure what we were looking at inside the container.

"It appears to be one of the Yuver," I replied.

FIFTEEN

"You found one? Is it alive?" This time, it was Karo asking the questions.

I glanced at the glowing yellow console, tried to decipher it, and failed. "I can't tell. None of this makes sense to me."

"We have to bring that on board," Suma urged.

"Suma, for all we know, this Yuver's skin is poisonous to us, or maybe it's carrying a virus that has the potential to wipe out all of Shimmal."

I may have been overdoing it, but she got my point. "We can't leave it. We can transport it home to Dr. Nick," Suma said, and I nodded.

"Very well. We'll bring it with us, but we're not opening this on our ship. We wanted to discover what the distress call was all about, and now we know. Let's progress out of here and focus on the task at hand." I was about to open the portal when Slate tapped me on the shoulder.

"Check this out." He'd picked up a flat tablet-sized device, and it activated as he pressed various buttons along its side.

"W, can you make any sense of this?" I asked the android through my earpiece.

"It appears to be a tracking map. Those two blinking lights are the transponders. One looks to be attached to your sleeping guest," W said.

The other blinking light was a ways away from the ship. How far, I couldn't tell by the alien tablet. "And the other transponder?"

"I would hypothesize it's attached to another Yuver," W said.

I was torn. There was another one somewhere under the surface of the asteroid, but what were the chances it lived? I didn't even know if this one was alive. I leaned over the glass, waving my suit's light away from the reflective surface. The Yuver inside had smooth dark-green skin and large eyes that were currently closed. The glass only framed its head, so I couldn't see the rest of the body or know how tall or heavy the creature was.

"Do we go after it?" Slate asked.

"I vote we take this thing and leave," Rulo said. The Keppe had become a star-hunting race, attempting to become more science-minded and exploratory than warrior, and she probably thought this discovery would be a good one for her people.

But what if there was another one? We knew nothing about them. It might be alive and trapped. Maybe they pupated or hibernated. "Damn it. Let's go look for it. It shouldn't take long."

"You know how you always tell me not to say that, because…" Slate started.

"Because any time I say something's going to be a quick detour, it inevitably winds up being a huge pain in the butt?" I finished for him.

"Yeah, that's what I was going to say." He tapped the blinking transponder signal on the tablet. "You really want to go after this?"

"I don't want to, but let's get this over with. First things first." I waved the portal open, and we could see the cargo bay of our ship through the yellow energy barrier. "W, can you give us a hand?"

We cleared a path between the cryogenically-frozen Yuver and the yellow-energy doorway to our ship, and by the time we were done, W had stepped through.

He walked over to the elongated box, which had to be some variation of a cryo tube, and spent five minutes around it, checking to see if it was self-sufficient or attached to the ship. "It appears to be sustaining itself, though I do not understand the science behind it. It must be a precautionary function in case the entire ship drains of energy, as this one seems to have done."

"Can we move it?" Slate asked, and W nodded.

"We can move it," the robot answered. I was never sure how to take his tone. Sometimes it seemed like he wasn't confident in his replies, but there was no way to tell.

I looked at the case containing the body. Did I trust bringing a potentially dead creature on the ship? This was part of what I'd signed up for with the Gatekeepers, and what the Keppe were doing with their exploration missions, so I resigned myself to adding the new guest on board.

"Slate, do you mind giving him a hand?" I asked, and Rulo stood beside me cross-armed as we witnessed W and Slate sliding the frozen Yuver through the portal doorway and onto our ship.

When they were done, W stood in the entrance, and I called out to him, "W, is there any way to collect data from this ship? Download their hard drive or something?" I said, knowing I wasn't articulating myself properly.

"I believe there may be a way," he said, heading onto our ship. In less than a minute, he was back, holding a box the size of a car battery; only this one was shiny silver and hummed with power.

He crossed the open space of the dark Yuver vessel and stopped near the front pilot's seat. I went over and helped him pry open a panel under the main helm console.

W opened a pouch he'd carried aboard and cut a wire before adding a universal plug to it. From there, he stuck the new end into the battery pack he'd brought with him. The ship remained dark.

"Give it a moment," he said, and as promised, the computer in front of us began to power up. Strange symbols filled the flat screen above an unfamiliar keyboard. It was along the same lines as the ones I'd used to build countless spreadsheets back home over the years, but the symbols were alien.

"Can we make this thing run again?" Slate asked behind us.

"Not at this time. We do not have the resources. The best I could do was power this particular processor." W pressed a datastick into the silver battery pack, and it glowed blue as he keyed in commands on the keyboard. "This will only take a moment."

I stood from my crouched position and wondered what secrets we'd find on the datastick later. There was something extremely exciting about it all: finding a new race, learning about them. It made me think of our time on Sterona, where we'd lived while Mary was pregnant after fighting the Iskios off. There was obviously so much we didn't know about the ancient race.

There was something haunting about them leaving their wonderful city behind. Part of me had to know where they went, and why.

"All done." W took the pack, disconnecting it from the ship. He linked the wire again, soldering it together, leaving everything as it was.

"We're going to check on the other transponder beacon. With any luck, we'll be done in no time," I told W as he crossed the portal and turned to face us from the Kraski ship's cargo bay.

"We will watch with you," W said.

"And W?" My gaze drifted through the energy doorway to the body in the cryobox aboard our ship.

"Yes, Captain."

"Don't open that, whatever you do," I warned.

"We will not open it," he assured me, and I closed the portal with the hand-held device, shoving it into a front pocket where I could easily access it.

Rulo was already at the exit of the ship, hopping out. Slate went next, and I took one last look into the strange round ship's interior, my flashlight casting unnerving shadows around the space before I joined them inside the cavern.

I called the light-drone to me and snapped it onto my hip. The whole cave was much darker without its beams shining on the ship, but our suits gave enough ambiance to see in the shadowy cavern.

Slate held the tablet with the blinking icon on it; the other icon now showed farther away, since the body was on our ship above the surface. He pointed to the edge of the cavity and that was where we went, guns raised and ready.

"You don't really expect anything to be living in here, do you?" Rulo asked from her lead position. The cave was massive, and the wall loomed before us. The edge of the cavern flowed to a hole, funneling us into a tunnel.

"How far do you think that icon is in there?" I asked before we stepped foot any farther into the asteroid.

Slate shrugged as we watched the tablet, held firmly in

his left hand. My suit's lights shone down the corridor, which was at least twice our height, and I figured all three of us could easily walk side by side into the tunnels. If it had been any tighter, I would have turned around and rushed back to our ship.

"I'd say it's no more than half a kilometer," Rulo said. "The other one was here" – she pointed to the spot that had indicated the cryobox not long ago – "and that was about three hundred meters away."

"You're right. Let's keep moving," I said, taking the lead now. My pulse rifle had a light attached to it too, and I kept it aiming straight forward into the rocky tunnel.

The entire underpass was pocked rock; fissures and smooth pebble-sized holes ran over the entire surface, floors, walls, and ceiling. It was rounded like a tube, and thankfully, it widened as we went deeper.

Soon we were inside another open cave, about a tenth the size of the one we'd come from. It was darker in here somehow; the area had a feeling of compression, as if the walls were slowly but surely getting closer with each passing breath.

"What the hell is that?" Slate asked, pointing a light at the room's far right corner. There was liquid on the floor; it reflected the light and rippled slightly as we walked toward it.

"Are you guys seeing this back on the ship?" I asked.

"Loud and clear," Suma replied.

We stood above the blob of liquid, which was a lot more viscous than I'd originally thought.

"Slime?" Slate asked, about to tap it with his boot.

"Don't touch it!" I warned, but it was too late. The toe dipped into the puddle of thick gooey mess, and Slate jumped away as if he'd been bitten.

"No one said you were smart. You remind me more

of Hectal with each passing day," Rulo said as she bent over to inspect the pile of slime. "There's more here," she said, motioning a few yards deeper into the cave.

"Great. Just great." My mind was picturing all sorts of things that could leave a mucus like that behind, and none of them were small, furry, or friendly.

We walked toward the blinking icon, sure we were on the right path. "Let's avoid bringing the alien gunk with us this time, Slate." I stepped around another pile of it, and Slate stayed even farther from it, hugging the far wall.

The cave led us to another corridor, this one a tighter cylinder, like the old volcano lava tubes in Hawaii. I could touch the ceiling inside and stayed in the lead, my rifle pointing forward like I was a man on a mission to clear the asteroid of all infestation.

"Dean, did you see that?" Suma asked in my earpiece.

"See what?" I planted my feet firmly, swinging my rifle and light around to look for anything moving.

"Over to the left," Suma said, and I moved my light to the left floor to find it empty.

"Nothing there."

"Above. Look up." Suma's voice held an edge of panic that didn't bode well for our situation.

I gradually moved my gun and flashlight up to the ceiling. There was nothing there. Then I saw the slime. It dripped from the exact spot where Suma had seen something moments ago. The warning from the Yuver had mentioned the ceiling. I hadn't remembered that part until now.

"Suma, can you rewind the footage and pause it?" I asked.

Slate was already moving forward, and so was Rulo, so I followed them while Suma did her magic on board our ship. I needed to know if there were indeed living organisms responsible for the goop more than I needed to find this missing Yuver.

"The Yuver should be right here," Slate said from inside a smaller cavern. He tapped the tablet where the icon blinked. He was right. This was it, only we didn't see anything inside the room but dark rock.

"We should go. I don't like this," I suggested, moving for the portal device.

"Did you hear that?" Rulo asked, taking a step into the cave.

"What?" I strained my ears but didn't hear anything but the soft plopping, like the kitchen tap dripping when it wasn't fully shut off.

I peeked up at the same second Suma warned me. "Dean, it's some sort of a slug on the ceiling!"

My voice caught in my throat as I stared at the cave's smooth domed ceiling. Dozens of the creatures were up there, and as soon as my light hit them, they began moving frantically. Slate glanced up, following my gaze, and he shone a light on them at the same time.

Rulo was directly under them in the middle of the space, crouching amidst the giant slugs' slime. She pulled something off the ground and turned to where I was shouting a warning to her. "I think I found the transponder." She must have seen the looks on our faces, because she tilted her head up and scrambled backwards towards the far wall. It all happened so fast that I didn't have time to react.

"Rulo, come now!" I finally shouted, but it was too late. The slugs began to drop from the ceiling one by one, landing with a disturbing squelching sound. One of the four-foot-long slugs landed on top of Rulo, and she shouted a primal sound as she batted at the soft creature with powerful armored hands.

Slate and I shot at them, pulse beams cutting through the dark cave. They screamed, a high-pitched wretched sound as we burned through them, sending pieces of slug all over the walls and floor. More were falling from the ceiling, slithering along the walls now, and before we knew it, there were at least fifty of them in the confined space, dozens moving in a pile between us and Rulo.

"Slate, we need to cut a path," I yelled, aiming for the middle of the room with my rifle.

Slate efficiently ended a half dozen of them before they retaliated. We were only a few yards apart, but soon Slate was cornered to my right. I backed up, trying to think of a way to distract the slugs. They didn't seem to like the light, and that gave me an idea.

I pulled the light-drone off my hip and activated it. The tiny drone rose in the air, heading for the ceiling, and it shot a bright beam toward the middle of the room. The slugs scurried away from the light, giving me the pathway I'd been hoping for.

"Rulo, now!" I yelled, and saw the Keppe warrior throw another slug off her. It hit the wall with a sickening splat, and she kicked at another. Now that her hands were free, she slung up her minigun and fired into the center mass of the slug horde.

She ran to me, spinning around and shooting more of them. Together we aimed at the slugs attacking Slate, and eventually, they were all a pile of guts. Slate was in the corner, his hands raised up in defense, and he was shuddering.

"Slate, they're gone. We killed them all," I said, stepping over a particularly large gray alien slug to get to him. I raised my hand and wiped guts off his helmet's face-shield to reveal his wide, fearful eyes.

Slate patted his chest and legs before giving one of his

patented grins. "And you were worried about me dipping my boot into some slime."

I laughed, and so did Rulo. Among a cave full of carnage, we chuckled like you could only do after a near-death experience.

Rulo held her palm out. "I think we found out what happened to our Yuver friend." A blinking transponder the size of a peanut was in her hand.

Suma was shouting in my ear, and I finally acknowledged her cries. "Suma, we're okay. It's over."

"No it's not, Dean." Her voice was thick with fright. "Look to your right!"

My gaze looked up and right, where piles of slugs were entering the cave from a crevice in the rock.

"Run!" I shouted.

SIXTEEN

I stepped on a slug's head and slipped, falling hard to the ground, face-first. Slate and Rulo were already over me, and my friends slowed to pull me to my feet.

"Thanks," I said, checking over my shoulder to see the slugs moving fast toward us. They were hungry, and I had it on good authority we were on the menu. I fired behind me, striking a few of them as we exited the cave into the smaller tunnel.

"Please don't be more ahead," Slate was whispering over and over. It was a mantra I could stand behind. If they were ahead as well as behind, we'd have to fend them off from inside this compact tunnel, and I didn't see that ending well for any of us.

"The portal," I said, remembering the device would open a doorway onto our ship. I grabbed it from my pocket and tried to activate it. Nothing happened, but I'd wasted a good ten seconds trying to get it to work. The slugs were almost at my feet, and I managed a good look at them.

They had no armor, probably because they had no predators out here on a rock in space. They had two forearm-sized tentacles emerging from the fronts of their tiny heads, and these wavered around, perhaps acting as eyes or noses, I wasn't sure which. Maybe both.

I shot one in the head, being rewarded with three

more taking its place. They were coming in droves, and if the portal wasn't going to work, I needed to run. Slate and Rulo were already long gone. Broker had warned there was a limited distance the portal encircled, and I seem to have stretched past that boundary.

I chased after Slate and saw the bottoms of his boots as he hurried ahead of me. We entered another cavern, and more slugs dropped from the ceiling. One landed on me, knocking me to the ground, but Slate was there to kick it off and offer me his hand.

They kept coming. Hundreds of them now. It was something out of a nightmare. I always thought slugs to be slow, methodical creatures, but those were the ones in my parents' garden, the slugs hiding under a two-by-four or a rock. These were something else: huge, fast, and with a mission.

We emerged out of the corridors and into the open cavity below the crater. I knew I could use the portal, but there wasn't time to stop and set it up. I didn't have ten seconds to spare. The mass of seething slime monsters was literally on our heels. None of us said a word as we pumped our legs, carrying our frantic bodies forward, past the Yuver ship and toward the ropes at the end of the room.

I glanced back, only to see the hundreds of slugs rising to the ceiling, covering the walls and the entire surface of the cavern behind us. There was no fighting them. There were too many to beat.

Rulo reached the ropes first, and she pulled them twice, the winch above doing its job, drawing her up quickly. Slate and I clipped in and did the same. We both fired at the ceiling and floor, where the slugs were approaching us as we were lifted toward the surface of the crater and our waiting ship.

Rulo grabbed us each under the armpit and tugged us up, making quick work of it in the near-zero gravity. The enemy was eagerly hunting us, and they scurried onto the surface in hot pursuit. The ship was a few hundred yards away and I ran for it, faster than I'd ever moved in my life, my weighted feet barely touching the ground.

"The ramp! Open the ramp!" I was shouting into my earpiece, and the incline began lowering. A quick look over my shoulder showed me we were cutting this close. There had to be a thousand of the creatures chasing us, tentacles wavering above beady heads, slime everywhere.

We arrived at the ship before the ramp was all the way open, and Slate jumped, rolling onto it. He spun and grabbed Rulo's and my arms, helping us up, and we scrambled up the ramp as it began to close.

I was on my butt, firing at the slugs trying to climb on board. Slate was doing the same, Rulo making quick work of them with her minigun. We had to be careful not to damage our ship, as the ramp was nearly closed.

One last slug pressed through just as the door sealed, cutting it in half. The top half of it kept moving, coming toward us. The tentacles reached forward, and it shrieked before stopping suddenly and deflating.

My heart was pounding so hard, I couldn't even hear what Suma was saying.

The ramp opened again, and I panicked before realizing we were above the surface, far away from the attackers. Slate kicked the slug through the containment field, and all that was left was a pile of ooze where it had died.

"Well, that was one for the books, hey, boss?" Slate gave my suit a light punch, and I forced a smile. It had been close. Too close.

"Are you guys okay?" Karo was there at my side, helping me take off my suit. I took deep breaths of the ship's air as the gore-covered helmet hit the floor. Slate and Rulo were likewise drenched in blood and guts.

"Remind me never to answer a distress call again," Rulo said as she piled her armor suit to the side of the room.

"We need to destroy that rock," I whispered, catching my breath.

"He's right," Karo said. "We didn't shut off the transmission."

"Someone else could be attacked by those things," Suma said.

"W," I said into my earpiece. "Bank toward the asteroid. I'm coming to the bridge."

I was in my sweat-soaked jumpsuit, my socked feet plodding down the hall on wavering legs. I hopped into the co-pilot's seat and W stared straight forward. "Good to see you, Captain. That was… unexpected."

"You can say that again." I activated the pulse cannons and took aim as we neared the asteroid. Even from here, I could see the writhing mass of slugs filling the crater. I fired at them and didn't stop until the entire asteroid was floating around in countless pieces. I wasn't sure if that would end the danger of these particular slugs, but it sure made me feel better.

"I need a beer," Slate said from behind me.

"I need a shower." This from Rulo.

"I need both." I laughed now and was joined by my teammates.

"Life is never dull around you all," Rulo said, clapping Slate and me on the shoulders. "I like that."

"I'm glad someone does," I said. "Hey, when we tell Mary this story later, can we not let her know how close we actually came to dying?"

"Speak for yourself. We were fine," Slate said, and I

recalled the look on his face when we rescued him from the attacking slugs.

"Sure. I'll tell myself that too," I said. "Suma, let's have a look at our new guest."

The Shimmali girl nodded with a smile.

A month passed without incident: just our daily routine of eating, working out, playing games, talking, and attempting to create a viable plan for a multitude of scenarios. That was the worst part, guessing what might have happened to *Fortune*. There were so many things that could have occurred, it was extremely hard to speculate any reasonable situations.

I spent most of my nights wide awake, staring at the ceiling of my room, thinking about my family back home. What kind of trouble was Jules getting herself into while I was away? Was Mary doing okay with my absence?

My thoughts often drifted to the Alliance of Worlds, and how the colony on Haven was going during its extreme growth period. Then, when I finally fell asleep, I'd have nightmares of Iskios, Lom of Pleva, and now I could add alien space slugs to the ever-growing fears within my restless mind.

I must have mumbled in my sleep again, because I was being shaken, someone softly saying my name. "Mary?" I asked, blinking my sleep-covered eyes to see Suma's silhouette.

"Dean, we're almost there," she said softly.

She didn't have to say where *there* was. Magnus had made a stop on his journey, and it was one of the last locations from which he'd been able to send messages to the Keppe. It was probably where he'd been the last time we'd spoken over our communicators.

My nightstand had the hand-held communicator on top of it now, and I tried it at least once a day, in the off chance I could reach Magnus with it. So far, I'd gotten no response. I hadn't let myself consider the fact that the entire crew of *Fortune* could have disappeared for good. I couldn't do it. Magnus, Natalia, Dean, and Patty were fine, along with the five hundred Keppe on board the exploratory vessel. They were alive, and we were going to find them at any cost.

"Thank you, Suma," I said, and swung my legs out of the blankets, sitting up. "I'll be right there."

She left me alone in the room, and I tried to remember the dream I'd been having. It had involved Mary and Jules being trapped on the other side of a portal stone. I shook the cobwebs clear from my sleep-addled brain and went to the Kraski bathroom, where I used their version of a steam shower. I emerged a few minutes later feeling like a new man, and donned a basic jumpsuit before heading to the bridge.

Everyone was present, and Slate passed me a cup of coffee, which I graciously accepted, smelling the roasted bean water before taking a sip. If there was one thing a two-month trip on a cramped ship needed, it was a good cup of coffee, and we at least had that. It was the one thing I'd remembered to bring with me from New Spero, and apparently so had Slate, because we hadn't needed to dig into the Keppe version yet. It was acceptable in a pinch, but not quite the same thing.

"What are we looking at?" I asked, taking a peek at the viewscreen. The screen showed a planet directly in its center, a space station between us and the world.

"This" – Suma was beside W, and she tapped the

console, zooming on the world beyond the station – "is where Magnus last sent any location information. We're far out in space and honestly didn't expect to find a space station here, let alone what appears to be the right class of planet for human, Shimmali, and even Keppe life."

"Maybe he didn't leave," I said. The surface was taupe, the color of a desert, but water filled half our view of the world now.

W shook his head from the pilot's seat, not turning around to look at me. "It is doubtful. They were gone when the last message was sent to the Keppe about the system with the missing star."

"But that was less than a month's travel from this location, maybe less given the unknown timeline. They could have returned damaged. The Keppe vessels have lifeboats, right?" I knew they did, because Hectal had shown them to Mary and me on *Starbound*. They were almost as big as the Kraski ship we were in now.

"Dean, you're a genius. The lifeboats have a locator built into them!" Rulo was excitedly explaining to Suma how to input the tracking into the Kraski computer.

"I'm amazed you know how to do that," Slate told Rulo, who shot an accusatory scowl at him in return.

"I've been on my share of rescue missions, and more often than not, we end up using these to track the missing boats after the warship has been disabled… or destroyed," Rulo said.

"Sorry. Sometimes I forget how much you and your people have been through." Slate offered the olive branch, and she took it.

"No problem. You're human. How can I expect you to act civilized?" Rulo's insult was punctuated with a sharp-toothed grin.

While they were working, I asked W to scan the station. It was circular, rotating of its own volition.

"I'm not picking up any life forms, Captain. There are also minimal energy readouts. It is dead as a doornail. I'll never understand human colloquialisms," W said.

"Neither will I, Dubs. So the station's dead. How about the planet?" I asked.

"We would have to send probes, but I do not see any on this vessel," he said.

"The ones on our fleet's ships now have been added as a modification. The original Kraski ships didn't have them," Slate reminded us.

"No sign of a Keppe lifeboat… wait… what's that?" Suma asked. "I'm getting a faint reading from the surface. It could match the signature, but there's something in the atmosphere blocking the readouts properly."

"I think that is one. I know we only got a flicker, but I recognized the nomenclature, I'm sure of it," Rulo said.

I was excited by the idea of discovering a real clue to Magnus' disappearance. Finding someone in space was like a needle in a haystack... if the needle was the size of a proton and the haystack was… well, space. We needed concrete leads to get us anywhere, especially since the trail grew dry after this stop along the map.

"We're going in, team. W, be careful with the descent. If the atmosphere is causing issues with the readouts, then I want you to exert extreme caution lowering us through it," I ordered.

"Yes, Captain," W answered, and flew us by the space station. I watched it grow larger in the viewscreen before our trajectory changed and we left it behind us as we made for the planet.

"You sure we shouldn't explore that space station? If I know Magnus, and I do, he'll have stopped there to check it out," Slate said.

He was right, but I didn't want the detour. "That can be a last resort. First things first. Check to see if this blip we got really was a Keppe signature."

Slate crossed the bridge. "Could it have been from *Fortune*?"

I watched Rulo's expression and caught something before she frowned and waved a dismissive hand at Slate. "No. I don't think so. It might be nothing."

If that was Magnus' ship, then I didn't expect it to be intact. The vessel was too large to land on a planet's surface without dire consequences. If they'd made an emergency landing through this atmosphere, that could be why they weren't able to leave or transmit.

Maybe they were down there. The minutes felt like hours as W traversed the distance to orbit. From here, the landscape below was much of the same. Sandy, desert-like, with oceans abounding.

"We're on the wrong side. W, take us around orbit, and we'll enter in twelve minutes," Suma said, and W nodded his agreement.

The twelve minutes went by slowly, and I found myself pacing the bridge like a caged animal. "I'll be right back," I said, and took off through the hallway and into the bunk room. The communicator was where I left it on the nightstand, and I picked it up, pressing the icon. "Magnus, if you're nearby, respond. It's Dean. Respond."

The communicator sat cold and soundless in my palm. "Damn it," I whispered to myself, setting it beside the bed. I had an inkling that if he was on the planet below, he might be able to answer, since we were so close now. It didn't mean the *Fortune* wasn't there, but it did make my mind spin in speculation even more than it had been.

The ship shook violently, throwing me against the

ceiling before dropping me onto the bed with a thud. I narrowly missed hitting my head on the end table, and after a few more shakes, the room calmed to a stop.

"Everyone okay?" I asked as I regained my composure and ran to the bridge.

Slate was on the ground, Rulo bent over him. "That's one hell of an entry, Dubs." Slate's voice was muffled, and I saw why. His nose was bleeding, and he tilted his head up.

Karo was in the far corner, rubbing his elbow. "You okay, Karo?" I asked the Theos, and he nodded.

"My pride is more wounded than my elbow, I fear," he said softly. "How about you?"

"I'm fine. And to think I always complain about how hard the mattresses are. I won't ever again," I said.

"I am sorry, everyone. The atmosphere was thick, the composition unfavorable to entry, but we are in the clear henceforth," Dubs said. I looked out the viewscreen, watching the dunes rising and falling below. It was an amazing sight. Wind blew, casting sand around, creating fog-like conditions the lower we drifted.

W lifted us above it, and we searched for a less blustery region to ground the ship in. We found it after a few minutes, and Suma was pleased with how close we were to the blip they'd discovered from above.

"It was nearby. Within two kilometers. Who wants to go on an adventure?" she asked.

No one replied, and Suma's shoulders sank as she stood solemnly. "I assume you won't be convinced to stay on board again this time, Suma?" I asked.

She shook her head and lifted her short snout. "You have to be kidding me. I need to stretch these little legs out. Slate's bleeding, so he should probably stay put."

"Hey, it's just a nosebleed. I'm as good as new…

see?" Slate removed his hand to expose a red and swollen nose.

"Uhm, Slate… you're out. Stay with W and be our eyes and ears on the ship." I was already moving to the rear of the ship and ignored his efforts to persuade me to reconsider. "And hurry up. I want to see if there are any clues and get back here within two hours."

SEVENTEEN

"I hate this world," I said as I stepped forward, my EVA boots sinking half a foot into the sand. There wasn't much worse than walking on sand while wearing a heavy space suit. The gravity was close to Earth's, but even stronger, making the venture all the more strenuous. The only one not complaining was Suma, who weighed the least, and therefore had the easiest time maneuvering through the endless sandy landscape.

"I do as well, Dean," Karo said. He pointed forward, and I squinted, attempting to decipher through the sandstorm. The winds had eased up, but not enough to make visibility a non-issue.

"What do you see?" I asked him. His voice carried into my earpiece. If we didn't have them, we wouldn't even have been able to hear one another a foot apart in the whistling wind.

"There's something sticking out of the sand ahead." Karo pointed again, and it came into my sight.

"I see it too," Rulo said. She bounded ahead of us, and I struggled to keep up as sand battered against my helmet. "It's one of ours. It's a Keppe lifeboat!" she yelled.

I spotted it then, an elongated rectangle. A corner of it was jutting out from the sand; otherwise, it appeared like the lower half was concealed. It was heavily damaged, broken on one side.

Even though we'd found it, the trek across the rolling dunes took another ten minutes, and by the time we arrived at its edge, my legs were screaming at me. It was a good thing we trained every day, because I'd be on the ground covered by sand if I wasn't in decent shape.

Rulo didn't waste any time. She was at the hatch near the front of the lifeboat, prying it open with a hard tug. Karo assisted her to pull it open, displacing sand into a pile beside us.

"Hello!" she shouted in her language, the word translating for me. We piled into the crashed vessel, one after the other. Suma was last, and I helped her up and in before tugging the door closed. I could hear the incessant shrieking wind, but at least inside, I was protected from it.

"Hello!" I said in English, shaking sand off my suit. Rulo was already checking the front of the ship, and Karo and I went to the rear, while Suma went to the side of the door, where a computer sat lit up.

The lifeboat was only big enough for ten passengers and had basic functionality. It was meant for its namesake function. If things were dire, the Keppe could send some of the crew out to be saved in the vessel.

Karo was ahead of me, and he stopped suddenly as he neared the rear section of the ship. I'd been looking at the ground, and I bumped into him.

"Oh my," Karo said, and I peered around him to see at least five dead. The ship was torn apart here, and sand was piling into the breach. The Keppe weren't wearing armor suits, or even masks. They hadn't survived the crash to the surface.

Rulo appeared and stepped around us, kneeling at the side of a fallen Keppe man. "This lifeboat is from *Fortune.* Why are they here, and crashed?" Her usually controlled voice wavered as she held the man's hand in her gloved fingers.

"No one up front?" I asked.

"No one alive. Three more bodies, though," she whispered.

"Perhaps we'll find answers in their computer system," Karo suggested.

"It won't do any good standing here." I glanced at the fallen Keppe and wished better for them. Rulo stayed behind, staring at her people's lifeless bodies.

"Suma, anything usable?" I asked.

She stared with wide black eyes, nodding. "Dead?"

"Yes," Karo answered, and she hung her head before tapping away at the console.

"The backup system is still working. I'll download it all, and I think we can find some answers. At least partial ones." Suma kept typing.

"Do you think we can determine where they came from?" I asked, and she nodded.

"It appears so," she said.

The lifeboat might have crashed, and lives had been lost, but at least their efforts allowed us a clue into where *Fortune* was. I had to count it as a win. A sad moment, but a win nonetheless.

"Karo, let's help Rulo bury her people and return to the ship," I said.

By the time we entered onto the Kraski vessel, we were exhausted, weak, hungry, and melancholic, but we held some important information on a datastick in Suma's possession. And none of us were willing to eat or shower until we knew where the lifeboat came from.

"Two hours, huh?" Slate gave me a playful jab with his elbow, and I rolled my eyes.

"I don't have the patience for this at the moment.

Can you grab us some coffee and see if W is done charging?" I asked, and watched Slate's smile dissipate into a frown.

"You got it. For once, I'm glad I stayed behind," he said.

Once we removed our dirty suits, we wound our way to the bridge, where Suma was already loading the stick into a port.

Data streamed onto the viewscreen with the tap of a button, and the group of us watched with keen interest as Suma made sense of it. Rulo sat beside her, identifying what files were important and what they didn't need to access.

"Captain, it is good to see you all aboard," Dubs said as he entered, followed by Slate with a carafe of coffee.

"Don't forget to tip your waiter," Slate said as he passed the cups around, each of us eagerly accepting the beverage with thanks. He set a plate of protein bars in front of us, and we chewed away at them as Suma found the map we'd been waiting for.

"There it is: the path this lifeboat has taken since being activated," Suma said.

A map appeared on the viewscreen. The trajectory of the boat showed as a dotted line, ending on the desert world we currently sat in orbit around.

"All we have to do is follow the line, and we'll find them," Karo said.

"Or at least see where they were when they felt the need to send a boat off. If they used this boat, things were dire," Rulo said.

"How many lifeboats does each Keppe exploration vessel hold?" I asked.

"Ten," she answered.

"That's not even enough for a quarter of the crew," I

said.

Her answer was honest: "In our experience, there's rarely an occurrence where everyone has time to vacate a ship in danger. So we play the percentages."

"What can we tell about the starting point?" Slate asked, pointing at the system where the dotted line originated.

Suma zoomed in, and we got a slightly better idea of the surroundings. "From this, we can see a few planets nearby, but the lifeboat's sensors were limited. There's no visible star near them."

"This is the system without a star that Crul was telling us about. Beyond the edge of the universe, where at least four other vessels have gone and never returned." I expected that number was a conservative one.

"I doubt it's really the edge. Most Shimmal astrophysicists don't believe there is an end…" Suma started, but I cut her off.

"I don't want to fall into a philosophical discussion about the expanding universe. My brain can hardly keep up as it is. Let's call it the unexplored side of the universe, then, for this purpose," I said, feeling every step in the sand at that moment.

"The image doesn't necessarily mean there's no star in the system either. It might be out of range of the inadequate sensors," Slate said.

"He's not wrong," Rulo said, not quite giving Slate's estimation full confidence.

"At least we have a starting point. W, how long until arrival?" I asked, and Dubs leaned over Suma, keying the location into the console.

"We can be there in eleven days, fourteen hours, and …"

"Thanks, Dubs. I think that's accurate enough." I

turned and slogged away, in search of a bed.

It had been under two months since we'd first left New Spero for Haven, but it felt like so much longer since I'd held Jules in my arms and kissed my wife. I sat in the kitchen with a tablet, scrolling through images of my family while eating dinner, when Slate came and sat down. His nose was almost healed, and he pulled a chair to the table across from me.

"What are we eating? Green or red tonight?" he asked, peering at my plate.

"Green. I can't stomach red anymore. I love the Keppe, but they have a limited palate, don't they?" I pushed the plate away, leaving a third of the slop. I wasn't sure even Maggie would enjoy this.

"I'll have a red, then. Reminds me of spaghetti." Slate got up and used the Kraski cooker to heat the food. "You miss them a lot." He didn't have to say who he meant.

"Yeah. It's so weird, Slate. Remember when we were running around the galaxy, getting into trouble at every intersection? I wasn't married, Magnus and Nat had just tied the knot, none of us had kids. Everything is so different now."

"Not for me. I got to basically grow up and watch everyone around me dive headfirst into adult relationships. I still haven't managed to do that." His food was ready, and he plopped the plate onto the table, his red sauce steaming.

"You were so young. I pulled up to the cloaked base in New Mexico with Leslie and Terrance cuffed in the back. You took the keys and drove into the base. You remember that?" I asked.

"Of course I do. I was working for General Heart. He was a good man." Slate looked older at that moment, with a bushy blond beard and a slight crinkling at his eyes as he smiled, thinking about the old general.

"He was a great man."

"You were a legend, Dean. You, Mary, Natalia and Magnus. When I found out you were coming to our base, I was nervous to meet you." Slate was eating slowly, his eyes distant and reminiscent.

"Nervous to meet me. If only you knew back then."

"What? That we'd become best friends? That I'd have to save your life more times than I can count on my two hands?" He laughed, and I joined him.

"Yeah. All of that. It's been quite a ride, hasn't it, buddy?" I stuck a fist across the table, and he clenched his big hand, bumping it.

"Wouldn't have it any other way," Slate said.

"Me neither. You ever think about trying to settle down again?" I asked. I'd tiptoed around the subject for the last few years, ever since I'd had to kill Denise. It wasn't an easy topic to bring up with him.

"I do. Maybe I should put myself out there again. Damn Denise. I can't even blame her, really. It was Lom. Him and his brainwashed hybrids. How did you get over it?" Slate asked, and I realized we hadn't talked about my previous relationship in a long time. It was easier that way, but I owed him this.

"I didn't get over it. I moved on. Janine will always be a part of me, but honestly, my heart doesn't miss any of it. It hasn't for a long time."

"It's easier when you have Mary," he said.

"You can find your Mary, then." I gave him a grin, and he kept eating.

"Maybe. I have had my eye on this woman on Earth. She's out of the New York complex. Maybe I'll go visit when we're back." Slate was finally opening up.

"We need to talk about things like this more, Slate. We're brothers. It doesn't always have to be about how many slugs we each killed or didn't kill. Sometimes it can be about these kinds of subjects," I said.

"I hear you… brother." He winked at me, and I threw a crumpled napkin at him. "You ready for tomorrow?"

Tomorrow was the day we arrived in the system of no return. "I hope so. With any luck, we'll find them sitting there waiting for us," I said, knowing that was a lot to ask.

"If only. Thanks for the chat. Any chance you want to lose another game of cribbage?" he asked with a smirk.

"I'd be happy to show you how it's done…again. You'd think you'd have learned by now." I picked up the tablet, took one last look at an image of my wife and Jules, and switched the screen to the crib board.

Slate was already shuffling, and we settled in for an evening of cards.

EIGHTEEN

"We are officially on the outer edges of the system we are calling UES, or unexplored side, as per our captain's orders," W said, making me sound like a dictator.

"I didn't… never mind. What are we looking at?" I asked, waiting for the system's radar scanners to advise us of any vessels nearby.

"Boss, may I suggest something?" Slate asked as he stared at the dark space beyond on the viewscreen.

"Slate, since when do you ask first? Go for it," I urged.

"We don't know what's here. Obviously there's something dangerous, and that could be an anomaly or an enemy. I suggest we go in cloaked, so we can investigate without being targeted." Slate rested his hands on his hips.

"Good call. W, cloak us. That will pull the power from our shields, but if no one sees us coming, they can't fire on us." The cloak also wiped our ID and electronics from sensors, so we were essentially going in dark.

"Cloaking drive activated. Shields at minimal protection, but it will be enough for small debris, should we encounter any," W said.

"We're picking up two of the system's planets from here, Dean," Suma said. "I've been tracking the closest one for as long as I could, and now have an estimation of its trajectory."

"What good does that do?" Rulo asked.

"It's going to tell me if the planet is indeed orbiting anything, or if they're now freely floating through space," Suma answered.

"Explain, Suma," I suggested.

"If the star actually disappeared, the planets would cease to orbit anything. They need the gravitational pull from the mass of the star for the orbit to function. If it's gone, they should be free in space. What I did find was interesting." Suma tapped on the console, bringing up an image across the right side of the viewscreen. "This planet still appears to be orbiting something."

"And that's bizarre?" I asked.

"If there's no star, then yes," she replied.

"Then we'd better check out the center of this solar system," Slate said.

"I concur. Let's find out what's waiting for us. If Magnus arrived here, that's where he would have gone," I said.

"That's where they would all have gone, and now *Fortune* is missing, along with at least four other ships, according to Kimtra." Rulo's arms were crossed, and she was frowning as she stared at the image of the planet moving along a plotted line.

"We will arrive in over three days," W informed us. The entire trip would have taken us a year if we'd flown from Keppe, but we'd had the luxury of cutting the trip's time by using the portals to navigate to the Traders' world.

The stones were failing, and we had no idea how long it would be before they failed completely. We either had to find a way to power them while deprived of the Theos inside or we'd end up living without them. There were still some ways of ascending from point A to point B, and I had the portals from Fontem to work with. Clare was trying to duplicate the system, but so far had come up blank. The technology was hard to deconstruct and reverse-engineer.

If the stones ceased working entirely, we wouldn't be able to move from Haven to New Spero to Earth with the quick jumps, and that was going to cause issues for our race. But maybe it wasn't such a bad thing. Mary and I could live out the rest of our days on New Spero, or even at the farmhouse on Earth. Maybe I was looking at it the wrong way. Perhaps the stones fading was a good thing for me.

I pushed the thought from my mind. It wasn't. We'd built too much, entrusted vast energy into our new relationships to let it slip away now. It was months to travel between Earth and New Spero, and we'd flown to Haven once, but only through a wormhole that stole years from us.

And what of the Gatekeepers? Their main function was traveling to portal worlds, exploring, cataloging, making contact with new races. Without the stones, they basically became inessential. I already wondered how many of our Gatekeepers had used the portals, only to end up on the wrong world. The "crossed wires" were likely wreaking havoc on the entire team.

We needed a solution, and fast.

"Dean, are you okay?" Karo asked.

I was standing in the middle of the bridge, rubbing my temples and muttering. "I'm fine. I was thinking about the stones again."

"We have time. Let's discuss this in the other room," Karo said.

"Call me if anything pops up," I told the rest of the

team and followed Karo to the kitchen.

We sat opposite one another, and I cut to the chase. "Karo, tell me the truth. The Theos are disappearing from the portal stones. What do you know about it?" I'd seen the way he stared at the glowing crystals, the profound sadness in his eyes. I used to think it was his loneliness, but there was more to it.

"The Theos are already dead, Dean. They don't sing inside the stones any longer. I cannot access them as we once did. With the Iskios gone, they're disappearing too."

"How much longer before they aren't operational?" I asked.

He shrugged and swept his long white hair over his shoulder. "There's no way for me to know that. I'm surprised they work at all."

"We have the device from J-NAK. That seems to work." I leaned my elbows onto the tabletop and rested my head in my hands.

"And it may continue to solve the issue. I'm not sure, though. I suspect they'll stop working eventually," Karo said. "Even with the Modifier."

"I think there are going to be some Gatekeepers out there unable to get home," I said, wishing there was more I could do.

"One thing at a time, Dean. We're here right now, and Magnus and Natalia need us. We can deal with the next thing once we return home with our friends." Karo's stare was hard and confident.

"What are you feeling about this? Planets orbiting nothing? It isn't scientifically possible. They need something with mass, don't they?" I asked him.

"As far as I'm aware, you are correct, but we've seen enough that goes beyond the scope of science for me to really judge what is and isn't possible. We have three days to travel and find out if *Fortune* is still there or not," he said.

"And what do you think?"

Karo gave as good an answer as I could expect at that moment: "I think there are too many unknowns to guess."

"Want to go work out?" I asked. My body was filled with nervous energy, and so was Karo's, judging by his fidgeting hands.

Karo gave me a good-natured mocking smile. "Sure. I'd be happy to give you another try at the mats."

"You're saying the star would be visible and taking up half of our viewscreen at this point?" I was encouraging W to reiterate what he'd said.

"That is correct. I don't know what classification, but we have used the size of the planets and their trajectories to determine what size and type of star would affect them in their current pattern. It is probably an orange dwarf."

"Does that help us in any way?" I asked, irritated that we were only a few hours from the position where the lifeboat had detached from *Fortune*.

"My father says it's always good to have all the facts," Suma said, hurt evident in her voice.

"Suma, it's fine, I was only wondering. Is there nothing showing up on the radars?" I asked, and W advised me that there had been no change.

"What happened to them?" I asked no one.

"Results are coming," Suma said, typing away at the console.

"What results?" I asked.

"We sent a series of transmissions out toward the location where the star would have been," she said.

"What would that do?" I stood behind Suma's chair and watched as data streamed onto the computer screen.

"I had an idea about the entire scenario." She rotated the chair to face me, while the data kept compiling. "I had a feeling that perhaps the star remained, but was invisible. That might give us a clue."

She turned and let out a series of Shimmali squawks and clicks. I picked up a few of them and leaned forward. "Good news?" I asked.

"I'm not sure. It appears as though the mass of the star exists, but the star itself doesn't. This makes absolutely no sense," Suma said, tapping away at the console.

"Perhaps the transmissions are false," W offered.

"No. It doesn't look like it. There's no heat being given off, so that rules out cloaking… maybe. There are too many variables we don't have the answers to," Suma said.

"W, don't get too close. What if Magnus set a course for the star that wasn't there, and it destroyed him? We can't let that happen to us. It's kind of ironic, isn't it?"

"What is?" Suma asked.

"We're cloaked and looking for an invisible star," I said without any mirth.

I went and woke up Karo, Rulo, and Slate, and advised them of what Suma had found. By the time everyone was on the bridge, we were closing in on the end of our planned journey: the starting point of the crashed Keppe lifeboat. This system was the epitome of black space, and if I had any choice, I would have turned around and raced toward the Traders' world.

"Captain, I'm picking up an anomaly on the sensors," W said.

"What is it?" Slate asked.

"I'm not sure." W zoomed in the viewscreen until we were able to see a colorful display some distance from our current position. "It appears to be a nebula."

It wasn't as large as some nebulae I'd seen before, but it was dense; dark green clouds of gas stared back at us. "Where did it come from?" Karo was walking past me to watch the image of the beautiful sight.

"We don't know. It wasn't there one moment; the next it was," Suma answered.

"This is it," I said, as if the entire mystery had been solved in a matter of seconds.

"What is what?" This from Slate.

"Things are vanishing from the system, and a colorful nebula arrives as soon as we reach the spot where Magnus' ship sat only two months ago. Either it's coming for us or it expects us to come to it." I was so sure I was onto something with my theory.

"It's an interstellar cloud of dust and gases, not an entity," Suma said.

"Would it be the strangest thing we've ever seen?" I waited for an answer, and when it didn't come, I continued. "If the star is still here, or at least its hidden mass is, then who's to say that Magnus isn't here as well?"

"How could he be here? Do you see *Fortune* on the sensors?" Rulo asked.

"No, and we don't see the star either. What if this nebula is causing vessels and stars, maybe planets, to disappear to sensors and to our eyes? I'll agree that it might not even be a nefarious supervillain, just an inert nebula with odd characteristics," I said.

I expected to receive a little flak for my suggestions, so I was surprised to get some positive responses. "You might be right, Dean," Suma said. "The lifeboat's tracking began from over there." She pointed to the viewscreen, and an icon glowed on it in the rough shape of a Keppe boat.

"Can you try the transmission test again to see if there's a ship there on some plane or another?" I asked, and Suma nodded.

We waited as she sent out a signal, seeing if it bounced off any object or if it pushed straight through. "Nothing," she said, "but his ship was a lot smaller than trying to hit a star. I'll keep trying. If the ship is here in this vicinity in some form, we'll find it."

I stared at the nebula in the distance, and it sat there in space, wide and unmoving. "Is that thing big enough to swallow a star?" I asked quietly.

"It doesn't look like it. Actually, now that we've watched it for a while, I'd say this is unlike any nebula on record. It's moving, and fast." Suma was right. The clouds were rolling, and it almost appeared that bolts of energy were flashing in its core.

"That can't be a good sign," Slate said.

Karo pointed at it. "This is no nebula. Dean was right in his assumption. It wants us. I can feel it."

That same feeling in the pit of my stomach began to grow as I watched it. There was nothing friendly or aloof about the lifeless cloud of dust. This was something more. Much more.

"Suma, hurry up with those tests." I said it softly, worried that alarm would ring out with my voice. If Magnus was nearby, trapped in a non-visible state, I wanted to know before the dancing dark green cloud raced toward us. "I really wish we had those probes now." I crossed my arms, trying to think of an alternative to send into the maw of the beast.

"Come with me. We might have something in the cargo bay that will work," Rulo said, and I followed her to the rear of the ship.

"I think I know where you're going, Dean. You want to send something into the nebula and see where it leads." Rulo began moving crates, opening a few before she appeared to find what she was looking for.

"A nebula doesn't have a mouth or opening to transport anything through it. If the object flies past the cloud and to the other side, we know it isn't related. What do you have in mind?" I was curious, and confused when she pulled out a small box.

"This is a tracker drone. We use them on ground missions. If we program a target into them, they follow it, above tree lines, underwater. Anywhere the target goes, this will follow," she said. It was even smaller than the palm-sized light-drone I'd used on the asteroid, and I watched as Rulo powered it up.

"That's tiny." It was the size of a field mouse. "Good for reconnaissance."

"It records everything, and this" – she held up an arm-strap console – "intercepts instant feeds from it, so we always have visual, anticipated body temp, whatever we need. Pretty great, isn't it?"

"And you can control it from there?" I pointed to the small strapped console.

"Yes."

I smiled. At least we had something to test the colorful space cloud with.

"Dean, you're going to want to see this," Suma's voice carried over the ship's speakers.

We jogged to the bridge, and if my eyes weren't playing tricks on me, our friend the nebula was growing larger on the screen. "What did you find?" I asked.

Suma spun in the chair and stared at me with her big dark eyes. "There was pushback."

She showed me an image on her console of a series of dots going out in a net. They hit a surface, and some kept moving above and below, but others remained stagnant. The end result was the shape of a space ship.

My heart beat quickly in my chest. We'd done it. "Can you run measurements?"

"I already did. The length matches *Fortune*."

NINETEEN

Two days had passed, and we weren't any closer to having answers than we'd been when Suma told me her discovery. It was so frustrating to be in such close proximity to them, without the ability to contact them or solidify their existence.

We were all cramped into the kitchen, W and Karo standing along the wall so we had enough seats.

"Are they really there? That's the question. Is that a stamp of what was, and for some reason, the imprint is still there, like the star?" I asked the theoretical question again. The truth was, none of us knew.

We'd approached the location of the ship and passed through it. Apparently, the shadow of the ship didn't give it substance. It was like *Fortune* had become a ghost.

Slate took a bite of the remains of dinner and ran his hands through his hair, leaning back in his chair. "We have to test the nebula," he said.

"I don't know why we insist on calling it that. It's clearly nothing of the sort." Suma was becoming frustrated too. This whole mission had us on edge; none of us had been able to benefit from a good night's rest since the discovery.

"Then what would you call it?" Slate asked her.

"I don't know. The Cloud. The Void. The eater of hopes and dreams!" She shouted the last bit, and I raised a hand.

"I know morale is low, and we're all tired. Let's not let our emotions get out of hand. Fine, Suma, for your sake, let's call the distortion the Cloud. Slate, I agree. It's time we send Rulo's tracking drone through the Cloud. I'm sorry it took me so long to make this decision. I was hoping to be able to contact the ghost ship before we attempted anything against the colorful adversary."

"You think it's responsible now?" Karo asked me.

"I do. There's no other explanation. It's coming for us, moving slowly over two days, but according to W, it's picked up speed three times, only to decelerate to a common drift toward us. That means it's capable of moving of its own volition," I said.

"And this tracking drone. Do you think it will be able to return to us?" Karo was full of questions tonight, but not many suggestions.

I shook my head. "No. I don't think it will, but maybe we'll learn some important information about it in the process."

"What if we learn nothing?" Karo asked.

I was fed up with his questions. "If you have something to say, spit it out."

The room was tense, and Karo's eyes softened. "Stay with me, Dean. I'm leading somewhere."

"If we learn nothing, we've neither gained nor lost anything. We stay for a while and try to find a way to contact Magnus." I drank the dredges of coffee from my cup. It was cold and bitter, but I didn't care. It was fueling my exhausted mind.

Karo asked another one. "And if it disappears inside the Cloud, never to return?"

"Then we know what happened to Magnus and the others. Probably the star too," Suma answered for me.

"I know where you're leading, Karo. You want to know if we'll be going into the Cloud if we think that's where Magnus and Natalia ended up." My cup lowered to the table with a louder bang than I intended. Slate jumped at the startling sound. "I don't know. That'll be a new discussion."

Rulo stood up, the chair battering against the kitchen wall as her bulky frame shrank the room. "What are we waiting for, then? No time like this moment to shoot off the drone."

Five minutes later, Rulo released it through the containment field at the belly of our ship, controlling it with deft fingertips. For a woman with substantial muscles and armored skin, she had a light touch on the controls.

After the ramp was closed and sealed, we moved the party to the bridge, where the massive Cloud loomed closer with each passing moment. We'd considered moving away from it, and W programmed the ship to do just that, should it settle within two thousand kilometers of our position.

"How far away is it now?" Slate asked W.

"It's twelve thousand, five hundred and eleven kilometers from us," W answered.

Rulo pulled a stick from the side of her armband console and passed it to Suma. "Plug this into the universal adapter you have jury-rigged on that thing. We'll push the feed onto the viewscreen."

Seconds later, we were intercepting a live feed from the miniscule tracking drone as it propelled toward the great Cloud. It was getting larger and darker the nearer it got to us, adding to the tension. It showed us nothing but the rumbling clouds and shades of moss green, energy within cracking sporadically. This was a big bad ball of energy, and it was coming for us.

Not much happened as the drone shot quickly across the expanse between us and the Cloud, until it was a thousand kilometers away. Rulo tried maneuvering it, but the drone began to spin out of control. "It's being sucked in now. I've lost control."

"I don't see a vortex or singularity. This is the strangest black hole slash nebula in existence," Suma said.

We all watched with fraying nerves as the drone's feed kept showing us the spinning colors and blazing lightning within the Cloud. For a second, I was reminded of the Iskios vortex, but this was different, far different.

"I'm glad Mary's not here," I whispered.

"So am I," Slate said.

"Drone is sending pressure and temperature data. It's cold. Colder than expected." Rulo's voice rose, even though we weren't hearing any sound from the stream.

I had to avert my eyes. The constant rotating was doing nothing to calm my already nervous stomach.

"It's entering the Cloud's perimeter," Suma warned. We'd determined the Cloud was five hundred kilometers deep, and twice as wide and tall. Not something to be messed with.

I glanced up, and the feed was now a mess of dust, debris, colorful gases, and crackling energy.

"It continues to send readings," Rulo said.

"Can we make use of anything?" I asked.

"Not yet, Captain. Perhaps once we have time to analyze the results." W was typing away on the console, his fingers moving faster than my brain could decipher.

Instantly, the room's mood changed, and the viewscreen side with the livestream went black before the Cloud took over the entire screen again. "It's gone," Slate and I said at the exact same moment.

"It's gone." Rulo unstrapped the control from her

arm and dropped it to the floor.

"What did we learn?" I was on the bridge with Suma, alone for the time being. We'd been through all our options countless times at this point, and we'd also moved away from the Cloud on three occasions. We were spinning our wheels out here, but the good news was, we hadn't been swallowed by the Cloud yet. I was clinging to the small victories.

Suma listed the items off. "We learned what the temperature was inside the Cloud, and what percentage of gases it's composed of, and the relative pressure within and around the anomaly."

"But nothing to help us learn what's on the other side." Our seats were facing each other, and Suma wasn't meeting my eyes as I watched her. "What is it?" I asked.

"I really thought we could help. I was so sure that if we assembled this team of you, me, and Slate, like the good old days, that we'd come out here and bring Magnus and Natalia home, along with the kids and the Keppe crew. But here we are, a week in-system, with no answers." Suma seemed ready to cry, and I reached across, grabbing her shoulder.

"Chin up, Suma. I'm sorry if I've been a little short lately. I want the same thing as you do; as all of us do. Under any other circumstance, I'd probably be storming inside the damned Cloud to see what happens and figure a way out after the fact," I said.

"But…"

"But I can't do that any longer, and I can't ask any of you to either. Plus, we only have one ship." I let go of her, and she finally met my gaze.

"We could leave and come back, then head in," she suggested.

I'd thought the same thing the night before as I stared at my ceiling instead of sleeping. It was all catching up to me. I had to cut the caffeine for a day and get some rest, or I wasn't going to last much longer.

"We could do that, but it might be too late then. Magnus is here. We know there's some weird stuff going on that we don't understand, but his ship's outline is there, as is the missing star's. If only I could figure it out." I squeezed the communicator in my hand. It was the same one we'd used when Leonard and I went to the Bhlat home world after we first landed on New Spero, and the others were in captivity above Earth after the Bhlat were threatening a takeover.

Now I had one side, and Magnus had the other; only they were proving useless across this Cloud barrier that seemed to separate us from each other's plane or dimension, or whatever it was really called.

Suma nodded to it. "Have you tried it today?"

I shook my head. "Hasn't worked any other day. Why should it now?"

"I don't know. We can't give up, Dean. That's all I know. Magnus would never give up," she said as her eyes went wide and she gave me a sad smile.

"You're right. Did he give up when we were stuck on Sterona?" I asked.

"Nope. He traded with the Keppe so he could come rescue us. And that very trade got him where he is today." Suma sat up in her chair, her posture improving as we chatted.

I flipped the communicator around in my hand. "What the hell. Can't hurt." I tapped the icon and smiled at Suma. She was such a great young woman, and Mary and my lives were much richer for having her around. Even now she was able to lift my spirits. "Magnus, come in. It's Dean. We're outside the anomaly and know you're nearby. Where are you? Come in, Magnus."

It stayed silent in my hand. "See. Nothing…"

"Dean! You're here…" The voice cut off, but there was no mistaking my Scandinavian friend's voice.

"Magnus!"

"…inside… can't leave… don't…"

"Don't what?" I was standing up, pacing the bridge, Suma right beside me.

"Dean. Don't come for us…" His voice was hard but fearful. I knew his protective tone like the back of my hand.

"We can't do that. We're coming for you!" I said into it, but the call was over. "Magnus!" I shouted into it, but the connection was lost.

The others must have heard my shouting, because they all raced to the bridge, surrounding me. My heart was in my throat, and I passed Suma the communicator like it might burn my hand.

"He's alive. They're alive!" I shouted, finally letting an ounce of joy press through the stress and pain.

"What happened?" Slate yelled. He was in his underwear, and Rulo rolled her eyes at him.

"I tried to reach him like I have every other day, but this time, he answered. He's alive. He said they were inside, and that they can't leave, right, Suma?" I was pacing frantically, and I was sure that my heart would never reach a normal pulse rate again.

"He also said, 'don't come for us'," Suma told the group.

"It doesn't matter. That was his papa bear mentality

kicking in. He's stuck on the other side, or in limbo in some unknown place, and doesn't want us to join them," I said.

"But we have to," Slate said.

"We have to," Rulo said too. It was her people's ship, and there were far more Keppe on board than humans. She would have been told by Lord Crul to bring them back at any cost. Rulo wasn't leaving until we did just that.

Karo broke his silence. He stood the farthest away, one foot on the bridge and one in the hall. "There are so many variables you haven't contemplated, Dean. What if the Cloud destroys us? What if it sends us to a different place than it sent *Fortune*? What…"

"What if we play the what-if game all night and never end up anywhere? Karo, we owe him this. At least I do," I said.

Slate's chin lifted proudly. "So do I."

"Me too. He's our friend," Suma said.

"Very well. I only want to be the voice of reason on an otherwise passion-fueled crew. I fully agree we should attempt this rescue." Karo stepped onto the bridge and put his big arm around my shoulder.

"Someone should go power Dubs up, I guess," Slate said with a laugh.

The entire mood had gone from devastation to hope, but Karo was right. Just because we got a communication from Magnus, it didn't mean we were going to be able to pull this off. Still, we had to try.

I walked to the corner of the bridge and stared at the Cloud through the viewscreen. It appeared to be moving faster, almost as if it knew our plans. "Forgive me, Mary. You'd do the same thing, babe. I know you would. It's Magnus and Nat. They need our help, like we needed theirs not so long ago. I guarantee they didn't hesitate to rescue us off Sterona. Little Dean, who isn't so little any longer. We need to see how he and Patty end up. We need to raise Jules beside our friends." I was talking to my wife, who was so far away at that moment, but I was sure part of her was feeling my urgency.

Dubs walked onto the bridge and turned his head, looking around at all our faces. "What did I miss?"

TWENTY

I woke up feeling well-rested for the first time in weeks. As much as I'd pushed for us to leave as soon as we were all assembled on the bridge, the crew wouldn't let me make that decision. Instead, they forced me to take a sleeping pill and go to bed. It had been the right call, because I had more energy and a calmness over my mind that had been gone for some time.

"Today's the day, buddy," I told Magnus. "We're coming to get you, Natalia." I pictured the reunion and imagined the look of consternation on Magnus' face when he found out I'd ignored his warnings.

I slipped into a clean jumpsuit, threw on my boots, and headed for the bridge, where everyone was already gathered.

"It's time?" I asked.

"We were going to leave without you, but Suma thought you'd want to be here for this part." Slate poked me in the arm with his finger, and I slapped it away.

"How long was I out?" I asked.

"Twelve hours," Slate said.

"You could have woken me up!" Twelve hours. If I didn't feel so well-rested, I would have complained more. "Any chance he used the communicator again?"

"Nothing. Squat. We've tried every ten minutes, but it hasn't worked," Slate answered.

The Cloud was massive in the viewscreen now. "We're going to head along the same path that the tracking drone took. It shouldn't take more than a few minutes to be in position."

I was glad I'd slept until that moment. Otherwise, I'd have been a nervous wreck in anticipation of traversing into the Cloud. No one spoke as we watched the approach. Suma and W were in the front two seats, and the rest of us strapped ourselves tightly to the rear wall. The drone had spun into the Cloud, and if that happened to us, we'd be thrown around, even with the inertia dampeners.

Our ship coasted toward the target and soon, the Cloud took up the entire screen. I stood at the edge of the bridge with straps wrapped around my chest and stared into the maw of the beast. An electrical storm raged around us, a few energy beams striking the shields. We'd removed the cloaking device because we already knew the Cloud was aware of our position. It had been following us.

"Remember to cloak as soon as we're through, unless we instantly see a need for our shields," I shouted, my voice loud over the silent bridge.

W was quick to reply, "I am ready, Captain."

As expected, the ship began to spin, caught in the power of the anomaly. It was like we were being flushed from one dimension to another. We spun slowly at first, then picked up speed. I had to close my eyes as the pressure built up, the straps digging into my body. Slate groaned beside me, and Rulo let out a war cry two spots over. Karo didn't make a peep on my other side, and I wondered if he'd blacked out.

Then it was over, the spinning slowed as W controlled the thrusters again, and I opened my eyes to see white dots dancing around the edges of my vision.

"Did we make it?" Slate asked.

"We made it. No initial threats, Captain. Shields activated." W's voice was thin in my ringing ears.

I unstrapped myself and fell to the floor in a heap. Slate had the decency to laugh at me.

On uneasy legs, I got up and pulled his strap buckles free with a smile. He poured to the floor much like I had. "I deserved that, boss," Slate said, taking my offered hand.

"What are we looking at?" I asked, walking in zigzags to the front of the bridge.

"It appears as though we are somewhere else, but at the same place. The location reads identically, but… as you can see." W rotated the ship, revealing a planet. A star burned hotly in the distance.

"Amazing. Suma, is that star…" I started to ask.

"In the same position as the missing star in our dimension? Yes. Yes, it is." Suma watched me with fear in her eyes.

I rested a hand on her shoulder. "We're going to be okay, Suma. This world" – I pointed to the red-tinged planet – "is populated! I can see lights from here."

"You are correct. This planet is occupied," W said.

"Occupied." Karo was beside me, watching with interest. "What's that on the radar?"

"I apologize, Captain. The telemetry scans did not activate. They must have been fried in the transport. I do see vessels. At least three of them, congregating close by." W was tapping on his console.

"Slate, where's the communicator?" I asked, and he pulled it from his pocket, passing it to me.

"Here goes nothing." I activated the line. "Magnus, come in. Dean here."

"It's a Keppe ship, Dean," Suma said as the readouts arrived. "It's them!"

"Dean Parker, I warned you not to come!" Magnus yelled through the communicator's speaker.

"We had no choice," I assured him.

"What the hell? How did you even find us? Never mind. We see you on the scanner. Come aboard. We have a lot to discuss," Magnus said.

"We're on our way." My hand trembled slightly as I held the communicator. We'd done it, only now we were trapped on the other side, and Magnus had been here for over two months without finding a way to return.

"We'll figure it out together," Suma said, as if reading my mind.

"Dean?" Magnus started.

"Yes?"

"Thanks. Thanks for coming," he said.

"That's what we do for each other, brother," I replied. "How long until we're there?"

W answered. "Twelve minutes."

"Good. Enough time to splash some cold water on my face and have something to eat." My knees were weak, and I had to give my stomach something before we got to Magnus and Natalia. "W, find out what you can about the other ships near *Fortune* while we're waiting."

"I am on it, Captain." W returned to work on his console, and I stared forward at the planet.

"We did it." Rulo clapped Slate on the back. "Somehow we found them! We should be celebrating!"

Slate hugged the big Keppe woman, and Suma was up now, joining in.

"You're correct, Rulo. Right now, we rejoice at having found them, and we'll deal with the consequences later. Great work, everyone. Magnus might be upset with us for his own reasons, but don't take his rebuking to heart. He would have done the same thing to rescue us." I beheld the crew, seeing the mix of characters at my side. This was how it was supposed to be done, not going rogue like I had when looking for Mary. Back then, I thought I needed to do it on my own, for selfish reasons.

But we were stronger as a group, and all of these people knew it. Rulo was crying, and I knew she had friends that she was going to reunite with aboard *Fortune*. It was odd to see tears streaming from her snake eyes, down the scar on her cheek.

We'd done it. But there was so much we didn't know about what *it* entailed.

We emerged off our ship and into the hangar on the Keppe vessel *Fortune*. It was a big ship, and our small Kraski vessel fit easily inside, nestled between two lifeboats. My boots met the grated metal floor of the hangar with a clank, and I was surprised to see Magnus and Natalia weren't there.

A Keppe crew member was by the corridor entrance, and he lifted a hand in greeting. Seconds later, Magnus' big frame pushed through the doorway, followed by Natalia. They ran to us, concern and relief radiating from their faces.

Slate and I met them in the middle of the hangar, and Magnus wrapped his thick arms around me, threatening to crush me in an embrace. Slate was spinning around with Natalia in his grasp, and everyone was laughing.

We switched, and Natalia pulled my face into her shoulder, and she finally spoke. "Dean Parker, I can't believe you made it here. Thank you. Thank you for coming to find us."

I held her at arm's length and smiled at her. "No thank yous necessary."

"Is Mary here?" she asked, and I shook my head.

"Mary's on New Spero with Jules. We thought it was a better idea if we waited until Jules was at least five to bring her on rescue missions," I joked.

"Where are we?" Suma was here, and the rest of the group greeted the married couple.

"We'll get into all of that inside. Dean, didn't you intercept my warning about not coming?" Magnus was frowning.

"Did you really think that would stop us from flying into the Cloud?" I asked.

"The Cloud?" Natalia asked.

"That's what we called the dark green nebula," Suma said.

"I guess I knew you were going to come anyways. I wasn't actually sure you got my communication at all. How did it work through…" Magnus pointed toward the exterior wall. "All this?"

"Sometimes the universe gives us a win. Come on, Magnus, let's find somewhere to talk. You can fill us in on what's going on." I was so glad to see them safe and healthy. Other than some sleep deprivation evident by the bags under his eyes, which I also had, Magnus appeared well.

The corridors of the Keppe ship were tall and wide, big enough to accommodate three of the large people consecutively, and I found the added space comforting. After being on the compact Kraski ship with so many crew members for the last few weeks, I could finally breathe.

Rulo stopped and chatted excitedly with a few Keppe along the way, and I knew she'd be getting the scoop from their point of view. I'd be sure to have her fill me in later.

We ended up in a room much like the one in which we'd first met Admiral Yope on *Starbound*, and I took a seat beside the head of the table, where Magnus plopped to a seat and swiveled from side to side in his chair while the rest of our crew got settled. Natalia was opposite me, and she kept staring at me like I was the last face she'd ever expected to see. The door opened again, and an old Keppe woman poked her head in. I heard the familiar jangle of dog collars, and I pushed off my chair, crouching low.

Carey ran at me, his ears flopping side to side, and he barreled into me, knocking me on my butt. "Carey!" The elderly cocker rubbed his head into my legs and climbed my lap to lick my face.

"We thought you might want to see your old friend," Nat said.

Charlie, Maggie's brother, bounced around, yipping and trying to make it past Carey to say hi to me. I stayed there petting the dogs for far too long, telling Carey how much I missed him, and how glad I was to see him so active and healthy-looking.

"He's had a few Keppe Nanoshots. They use them for animals, keeping their pets healthy for longer than they'd otherwise have been. He was sick a year or so ago, and we had no choice. He's like a puppy again," Magnus said, and I could see it in the dog's gait. He was in amazing shape for such an old canine.

"I can't believe I'm here with you guys. Mary would love to see these pups." Saying her name, and seeing Carey, was giving me all the more drive to find a way to go home.

Eventually, I had to pick myself up off the floor and settle into my chair. Carey found a spot to rest between Magnus and my feet. Charlie sat directly on Nat's feet across from us.

"Did you bring the dogs to double-check if it was really me?" I laughed, and Natalia didn't quite deny it with a smile.

"*Da*, I know, Dean. It's… been a hard couple of months."

"How are the kids?" I asked, anxious to hear about them.

"They're fine. Everyone on board is fine, Dean. But we have no way of escape. We're stuck. There's no Cloud on this side to send us away," Magnus answered.

"Who do the other ships belong to?" Slate asked.

"They're explorers like us," Magnus answered.

"How many?" I knew there were a few ships.

"Hundreds. Hundreds of vessels have arrived here over the centuries." Magnus grabbed a device from the tabletop and brought up an image on a wall screen. Everyone turned to look at the feed of the nearby planet. "This is where they end up."

"On the planet?" I clued in, finally. "Wait, are you saying that the Cloud sucked hundreds of ships through it, and now they're populating the planet?"

"That's exactly what I'm saying." Magnus tapped the controls, and the image slowly zoomed from a vantage well out of orbit, until it showed us a city from above. "The various races ended up accepting their fate and elected to populate the system. Recent records show over a billion various beings on the world today."

Slate let out a low whistle. "And how many alien races?"

Natalia shrugged. "We don't know. Over a hundred. There are Deltra, Padlog, Terellion, and even a race of telepathic bird-people, like Regnig. It's quite amazing. Suma, there's an entire Shimmali population down there."

"There is? Wait until my father hears…" Suma stopped after realizing he might never find out. He might also never know what became of his daughter.

This was huge news, but I didn't know what to do with it. My shoulders slumped as my thoughts drifted to the future. "All of these beings, all of these minds, and no one's ever found a way to leave? How can that be?"

"There *is* no way to leave, Dean. That's why I was warning you." Magnus clicked the screen off and turned to me. "Our lifeboat, is that how you found us?"

"In a matter of speaking. Why did you send them off?" I asked before telling him their fate.

"We were on the other side, trying to understand where the damned star went, and the nebula, or the Cloud as you're calling it, jumped right in front of us. It moved so quickly, we had no time to escape its clutches. We fired off a lifeboat, hoping it would be able to break free and search for help."

Magnus' explanation made sense. "That's why it was damaged. We found it crash-landed. I'm sorry, they were dead." I told him the news, and Magnus banged his hand against the table with a thud.

Suma spoke up, breaking the tension. "We used their trajectory to determine the starting point of their trip, which brought us here."

"Good work, but now I'm afraid you're stuck on the other side with us." Magnus rubbed his temples, and Natalia rubbed his forearm gently.

"This isn't over. We'll figure it out." Everyone in the room wore somber faces, as if the idea of never going home had struck them at the same time. "What about flying away?"

"We haven't tried, but that's only because we've heard countless times that there's nothing else out here. Only the darkness of space. It's almost as if someone created this place: a star, a planet, and a ship-sucking nebula on the other side to send patrons their way," Magnus said.

"Who is this someone?" Karo asked.

"No one has ever seen signs of one responsible for creating this dimensional shift. Maybe the Cloud is a naturally-occurring disturbance. Who knows? Or perhaps some being set it up a million years ago and died a long time ago," Magnus said.

"We were considering heading planetside eventually. We've already been down there to one of the cities. It was… interesting but liveable," Nat said. If she'd given up hope, then I could understand why the fire was blown out of Magnus.

"You said there are many races on the surface. Are there any… Theos?" Karo's eyes were wide, and I could feel the hope emanating from his chest.

"I'm sorry. I actually checked. No one matched your description, and there's nothing on record regarding your people," Magnus told him.

"I understand. I was expecting that answer," Karo said.

A light bulb went off in the dark corners of my mind. "Wait. Is it possible there's a portal stone on the planet?"

Magnus straightened in his chair. "I knew you'd ask. It took me three weeks to think of that. I have some inquiries in with the locals, but nothing's come up so far. If no one has ever seen it or used a portal stone, it's not going to be on record. I was going to start searching, but where would we even begin?"

I couldn't answer that. "We'd probably be grasping at straws anyway."

"Well, we can't do anything today. How about you all settle in crew quarters, and we'll revaluate in a day or two?" Magnus asked, rising from his seat. He tapped a button on the table, and a small, robed Keppe walked in. "See they're all assigned quarters, please," Magnus said, his orders translating for the Keppe crew member.

My team was funneling out, following the porter, and Magnus grabbed my arm, urging me to stay behind.

"I'll help them get settled," Nat said as she hugged me again, whispering in my ear, "It's good to see you."

Seconds later, Magnus and I were alone in the room with the dogs. His brow furrowed, and he stood inches from me. "Dean, what were you thinking?!" he yelled, and I stepped away from him, startled by the sudden occurrence. Carey let out a bark.

"What do you mean? I was thinking about helping you home."

"You had a grasp of what was going on, didn't you? Don't you think I would have come through if there was a way? Are you really that egotistical that you figured you'd be able to come save us? That you alone would have the ability to bring us back from the other side or whatever godforsaken dimension we're in now?"

Thick cords stuck out on his neck, but I stood my ground. "You can insult me all you want, Mag, but you know damned well that you'd have done the exact same thing. Are you saying you're that egotistical, then?" I stepped forward, and we were chest to chest.

Something deflated in him, and he shook his head, lowering his voice. "No, but I might be that stupid."

We stared at each other for a second before Magnus let out a bark of a laugh, making me join him. We both relaxed, and sat heavily on our chairs. "What are we going to do?" I asked.

"Honestly? I don't know." Magnus stood and headed for a cabinet at the far end of the room. He pulled out two bottles, and I instantly recognized them: a micro-brewed beer from his favorite place on New Spero. He took a sip and passed me one.

I winked at him. "I can't believe you have any left."

"I do, but that's only because I brought a lot of Scotch." Magnus leaned forward and clinked his bottle against mine.

"Cheers." I tasted it, and instantly, it felt like we were back on his porch on New Spero.

"Dean, I may be upset that you're here, but you want to know something?"

"What?" I asked.

"I'm more upset with myself." He took a drink from the bottle and fiddled with the label.

"Why's that?"

"Because I actually believe you're going to find a way for us to get home." Magnus laughed again, but this time, I didn't join him.

"Cheers to that, because you know what?"

It was his turn. "What?"

"I *am* going to find a way. Mark my word."

TWENTY-ONE

"These are the sections of the world with mountains, hills, underground caverns, or any other attributes similar to the locations of the portal stones we know about. Earth's was under a monument, but we don't know what the terrain looked like before the Egyptians built Giza. New Spero's is in the mountains, Haven's is in a hilly region underneath the surface, and the ice world's was in a frozen cavern on a cold snow-covered peak. We're using the same mapping here." Magnus was operating a console on his desk to highlight the five regions on the nearby world that fit these descriptions.

"These are pretty big areas to cover. What's the plan?" Slate asked.

Karo stood and walked over to the screen, hovering a hand over its surface. "If there is a portal, I can find it. They are, after all, powered by the Theos. I spent some time with J-NAK by the stone, and I might be able to track it."

"But you're not sure?" Magnus asked.

"I would have to be close, but I would feel or sense their vibrations," Karo said, as if that explained anything.

"Why didn't I think of this sooner? I have something in my pack on our ship, Magnus. Do you remember the device Clare made to help me find Mary?" I asked.

He made a methodical exaggerated nod.

"We could find a way to program it to Theos DNA, right? Then maybe we'd be able to track a portal stone, if there is one." I was on my feet, ready to go grab it. When it came to contraptions, I preferred to bring everything I had when I traveled on missions. You never knew when something was going to come in handy.

"That might do it," Suma said. Rulo wasn't with us, and W had stayed on our ship. The Keppe warrior had been spending a lot of time with one of Magnus' crew members, a male she'd mentioned to me a few times on our journey here. "I think I could rework it to operate successfully."

"What do you think, Karo? Willing to give a sample?" Suma's snout twitched toward him.

"Yes. Will you require stool?" he asked, straight-faced. Magnus stared hard at me, his expression threatening to make me laugh.

Suma's gaze darted away from the Theos. "Uhm, I think blood would work just fine, Karo."

If I didn't know better, Karo was making a joke at her expense. It was good to see his spirits return.

"Then it's a plan. Let's move on this. Suma, how long do you think?" Magnus asked.

"No idea. I'll have to take it apart and see. Could be a day, could be a week," she answered.

"We'll leave you to it. Magnus, how about we finally go see my little niece and nephew?" I suggested. I was excited to see the kids. It was only our second day here, and it had been too late last night to wake them.

Magnus led me down the corridors, and we talked along the way.

"Other than the obvious, how was the rest of the three years?" I asked him.

"I loved it. Captaining a real exploration vessel, with a

full crew, resources, food, schools… what more can you ask for?" Magnus greeted dozens of Keppe by name as we walked, and I was proud of him in this role. Today, he was in full Keppe uniform, which consisted of a gray robe with black stripes along the sides, and short pants that only went halfway down his shins. It looked a little amusing on a human, but on the warrior race, it was natural and classy. Magnus was lucky he was almost as large as them, because it helped him pull it off. I suspected I wouldn't look quite as comfortable in the outfit.

"And when we get home?" I asked.

"One thing at a time there, Parker. The kids have been great, though. They speak Keppe now, which is impressive. I do okay with it myself, but I prefer to use the translators anyway, in case I say the wrong thing and cause an explosion as a result." Magnus stopped at a doorway on the third floor. The ship's features were quite similar to Lord Crul's home base on Oliter. The walls and floors were shiny white, though they were made of some composite material here, not the marble-like stone that Crul favored.

"You still think you'll solve this, do you?" he asked before opening the door.

I had to tell him the truth. "I do."

His face broke out in a smile. "Good. I wouldn't have it any other way." He tapped a code in a control panel on the edge of the wide white door, and it slid open to reveal thirty or so Keppe children sitting at desks. "The Keppe try to only allow a certain number of married couples with children on each vessel, because of the additional costs. Plus, it's dangerous work, so there's always the added risk," Magnus whispered to me. "This is the entire juvenile population on *Fortune*."

They ranged from small Keppe, with sprouts of armor growing under their dark skin, to big ones, almost fully grown. I was sure a boy and girl at the front of the class were at least as big as me. Then I spotted their heads: a mess of short dirty-blond hair and the darker long hair of a human girl. I cleared my throat, and the entire room turned to look at the doorway.

"Dean!" Magnus' son yelled and ran across the room, jumping into my arms. He hugged me tightly around the neck, and I returned the hug, laughing as I held him.

"I wasn't sure you'd remember me." It had been almost three years, and he wasn't even five when they'd left.

"Mom and Dad named me after you. How could I forget you?" I set him on the floor and was astonished at how big he was.

"You're so tall. I guess you take after your dad." I rubbed his naturally messy hair, and he stepped to the side, attempting to fix it.

My gaze drifted over to Patty, who'd walked over but hadn't said anything. She stood a good five feet away, her dark brown eyes assessing me.

"Hi, Patty. I'm Dean Parker. You wouldn't remember me, since you were only just walking when you left home." I crouched, and she came closer.

"What do you mean? I *am* home," she said defiantly. I glanced up at Magnus, who rolled his eyes and crossed his arms.

"Her mother through and through. I haven't won an argument with her yet," Magnus said, and Patty stood up taller.

"I'm glad you're enjoying it here, then, Miss Patty. My little girl is going to love spending time with you," I said.

"Is she here?" Patty asked, her head cocked slightly to the side.

"No."

"Then I'll probably never meet her."

"Why's that?" I asked.

"Because Tipo told me we're stuck, and we aren't ever going to leave, and that we're going to die here." She said the words in one breath, fast, so I had a hard time keeping up.

"Is that so?" I asked, and glanced around the room, wondering which one was Tipo.

Patty nodded firmly.

"We'll have to see about that. Patty, it's been nice to see you. Dean, are you doing well in school?" I asked the boy.

He glanced at his dad before answering, "I think so."

"Would you guys mind if I came over for dinner tonight? We could talk more that way, instead of interrupting your class." The teacher was waiting at the front, hesitant to break up the reunion. I waved an apologetic hand in his direction, and he nodded his understanding.

"Yeah, come for dinner!" Dean said with excitement.

"I guess that's okay." Patty turned away and stalked to her seat.

"See you later, Dean," Magnus's son said to me, and we left the schoolroom.

The door closed, and Magnus and I were alone in the hallway once again. "That was intense."

"I don't know where she gets the attitude," Magnus said, and I laughed.

"Right. As if the offspring of Magnus and Natalia could be any other way," I accused him.

"What about Dean? He's so outgoing."

"It's the name." We kept moving through the corridor. "Every Dean is meant for big things. I hope you don't mind me inviting myself over for dinner."

"Not at all. We were going to anyway. Tonight, we eat like a family, and tomorrow, if Suma's done her modifications, we head to the surface," Magnus said.

"Perfect. I hope you don't mind, but I invited the others to dinner as well," I said. I really hadn't, but I was feeling him out.

"Even Slate?" Magnus asked with mocking disgust.

"Even Zeke," I replied.

"The more the merrier. Dean, I really hope we can climb out of this mess. I admit I'm angry that you're here, but if I'm going to be stuck in another dimension with no way home, part of me is glad you're by my side," Magnus said.

"I won't tell Mary that part when we get home."

"Good idea."

Karo rubbed his arm as we walked in, and Suma was inserting the blood sample into the Locator device Clare had given me.

"Good work, Suma. I knew you could do it. Karo, how do you feel?" I asked the Theos.

"I'm fine." He turned around and picked up a slice of pizza, admiring it before he took a bite.

"I don't know how you stay in shape," I told the ancient being.

"Something Suma calls 'metabolism'," he answered in between bites.

"I'll have to find one of those." We were in an office inside *Fortune*'s engineering room. The ship's hyperdrive was massive, and the core energy tubes ran vertically for two stories inside. It was warm in here, and I undid a button on my borrowed shirt as I sat beside Suma.

"What's the verdict?" I asked as she fiddled with the device.

"It should work. We'll have to test it out first." Suma clicked it shut, and I saw the screen go blank, then reset, glowing yellow and then orange. It was just the three of us; the others were aboard our ship, waiting to go to the surface when this was ready.

"Should I move farther away?" Karo asked, holding another slice of pizza.

"I don't think it matters." Suma tapped a command, and it began searching. I'd kept it probing for Mary the entire time I was looking for her. The light on the screen blinked, identifying Karo in the room with us, which was expected, but what really excited us was the second blinking light.

"There's a stone!" I shouted.

"This reading is strong," Suma whispered, and I didn't quite take her meaning.

"When do we go?" Karo asked.

"Right now." I moved for the door, but Suma grabbed my arm, holding me back as Karo headed toward the hangar where the others waited. "What is it?"

"I'm surprised by the strength of the signal, that's all. This stone must have a lot of Theos powering it." Her voice was quiet, cautious.

I led Suma down the hall. "Maybe it's been affected by its interaction with the Cloud."

"That could be it." That ended our conversation, and a minute later, we were climbing into our Kraski ship, giving the crew the news.

"Where's Rulo?" I asked.

"She headed to the surface with her boyfriend," Slate said.

"I would have preferred that she come with us." I didn't want to go in with no firepower. I really had no clue what to expect at the portal stone.

Footsteps clanged out behind me, and when I turned, Magnus was there, holding a pulse rifle and giving me a sideways grin. "Then I guess you have room for one more."

"Always. Get on board." I waited for him to enter into our cargo bay and shut the ramp.

"I haven't been in one of these for a while. I sure prefer our modified versions." Magnus' gaze moved around the room, nostalgia clouding his eyes for a moment. "Enough of that. Let's find this stone and see what's what."

W lifted us up and out of the hangar while we entered the bridge, and he headed for the nearby planet. It was a beautiful sight: water, red clay ground, and the lights of a few bustling metropolises brightened the view from out here.

"All of these people were brought here against their will through the Cloud, and they formed a city." It was still hard to believe.

"An old race of Panthera people was the first to arrive, or so the tales say. After a generation searching for something else beyond this world, their ship came back, and they settled the land. It wasn't long before the next interstellar vessel was thrown here, and then another. Soon the cities were expanding, a melting pot of castaways. It's pretty amazing if you think about it." Magnus told the story, and we all listened intently.

"Except now we're castaways too," Slate said.

We flew in orbit as W circled the planet, heading toward our final destination. "Unless this portal stone works and we can offer everyone a way home." I really hoped the stone would function from here.

Magnus shook his head. "I have a feeling a lot of these people will stay even if we have a way home."

Slate looked surprised. "Seriously?"

"Think about it, pup. Some of them have been here for fifty generations. They don't know anything but this life. Imagine the inhabitants of Haven in a thousand years. It's going to be something like that."

"They can stay. We're leaving," I told them firmly.

We broke through the atmosphere with hardly more than a bump, and moved toward the hard clay mountains in the distance below. There was no body of water near our destination, only dark red clay and sparse vegetation. "Where's the nearest city?" I asked Magnus.

"Not close. This ground is terrible to grow anything in, and the water supply is meager. That's why most of the population lives in the other hemisphere." Magnus leaned against Dubs' seat as we lowered the ship toward the base of the mountain.

Suma held up her device, and it showed the blinking Theos light roughly a kilometer away. "Guess we're walking," she said.

"It appears so. W, stay with the ship and be ready to pick us up if necessary. We'll keep you posted on our progress. With any luck, we're going to find an active portal stone, and judging by the intensity of the readout, it will be *very* active." I glanced at Karo, who was moving for the cargo bay. He was obviously eager to find out if there actually was a stone. He really didn't seem to want to be on this side of the Cloud, and I couldn't blame him. I was of the same mindset.

"You're sure we don't need the EVAs?" I asked Magnus. He was in a jumpsuit, not wearing armor or a helmet, and certainly not an EVA.

"Air's fine. I don't know what these geniuses did, or how they managed it, but eighty percent of the races here are breathing the same air successfully. Looks like we aren't all so different after all, hey? Makes you wonder," he said.

"Wonder what?" Suma asked.

"How we can all be so similar." Magnus shrugged as he spoke. He slung his rifle on his shoulder. "Let's go."

"Should we expect trouble?" I asked.

"Doubt it. This world has a few predators, but they're mostly in the water. We should be safe here. I don't expect any surprises," Magnus said.

Slate was pushing a pistol into a holster on his chest. "I'm not taking any chances."

I agreed with Slate. "Whenever someone says they don't expect anything out of the ordinary, that's when things go awry."

"Not this time." Magnus led the charge, and the ramp lowered, letting us off the ship and onto the hard clay surface. The air was crisp, cool; refreshing. I took a deep breath and noticed the unique scent of the world. It reminded me of my mom's garden after the spring thaw.

The red peak rose nearby. It was more of a hill than a mountain, but it was sharply protruding from the surface. "Suma, is it above or below ground?" I asked, and she used the device to 3D map the region.

She pointed to the top of the incline. "Up there."

"We better get going, then. We have about five hours of light left." Magnus took off after Karo, who was already a hundred yards ahead of us.

"Suma, how does it look?" I asked her, out of earshot of Karo.

"I don't know. It's glowing as brightly as Karo on the screen. I have a strange feeling about this," she admitted.

"Maybe it's not working properly. Could you have messed it up when you opened and reprogrammed it?" We were walking now, Slate ahead of Suma and me. The entire area was bereft of trees or foliage. It was as if this side of the planet was roughly sculpted by a giant child from a ball of red putty.

"It's possible. I didn't think so, but I may have miscalculated. I hope we're not out here for no reason." Suma tapped the edge of the small device, but the light didn't disappear. It kept blinking where it was. The other indicator light showed us Karo's position ahead of us, slowly moving along a path on the compact screen.

The air was thinner than I was used to, and I thought it might be a combination of the world's oxygen levels and our altitude. I took deep breaths as we went. We chatted idly along the way, Karo taking the lead, but he slowed his speed so we could catch up. When we were almost to the top, I turned, looking at the horizon. More red clay, more hilly landscape.

"Almost there," Slate said as he neared the precipice of the hillside.

"Is there an easier way up?" The edge was at least ten feet high, but there didn't seem to be an opening in the cliff face or a better way to climb over it.

Slate pulled off his pack and activated a small drone. "Pretty cool, isn't it? Clare gave it to me before we left. It's like a new grappling hook, only kind of foolproof." We watched as the drone rose in the air, heading for the top of the cliff. It had a thin but strong rope attached to it.

"Does that mean even you can use it?" Magnus loved busting Slate's chops.

"We'll have to find out." The drone lowered, and we heard it shoot a peg into the surface, latching itself into the hard clay. Slate motioned Magnus to the rope. "How about you test it out for us?"

"Dean, I don't know how you put up with this guy. Fine. I'll go first." Magnus grabbed the rope and made quick work of the short ascent.

Slate grinned at me and climbed up. "Go ahead, Suma. I'll grab you if need be."

"I can climb a rope," the girl shouted, and a few seconds later, she supported up her claim, leaving an impressed Slate looking at Karo and me.

I waited to go last, but when I got to the top, I didn't see an opening. "Where's the portal room?"

"It looks like it's directly below us." Suma pointed a short distance across the flat surface of the clay mountaintop. "Over there."

"Scour the top. There has to be an opening somewhere nearby," I ordered, and we spread out, searching for anything out of the ordinary that could lead us to a portal room.

"Here!" Karo was across the top, kneeling on the clay. He pulled a hidden door open, revealing a hole.

"That door isn't natural. It's metal, painted to match." Slate knocked on it, and the metal reverberated.

TWENTY-TWO

I peered inside the dark hole, seeing metal rungs leading below. "The plot thickens."

"Someone knows about this portal room. Or at least, someone did at one time." Magnus lowered to the ground and stuck his head in the hole while aiming a flashlight inside. "Can't really see much. We'll have to go in."

Like there was really a choice in the matter. "I'll enter first," Slate said, moving in front of Magnus.

"Go for it." Magnus stepped to the side. "But be careful."

"I always am." Slate started down the metal rungs, a flashlight beam jostling around with each step down he took. "They go on for a—" His voice cut out.

"Slate!" I shouted, with no reply back.

"I'm going after him," Magnus said, moving quickly to the hole. I didn't have a chance to stop him, and Karo was right behind Magnus.

"Suma, stay here," I warned her, and she shook her head.

"No. If he's in trouble, I want to help." I knew there wasn't going to be any talking her out of this.

"Fine, you go next, then. Magnus, what's happening?" There was no answer. "Damn it. Suma, stay close to me." I glanced down the hole as I placed my boot sole on the first rung. I spotted a flashlight shining sideways on the floor. One of them had dropped it and left it there. That didn't bode well. There had to be someone or something inside.

Suma made it to the bottom of the rungs first, and I hopped beside her, aiming a pulse pistol forward with the Shimmali girl behind me. Magnus and Slate were frozen, trapped there in a glowing green energy. I saw their feet lift off the ground. Karo was standing near us, staring at our two trapped friends.

"Magnus! Slate! Can you hear me?" I asked, tentatively stepping into the room.

They didn't move, their expressions unchanging. I thought I saw Slate's eyes move, but it could have been a trick of the light. "Karo, what happened?"

"They were like that. I don't know why..." Karo let out a mangled shout as a blast of green energy enveloped him, lifting him from the ground. His face was twisted in agony, sticking in that position.

"Stop it! We're not here to harm you!" I called to whatever was attacking us.

"Over there." Suma pointed across the dark room, and I picked up the flashlight, aiming it in the direction she indicated.

"We're not here to hurt you," I said again, this time more calmly.

A voice rang out through the room in an unfamiliar language. It was a quick, clipped phrase, and it repeated, but now in a different language. The sound echoed through the dark room, but from what I could tell, it was never the same dialect twice.

"Do you speak Shimmali, or English?" I asked.

"But of course," the robotic voice said in clipped squawks and chirps.

Suma gripped my arm tightly.

"Also English, if that suits you better," it said with a slight drawl.

"We're not here to hurt you." I stepped forward with my hands raised in the air. My three friends were hanging weightlessly, covered by the glowing green energy, each stuck in place, unable to move.

"Hurt me? You cannot hurt me." The voice was coming at me from all around the room, almost as if ten voices were speaking with a split-second delay.

"Then you have nothing to fear from us. Let my friends go," I said, more forcefully than I intended.

I still couldn't see our attacker in the dark room. It was almost as though my flashlight beam dissipated faster the farther into the room the rays stretched.

"Fine. Three humans, a Theos, and a Shimmali. I already have one of each anyway." The three of them fell to the ground with a thud. Lights began turning on, slowly, until the entire room was lit up. Suma gasped as she clutched my forearm, and I wasn't far off.

It appeared that we were in a high-tech building, and I had to blink while my eyes adjusted to the sudden brightness. My friends were starting to move now, Slate the first to sit up, rubbing his head. The room was narrow but appeared to go on for miles.

I walked to the wall, where a being was encased behind glass. It was frozen in place, the same green energy surrounding it. I'd never seen anything like it; tusks rose from its cheeks, arcing up. Thin lips gave way to thick teeth, and knowing eyes stared straight forward, wide open.

I couldn't help but notice that the specimen was naked. Below it sat an ID tag, but it was in an unfamiliar language. I stepped to the side to see another alien creature enclosed in another display case, this one far different-looking but frozen just the same. I spun around and saw the same thing on the opposite wall. The pods were a few feet apart from each other, but they were constant.

"Dean, where's the attacker?" Slate asked, holding his gun up.

"I haven't seen him yet." I didn't turn to look at Slate, but I heard Karo and Magnus moving. I was transfixed on a pink jellyfish-like creature floating frozen in a viscous liquid.

"It's like the animal displays at the museum," I said, walking over to another enclosed person. My hand pressed against the glass, wondering if they were able to see me.

"Are they alive?" Karo asked.

"I don't know. I think so," I answered. "What is this?" I shouted to the unseen voice behind it all.

"Why, this is my personal collection. Do you like it?" the voice asked; the English was spot-on now, as if it was learning from us.

"Not really," I muttered. "Should we get out of here?"

Magnus stepped toward the exit. "I'm not sure it's going to let us."

Suma hadn't said a word, and I scanned the room for her, finding her a few pods over, mesmerized by a tiny fairy-looking creature in its display. It was palm-sized and had translucent wings.

Karo walked down the center of the room, his fists clenched in sudden anguish. "You said you have one of each of us. What does that mean?"

It had taken me a moment to understand what he was asking, but it clicked quickly.

The voice spoke before I did. "Just as I said. I am a Collector, and I do not need another Theos, human, or

Shimmali, because I already have one of each. Though the Shimmali girl is a better specimen than the one I have. Perhaps the young healthy human is too. You've given me a lot to consider."

"I don't like the sounds of that. Suma, come closer," Slate said. "Boss, was he talking about me?"

I nodded. "We leave. Now." I said the words so quietly that I didn't think any of them heard me, but Magnus started for the exit.

"No, Dean. The locating device Suma has. It found a Theos here. That's why we came. It wasn't a stone; it was a full-blooded Theos." Karo's eyes were wide and pleading as he stared toward us. He was such a great friend and strong person, who was constantly overshadowed by his loneliness at being the sole remaining Theos alive.

"I knew something was wrong with that readout," Suma said. "Where is the Theos?" she asked loudly.

A pod began to grow brighter, far into the room. It was at least half a kilometer away, but the illumination would lead us there. "Karo, I don't think…" I began, but it was too late. He was already stalking forward with purpose.

Magnus shrugged and started to follow Karo, and the rest of us joined him. We came together, we'd leave together. I stared at the various captive creatures along the way, my mind hardly able to process the sheer number of different beings I'd never seen before. By the time we reached Karo, I'd only managed to see a Padlog and a Motrill that I recognized, and I had to have walked by two hundred pods.

Karo let out a sound between a sob and a laugh. Both of his hands met the glass casing, and I leaned over to see the Theos beyond. She was striking. Piercing blue eyes, long white hair floating in the tank; her gray skin was a little paler than Karo's. She was tall, almost matching his seven feet.

"I'm not the last one," he whispered.

"Show yourself so we can talk and learn of you," I said, trying to sound powerful and level-headed.

"I should kill you all for trespassing."

Slate and Magnus held their weapons up, and they spun slowly, back to back as they scanned for a target.

"But I'll make an exception. Perhaps I've been here too long, or maybe I'm getting old," the voice said. It echoed from unseen speakers. A hiss carried to us from farther down the long display case, and a figure plodded toward us in choppy movements.

"What is that?" Suma asked, but none of us had an answer.

As it neared, I tried to decipher what I was looking at. It was a beige figure, roughly formed into a humanoid shape, not unlike the clay outside. It had a round head, but there were no distinguishing marks like eyes, a nose, or a mouth. It moved like it was being tugged along by a puppeteer, lifting arms and legs one after the other and slowly arriving to stand a short way from our group.

It was an unnerving sight. And that was compared to the hundreds of staring, lifeless creatures behind their display cases.

"There. I have shown myself," it said through the unseen speakers, not through the figure.

"You don't have your own body. What are you?" Suma asked, and it laughed, a shrill sound.

"You aren't privileged enough to see me. I am a god, and you a mere carbon-based animal. I collect you, and that is more for my own posterity than for any other reason. I have the largest collection in the universe," it said, the head on the golem tilting as it spoke.

"There are others like you?" I asked it.

"There are no others like me, no. There are other Collectors, though."

"I need her. Release this beautiful creature to me now!" Karo shouted, stepping toward the molded man.

"You cannot have one of my specimens. Do you offer yourself in her place?" it asked.

Karo hesitated a moment before looking once again at the trapped Theos woman. "I do," he softly said.

"Karo, you can't do this. There has to be another way," I said, pulling on his arm.

"I will make this bargain," the voice said.

"No!" I shouted, facing the golem. "Karo stays with us."

"Very well. It is your choice, human."

"You said you have a human here. How did you happen by them?" Magnus asked, his gun gripped so tightly I could see his knuckles whiten.

"I am a Collector. I've traveled the universe extensively, gathering one of each worthwhile race." The roughly-shaped body waved an arm through the air.

"Why are you here, then? On this side of the nebula?" I asked it.

"Likely for the same reason as you are," it said, surprising us all.

"You aren't in charge of the Cloud?" Suma asked it nervously.

"The Cloud?"

"The nebula sucking ships into this… purgatory," I explained.

"I'm powerful, but not that powerful. No, I believe that to be a sentient being. And this is its construct." The golem walked toward us, stopping in front of Karo. Magnus appeared ready to fire, but I didn't think shooting this molded man would accomplish anything useful. I shook my head at him.

"So you were sucked in here too, after you had most of your collection." I wanted to keep it talking, to learn more about the situation.

"That is correct. Conveniently, this Cloud, as you call it, brought me more specimens. Hundreds over time," it said.

So that was what it was doing perched here in hiding. "Are we in a ship right now?"

"This is a space vessel, yes."

"And all of these specimens are alive?" Suma inquired. I could see where her mind was going, but we didn't know enough about this Collector to hijack its ship and free the isolated beings.

"They are alive. You never know when one might be needed," it said, though I didn't quite grasp the meaning behind the words.

"You've been plucking away 'specimens' as they arrive in-system?" I asked.

"They've been so kind as to come all the way to me; why not add them to my collection?" the voice admitted.

"How many do you have on board?" I asked it.

"Twelve thousand, four hundred and thirty-seven unique specimens," it said.

"Twelve thousand!" Magnus barked. "I guess there's a lot we don't know about out there, Dean."

The number was huge, and I didn't know what to do with it. I needed to win it to my side, somehow. "Can you show me the human?"

"Very well. I don't often have company." It let out a shrill laugh, one that assumed we weren't dealing with a rational being here. It was clearly maniacal. "Right this way." The marionette creature moved on invisible strings, leading us through the display hall past countless unfamiliar people behind their glass cases, until we arrived at a circular platform in the floor.

"Dean, I don't want to leave her here," Karo said.

I was trying to think of a plan, but it hadn't clicked quite yet. "She's coming too," I assured him with a low whisper. He nodded his understanding, and as we stepped onto the platform, his gaze lingered over toward the frozen Theos.

"Going down," the voice said, and the golem lifted its arms. The platform lowered silently as the floor opened up, allowing us to drop through. We saw another level lined with display cases, then another.

"How many levels are there?" I asked.

"Eleven." This ship was huge, stuck within the mountain. The Collector must have formed the clay over it to make the misshapen mountain we'd climbed to find this place.

We stopped a few floors later, and the lights flashed on one after another, all the way over the expansive display corridor. I was looking for any signs of another room, something other than the level after level of showcases. So far, I'd come up empty.

My plan formed, albeit it was a long shot. Either way, a backup was always a good idea. I stepped off the lift and tapped my earpiece. "W," I said as quietly as possible.

"Captain, what can I do for you?" he asked in return.

"Bring the ship. There's space to land it on the top of the mountain. Stay there until further notice. We may be in danger," I said, not waiting for a reply. I tapped the earpiece off.

The golem was leading my friends deeper into the corridor, toward a well-lit case. It was speaking to them about the time it found the human, and how funny a creature they were. "No offense," it said before laughing again.

"None taken," Slate muttered.

We stopped in front of the human's case, and there he was, green energy circling his body, freezing him in place. He appeared to be almost Neanderthal-like in features, and it made me wonder how many years ago this Collector had been to Earth.

"Kind of looks like you, Magnus." Slate broke the tension with a joke, and nudged Magnus in the arm with a fist.

"Me? If I didn't know better, this could be your long-lost twin," Magnus joked.

Since it was willing to accept my request, I thought about the ace up our sleeve. Eccentric Collector types always liked a good bargain. It might be the only way to escape out of here alive, and with the Theos. It was worth a try. "Interesting." I pretended, of course, that it wasn't all that interesting. "How about you show us your Yuver?" I said.

The golem turned slowly, and I knew I had it in my grasp. The voice carried in its echo from the walls. "A Yuver, you say? I'm afraid I do not have one of these."

"Oh, really? That's because they've been dead for some time," I lied. Truth was, I had no idea where they were from or if they were still around. The one we'd found had been on that asteroid for a very long time, by our estimation.

"Yes, a Yuver." The name sounded strange out of the Collector.

"You know," I casually said, "the Theos are thriving. We had a ship full of them following us a week ago. I'm expecting they'll be sucked through to this side of the Cloud any day now."

Karo frowned at me, not quite picking up my motives. The golem stepped toward me. "Is that so?"

"That's correct. But, you see, my friend here has his heart set on getting a new wife." I lifted a hand up to stop Karo from interrupting, because he was clearly on the verge of cutting in.

"I understand being lonely," the voice said.

"Karo here is… how do I say this delicately? He's an extremely undesirable mate. Perhaps someone out of the game a few thousand years will find him fetching." I grinned at Karo, who was shooting daggers at me.

Slate chuckled but didn't say anything.

The voice got louder. "I do not give away my collectibles."

"I wasn't expecting you to. Like any great collector, you must be willing to trade up for a specimen? Surely a barter for something you don't possess would be of interest to you." I played up to its ego, which had to be huge for all its elaborate displays. I didn't forget the fact that it had called itself a god when we first met.

"What do you propose? As I said, I already have each of your…"

"A Yuver. I have a Yuver," I said plainly.

The golem started to shake: slow vibrations at first, then jerky motions. "And a ship of Theos is arriving soon?"

"Yes. The outside galaxy is teeming with them. Infested, really." I knew I was pushing Karo's buttons, but I had to be convincing that the Collector was receiving the better end of the deal.

"And you have a Yuver?" it asked.

"That's correct. What do you say to a bargain?" I asked, extending my hand. The golem's head didn't move, but the arm extended in a mirror action of mine, and I took the lumpy rounded hand and shook it. It seemed confused by the whole ordeal, but it was hard to tell, since the head held no face.

"We have a deal. I never much cared for the Theos. As you said, they're little better than an infestation." The golem turned, and I grabbed Karo's arm, holding him back from attacking the strange figure.

"Don't. It's only reacting to what I said about the Theos. He can't have her any longer," I said, pulling him close to whisper privately.

A few minutes later, we were once again at the top level where we'd arrived, and we stood in front of the display case where the Theos woman was suspended.

"Where is the Yuver?" it asked.

I walked away from the rest of the group and pulled out the portal gate device I'd gotten from the Traders and activated it. The yellow doorway opened, which meant W was directly above us in the Kraski ship. "Slate, Magnus, can you give me a hand?" I asked.

We walked through the energy doorway and onto our ship. Suma and Karo hung back, and I had the urge to shout at them to join us so we could escape. But there was no way I could leave without freeing the trapped Theos. Karo would finally have another of his kind around.

"What's the play?" Slate asked once we were in our own cargo bay. I glanced through the doorway, seeing the golem stare toward us with interest.

"The play? We trade this for her." I kicked the box where the Yuver sat inside, cryogenically frozen by some unknown technology.

"Is that fair to the Yuver?" Magnus asked.

"Look, it's not ideal, but what were we even going to do with it? We can't even be sure it's alive, and we sure as hell don't know where it comes from. It's all we have," I urged, and they nodded.

"Like you said, we don't have much of a choice. If we didn't stumble upon this Yuver, it would have been on the asteroid forever, or at least until a slug broke in and ate it. At least we're giving it a chance someone will release it one day," Slate said, convincing himself more than anything.

Magnus grabbed a handhold, and Slate and I each took another. We dragged it through the portal door, into the Collector's ship.

"There it is. One Yuver." I pointed to the window, where its face was visible.

The golem shook again, which I now took as a sure sign of excitement. I peered around, trying to find cameras. Where was the real Collector located?

"Very good. Yes, very good indeed. A deal's a deal. Take your mate, oh hideous one," the voice said, and the female Theos' display case opened with a hiss, the green energy around her vanishing. Karo caught the woman in his arms.

"Take her through the portal," I said quickly, and Karo didn't hesitate. He was gone in a flash.

"How did you do that?" the Collector asked, obviously meaning the doorway portal.

"I'm also a god," I lied. Maybe if I got it on an even playing field, the Collector would reveal more secrets.

"But you are human," it said. "Maybe something a little more?" The head moved, like it was sniffing the air.

"This is merely a vessel, like your golem here," I said. "Where are you hiding?"

The golem shook again. "I am not hiding." It fell to the ground, and Slate raised his gun as the entire ship trembled.

"I think it's time to go, boss," Slate said, backing away.

Something lifted through the floor; it was red, misty. A blob of energy. "See me for all my glory. What is it you look like? Bare yourself to me so I can decide if I should keep you for my collection." The voice emerged from all around the room.

It was moving closer, and I shoved Suma behind me. "Get on the ship!" I yelled as the Collector's display cases rattled.

"Do not leave! I do not permit it!" The red wraith pulsed in anger, and I followed the others through the portal, tripping as I entered our Kraski ship's cargo bay. The portal control flew from my hand, bouncing along the floor.

"Grab it! Shut the portal!"

Suma was already running for the bridge, and Slate grabbed for the control, trying to figure out how to use it. I rolled over, stumbling backwards as the Collector raced toward me in its wraith form.

"Shut it!" I yelled, and the yellow doorway vanished just before the red wraith entered. I lay on the ground, the air from my lungs pushing out in great uneven gasps. "Thanks, Slate."

"I didn't do anything!" he said, gaze transfixed at the controls.

Suma returned from the bridge, smiling. "I told W to fly away. I remembered the portal was only good for short distances, so he blasted us off the surface."

"Good thinking, Suma! That was a close call. We didn't expect that." I got up, looking around for Karo. He was nowhere in sight.

"We didn't solve our problems," Magnus said. "We're still stuck here."

"No. I guess there's no portal stone here." I walked away, heading toward the bunks.

Karo was inside, leaning over a bed, where he'd covered the nude Theos woman. He tilted out of the way, smiling widely. "Everyone, meet Ableen."

She sat up, holding the covers to her chest. Her eyes were sparkling, jumping back and forth between us, trying to decipher what was happening.

"It's okay. You're safe now. Let's get you to *Fortune* and find you some clothes and food. Wait until you try pizza," Karo said, and we ushered ourselves out of the room, leaving him to comfort the only other Theos alive.

TWENTY-THREE

We were on Magnus' ship a short way from the planet, sitting in his office, off the elaborate bridge filled with Keppe crew. Magnus was typing on a screen on his desk, and the words appeared on a digital whiteboard.

We still don't have a way to leave this godforsaken dimension!

He deleted the words after glancing at my admonishing look and started again.

"We're no farther along." Magnus rested his face in his hands and let out a deep sigh.

"We found a Theos! I'd say that's a win." This from Suma, from her chair beside mine.

"You're lucky you got out of there. What are we going to do about this Collector?" Natalia asked. It was just the four of us. Rulo was planetside with her partner, and Slate was sleeping when I checked on him. I thought it would do my buddy good to rest.

Karo was getting Ableen caught up on the history and current status of the Theos. She'd been taken from their home world three thousand years ago. I didn't think she looked a day over thirty, personally. But you could never tell in a universe of ancient races and energy-induced cryogenic freezing by maniacal red wraiths.

Karo was worried how she would respond, so he was trying to ease her into it. I wasn't sure what that entailed: *Here's some pizza. Also, our race is long dead after a battle with the Iskios, and I was left behind to guard the Theos history, awaiting someone to arrive, who happened to show up as our nemesis was destroying solar systems with a powerful vortex fueled by their souls and piloted by the very same Recaster's possessed wife.*

"What are the plans for the Collector?" I repeated.

"Nothing. I'm not going back there."

"We could figure out a way to kill him, maybe? Release the trapped people?" Suma suggested.

"I don't know if we can…"

The door buzzed, and Magnus told them to enter.

"Sir, you wanted to know if anything occurred from that region you came from earlier?" the Keppe woman who entered asked, and Magnus' desk translator relayed it into English for us.

"Yes, what do you have?" Magnus asked.

"A ship left."

"A ship?" Nat was at the wall, keying something into a console.

"Yes, I've patched it through." The Keppe pointed to the whiteboard, and the video began to play. It was an aerial satellite shot from above. The red clay mountain erupted as a long vessel tore from the earth. It rose straight up, appearing larger every second in the center of the screen. The Collector's ship was slick, smooth, and long like a pencil.

"There go twelve thousand of his *specimens*," I said as we watched the vessel propel forward slowly, beyond the atmosphere.

The Keppe officer spoke again. "It's moving away from us and the planet."

Nat changed the camera angle to one from *Fortune*, and she zoomed to show the thin cylindrical ship rotating before a bright powerful thruster kicked in, and the Collector vanished.

"One less thing to think about," I said, and Nat shut the screen off.

The Keppe officer left with a bewildered look on her face, and the door shut, leaving the four of us to ponder what had just happened.

"These people on the planet below have been here for so long. If there was a way to leave, don't you think one of them would have figured out a way?" Magnus was getting frustrated, and I didn't blame him. It was hard not to be upset while thinking about our predicament. Mary would be worried sick about me, about all of us. There had to be a way.

"I wonder what happened to Sergo," Suma said out of the blue.

"Sergo? You mean that insect guy from Volim? If I ever see that Padlog again, I'll hit him with a flyswatter," Magnus said.

I laughed and decided to fill them in on our encounter with the runaway thief on the day of the Gatekeepers' graduation. "He'd stolen some Inlorian bars from the Inlor mine, and thought he could use my Relocator to sneak out of there, grabbing millions of credits' worth of the sought-after metal."

"What a scammer, using your device to steal from people," Natalia said. "It's probably a good thing he couldn't jump to Volim. You got to make a new alliance with the Inlor. Also, belated congratulations on joining the Gatekeepers, Suma," she said with a caring smile.

I felt so far removed from the Gatekeepers and the progress with the Alliance now that we were trapped here, so driven the last couple of months to find Magnus. Now that we were here, there was nowhere to go. Something niggled at my brain about what Nat had said. "Natalia, say that again?"

"Congrats, Suma," she said.

"No. The part about jumping to Volim." My mind raced, and my eyes sprang open.

"Dean, are you okay…" Natalia started.

"The Relocator! I have it with me. What if it's not really broken? What if we can use it to travel back to the last location Sergo had embedded into it?" I was off my seat, raw energy coursing through my body.

"What if it doesn't? What if it's broken? What if it does work, and it tries to send you to Volim or wherever he had programmed, and it doesn't recognize it over on this side of the dimension, and you arrive into deep space with nothing but an EVA and a tank of oxygen?" Magnus was always so articulate and supportive.

"Now that you've managed to remind me of my biggest fear…" I ran a hand through my hair and paced the room. "Seriously, this might work. Suma, meet me in the engineering office again, and let's see if we can make this Relocator function again."

I ran out of the room before anyone could argue, and for the first time since arriving, I felt real hope flood in my chest.

Suma set the Relocator on the table. "I don't know what to tell you, Dean. It won't activate."

I picked it up and flipped it around my palm. Kareem had gifted this to me so long ago, and I'd used it to sneak out of some really dicey situations. I'd been so sure we could figure this out, but Suma's abilities could only be stretched so far.

"I know. Thanks for spending the last week on it." I

spun in my chair in the office that connected us to *Fortune*'s engineering room.

Magnus appeared at the door and gave me a dour expression. "You two are still in here. God, Dean. When are you going to give up on that Relocator?"

"I'm not. Did you acquire that contact for me?" I could tell from his face that he had.

"Sure I did. I don't think it's going to do you any good. If Suma says it's dead, then it's dead, right?" Magnus nodded to Suma, who shook her head.

"Not necessarily. The power core is shot, but I don't know how Kareem or the Deltra managed to make it. It's unlike anything I, or your chief engineer, have ever seen. If we could find another power source, we might make a go of it, but…"

"But what?" I prompted.

"But I've tried at least three other cores, adapting them to fit, and nothing has worked." Suma pushed away from the table and let out a classic Shimmali squawk. I knew she was missing home and her father. Sarlun was going to have some words with me when we got home. I closed my eyes and amended the thought. *If* we got home.

"W," I said into my earpiece. "Are you at the ship?"

"Of course, Captain. Where else would I be?" Dubs answered.

"Good. We'll be there in a few minutes."

"And where are we going?"

"To the surface of the planet. We have a meeting with a Deltra." I grinned, and Magnus passed me a tablet with the woman's location on it. "I never thought we'd be meeting more Deltra, did you?"

"Nope. These ones don't even know about their captivity by the Kraski, or the subsequent betrayal. It might be best if you don't bring it up," he said.

"Thanks again. I'll see you when we get back. Hopefully with some good news." I clapped Magnus on his shoulder with a palm, picked up the Relocator, and left the room.

Suma was already out the door, and I walked with her toward our quarters. "I need to grab something," I said. I had an urge to take my pack with me. There were times I felt this nudge, as if the universe was trying to guide me. I thought to what Regnig had called me while we were under Bazarn Five: *Recaster.* I was there to change things up, to right wrongs, or maybe wrong rights; it wasn't so much about good versus evil, or anything like that, but more about equilibrium.

The intuition, as Mary called it, had proven useful on many occasions, and I wasn't about to ignore it now. I cut into my quarters, grabbed my small pack, slung it over my shoulder, and carried on until we arrived at the hangar where W awaited our arrival.

"Should we bring back Slate?" Suma asked.

"He's already here," a voice shouted across the half-empty hangar. "Thought you could get rid of me so easily, did you?"

"Had enough working out with the Keppe?" I asked him. He had obviously just left the gym because he was drenched in sweat and had a towel draped over his head. "Do us a favor? Shower before we land."

Slate rolled his eyes, and we hopped into the ship before W lifted us out of *Fortune* and headed for the surface, this time smack-dab in the center of the largest metropolis on the planet. There were nearly a billion various people on the world, and judging by the immense sprawl of the city, fifty million of them lived here. The directions Magnus gave me took us between two skyscrapers, each at least a hundred stories tall, and narrow. The landing pad flanked by the buildings was almost full, and we had to squeeze between two unfamiliar vessels.

"I'll wait here, Captain," W said.

When we exited the ship, I was instantly amazed at how fresh the air was. With all of the combined technologies of the different alien life on the world, it appeared as though they'd found a way to prevent emissions. It was the freshest air I'd ever inhaled in the middle of a city.

"Dean, look." Suma pointed above us, where small vehicles flew through the air like regular traffic. There were floating buoys separating lanes, and in the span of a minute, at least a hundred small ships must have flown by.

"I wonder if this is rush hour?" Slate asked, and then I noticed there were at least five more lanes above the ones closest to us.

"I don't want to be a commuter here. This looks intense," I said as a hover train soared between the skyscrapers, fifty yards overhead: their version of the subway. "Maybe we should take some notes for Haven. It looks like they've built quite the utopia here," I said, and finally glanced at the tablet, my eyes spinning from staring at all of the hovering traffic.

"First things first. Let's see if the Deltra can help us." Suma took the lead and made for the tall glass building.

A purple gelatinous blob met us at the entrance, and it said something in its own language, which sounded like a series of burps. "Names," it translated.

"Dean Parker to see Braylam of the Deltra," I said, and my translator burped my response at the blob. It was semi-transparent, and I spotted organs through its surface, two hearts beating. "Are you a Cib?" I asked, recalling a similar creature with Cee-Eight.

It replied that it was indeed a Cib and directed us inside before telling us to go to the ninety-ninth floor.

"Kind of a posh place," Slate said. "I wasn't sure what to expect, but it was surely different than this."

We crossed a grand foyer; a couple of aliens loitered, chatting, by the far wall. I felt like I was in a New York Upper East Side apartment, complete with a gelatinous blob for a doorman. We made our way to an elevator and I scanned the console with my tablet, translating it to English before pressing the correct button.

We were on the far wall, and the clear glass wall of the elevator allowed us to see the impressive view as we rose high into the building. Another hover train raced by, sending Suma jumping backwards into Slate.

I hefted my pack on my shoulder and checked my collar, making sure it wasn't janky. I'd been able to use the Keppe ship's computer to print my own clothing, and I almost had a passable shirt and blazer to go with a pair of almost-jeans. It all felt a little off, like I was a card-board doll with folded-over paper clothing.

The elevator stopped, a soft chime alerting us that we were at our destination. The doors slid wide.

The layout was an open floor plan, and a few Deltra were walking around, tablets in their hands. It appeared as though the city had fully-developed commerce going on. It was off-putting, but realistic.

I adjusted my translator to relay Deltra, and I waved down a tall bald man that reminded me of Teelon from so long ago. The memory stuck in my throat, and I cleared it before speaking. "We're here to see Braylam."

The man stopped, staring at us with wide eyes, and nodded. "This way."

We followed him to a corner office, and he knocked before letting us in. A Deltra woman hovered in a chair, facing a wall-sized screen with 3D images scrolling over it.

"I've been expecting you," the woman said in English. She had the same unaccented monotone voice that the Deltra I'd stumbled into on Earth during the Event had. It was unsettling.

"How?" I started, then saw her point to her throat.

"Modifications. Most of us have them now. There are too many races and languages to worry about translators. It's already loud enough out there, we don't need any more noise pollution. Have a seat." She was bald too, tall and heavier-set than any Deltra I'd ever met. She wore long, dangling earrings and had multiple piercings on her face.

"We need to see if you can help us with something," I said.

"I was briefed, but not clearly. What can I do for you?" she asked as she lowered to the ground and walked over to us.

I slung the pack off my shoulder and passed her the Relocator, almost not wanting to drop it into her outstretched hand. "I got this from one of your people. He was a good friend," I said.

"Was? Is he passed?" She inspected the device.

"He did. A few years ago. We need to activate this device," I told her.

She set it on the desktop. "I don't know what it is. Are you able to share?"

I hesitated, but Slate nodded to me, giving me the boost I needed. If I couldn't trust her with the information, I had no hope of finding out if it could be fixed. "We call it a Relocator. It saves a location, and the device transports you and anyone you're in contact with to that spot."

"Really? That's interesting, and extremely handy. You

say a Deltra came up with it?" She held it again, looking closely.

"Yes." I didn't tell her they'd also created the *Kalentrek*, a device capable of wiping out an entire species with the press of a button.

Suma cut in. "The power core is shot, as far as I can tell, but we can't access one to work. We thought it might be a Deltra trade secret."

The woman leaned in, her gaze lingering on the doorway for a second before she quietly asked a question. "What are you hoping to use this for, seriously?"

I decided to be honest. "It has a location saved in it, one from beyond this dimension."

"And you think you can wield it to traverse the dimensional shift caused by the nebula?" she asked.

"Pretty much," Slate said.

"Impossible. To do that, you'd need a conductor far more powerful than anything we have here."

The intuition was paying off again. I opened the bag again and pulled out an Inlorian bar. "Test this. Could you make the power core out of this?" I passed it to her, and she grinned.

"I don't know, but now you have intrigued me. Leave this with me and return tomorrow." She set them both to the side and crossed her arms.

"I'm not sure…" I started to say.

"It will take time to analyze. I do not wish to steal, break, or do anything reprehensible with your device. I'm more curious than anything, and this is definitely Deltra, so it interests me. Also, I'll duplicate the technology to a scalable device and make a fortune. In the meantime, I'll see about getting you home."

She seemed honest about it. "You have no interest in leaving this world?" I asked.

"All I know is here. My life is good. We have food, shelter, and everything we could possibly need. There's nothing on the other side for me." She sounded so sure of her answer.

"So tomorrow, then?" I double-checked.

"Tomorrow," she replied, keeping her gaze on the Relocator. She ushered us out of the room and called a few of her staff into her office, barking commands as she shut the door.

"I guess we have no choice but to trust her," Slate said. "We're in the city, we may as well enjoy ourselves."

TWENTY-FOUR

"Are you sure Ableen's up for this, Karo?" I leaned to whisper the question in his ear. The group of us were seated at a rooftop restaurant, overlooking a great ocean. I could understand why Braylam wouldn't consider leaving for a galaxy she'd never even seen.

Ableen was staring at the food with wide eyes. She only spoke in an ancient Theos dialect that I'd never heard. Karo had always used English with me. He turned to her and softly spoke a phrase, and she nodded.

"She said the food is very good." Karo was smiling, and I'd noticed the instant shift in his personality. He'd been brooding of late, and for good reason. Now we'd managed to find another of his kind, and he couldn't have been happier.

The restaurant was busy; dozens of tables were occupied by all sorts of beings. Some were familiar, others far off my radar. But what struck me as amazing was how well they all got along. They'd really built something special out of necessity. The open-air space was a cacophony of alien chatter and laughter.

Our table was its own mix, with two Theos, Suma the Shimmali, Slate, Magnus, Natalia, and I rounding out the humans, and Rulo had a hulking Keppe with her who gave me the impression he wasn't her cousin.

"Can you ask her to tell us her tale?" Natalia asked

from her seat beside Ableen. She reached out and set a hand on the Theos woman's forearm.

"I know much of it, but will translate for you now." Karo spoke softly to Ableen, and she met our gazes with a smile of her own. I couldn't imagine being abducted then waking thousands of years later, and a day after, sitting with a view like this, with a bunch of strange people asking about you.

She talked, and Karo recited her story.

"Ableen was born a quarry miner's daughter. This was before the Iskios were even banished. Then she'd had many Iskios friends, so she was shocked to hear when I told her about our race being extinct, and about the portal stones.

"She grew up as any other child on our world, taken care of and not lacking anything. She excelled in classes and quickly rose above her parents' rank, venturing into engineering in the capital." Karo raised a hand; his eyes were full of wonder. "I was there once as a child, before they extended my life to watch over things and await the Recaster's arrival." He shot me a look, and Ableen glanced over at me, averting her eyes. She seemed to think I was someone important.

Karo kept speaking. "The capital was being vacated when I was there, lines of Theos leaving to pour themselves into the stones. It was a sad sight. A majestic place with no one to walk the streets any longer. Anyway, enough about me; I'll continue with Ableen's story.

"She lived a simple life, even finding love after some time. She doesn't recall much about the night she was taken by the Collector. Her last memory was walking home after a long day working on an experimental project. She saw a red energy bear down on her; green light zapped overhead, and the next thing she knew, we were pulling her from the display case on his ship."

Ableen stopped talking and took a few absent bites of her dinner. I was sure there was far more to the Theos, but at least we understood the basics now. Karo would learn things in due time.

"We don't know how long ago this was, then?" I asked.

"It would be hard to tell. Imagine what she's feeling, Dean. I want to comfort her, but her wounds and losses are fresh. Her love, her family, all gone for thousands of years, and now she learns we're the last two Theos in existence," Karo said. "I'd be reluctant to pressure her, but I do hope she stays close to me. I would love nothing more than to reconnect with my own kind, even in a strictly platonic way." He said this all in English as Ableen pecked away at the foreign food on her plate.

"Does she know that, Karo? Because she's been giving you some serious sideways glances," Slate said, and Suma threw an elbow at him.

Magnus ordered another Padlog nectar drink for the table and winked at me. "You sure love those things. I bet you were thrilled to hear they had it," I told him.

"If we're stranded here, there could be worse places," he said. "At least there's a city. I couldn't image having been stuck on Sterona like the four of you."

Three of that group were at dinner now; Mary was the only one back home. "Mary would have preferred this, that's for sure," Slate said, and I nodded.

I wished she and Jules were here with me. Maybe I should have brought them. Wouldn't it be better to be stuck in a dimensional purgatory together, than to be apart? I decided I wasn't sure, but I knew where my vote would lie.

"You must miss her," Natalia said.

"I do," I said as our Cib waiter came by, drink trays balanced on outstretched gelatinous hands. He passed my nectar over, and I took a long pull. It was really good.

"What about this Braylam? Even if she gets this Relocator to work, will it take you out of here?" Magnus asked.

Slate stuck his hand in the air, like a student waiting to talk. "I'm going to test it."

I shook my head. "No, Slate. It's my responsibility. I brought us here, I'll test it." I knew that even if Braylam suggested it was operational, our being across the dimension might affect it. There was a distinct chance I could be Relocated into the middle of space… or worse.

"That's not fair," Suma said. "We came here as a team, and we all voted on traveling through the Cloud. As one."

"I know, Suma, but I'm going to be the one to try it. End of story." I rested into my chair, letting a thin robot porter clear my plate. Suma didn't argue, but I knew she was pouting about it. "We'll go together in the morning and check on progress, is that better?"

"Sure thing, boss. But don't make it too early," Slate said.

"Why's that?" I pressured.

"Because Magnus and I are going to stay up drinking these bad boys for a while," he said with a laugh.

"You know what? I'm starting to enjoy this, pup," Magnus said, lifting his glass in the air. Natalia rolled her eyes but raised her own glass.

"What are we raising a glass to?" I pondered.

"To us, Dean. To friendship!" Magnus stood, and the rest of us followed suit, clinking our metallic cups in unison, nectar splashing over our dirty plates.

"To friendship," we chorused, but the whole time, I

had a sinking feeling in my gut that I was never going to be able to leave this purgatory to get home to Mary.

The suite was opulent, but even though it was well past the middle of the night, I lay awake, sitting up in bed staring out the window at the picturesque view. I'd managed a couple hours of uninterrupted sleep, but the second my eyes sprang open during a bad dream, I hadn't been able to fall back under.

There were far too many thoughts bouncing around the inner reaches of my mind, including the bizarre Collector. What other races did he have on that ship? What could all of those beings teach us about the universe we lived in, or used to?

My ears perked up like a dog's on the hunt as I heard light footsteps attempting to conceal their presence. My head jerked to the side, seeing my pulse rifle propped against the wall twenty feet away. Slate was next door, and I thought about yelling for him, but with the quality of this hotel, I doubted they made the walls paper-thin like a seedy motel.

"Who's there?" I went for the direct approach. I moved to the ledge of the bed, a little closer to my weapon.

No answer came, but I saw the form lingering in the shadow by the suite's entrance.

I didn't wait any longer. I rolled from the bed, over the hard floor, and arrived beside the chair, grabbing my pulse rifle firmly. I hopped to my feet and jumped away, holding the gun toward the figure I'd seen seconds ago.

"Don't be alarmed, Dean," a voice said behind me.

I spun, and a slim hand waved in the air, knocking my gun to the ground. I bent to pick it up, but it stuck to the floor as if someone super-glued it there. I scrambled away until my back pressed against the far wall. "What do you want?" I asked.

"Dean." The figure removed a hood covering their head, the shadows dissipating from her face. It was Braylam, the Deltra engineer. "Relax. It's only me."

"Relax? You sneaked into my room in the ungodly hours of the night!"

"I finished the Relocator." The small device sat in her palm now, and she held it outstretched to me.

"And you came over here with it?" I asked, her story not quite adding up.

"Dean, I think you're right."

"About what?"

"The power of this thing. I replicated it, testing it with a normal power core. It worked fine, but when I used the Inlorian bar to make wire for the coils, my replication exploded. So I had to brace the original to withstand the power inside the new core. It worked." Braylam's usually monotone voice was filled with emotion I'd never heard from a Deltra, even from Kareem on his deathbed.

"What are you suggesting?" I stepped toward her, accepting the outstretched device.

"I'm suggesting this might just take you where you want to go: to the pre-set location saved inside it." She smiled thinly, and her hand shook slightly. She seemed to notice and shoved her hands into deep pockets inside her cloak.

"And you came here now to tell me this, why?" I pressed her.

"Don't you see? If anyone here finds out you have the power to leave this place, there will be pandemonium."

"I thought no one would ever want to leave this utopia?"

Braylam shook her head. "There are factions that do. But there are others that would smell profit in this." She pointed to my hand. "They'd kill you ten ways to tomorrow for that thing."

"Then why did you bring it to me?" I wondered if this even was the original. Braylam could have duplicated it and, when it failed, blamed the device, not herself.

"Because it's too dangerous for me to have, and because you were given this by one of my people. We aren't a very trusting lot, so that means something to me. The Deltra are an honorable race, Dean Parker." Her eyes were wide, and I thought about all the real Deltra had been through. Betraying the Kraski, then us; but through it all, it was only about self-preservation, and I couldn't blame them. They weren't all that different from us.

"Thank you." I peeked at it, seeing a glowing ring around it that was never there before.

"The core is strong, that Inlorian bar intense. A jump like the one you're describing, taking you across this dimensional shift and countless light-years after, could fry it. If you're lucky enough to end up at the right destination, the core may need time to recharge. I added a display bar inside." She showed me, flipping it open. It had ten glowing green bars in a row. "If you use it to come here again, make sure all ten bars are charged first."

"Do you really think it might work?" I asked, suddenly nervous to attempt it.

Braylam stayed silent for a moment too long, and her hesitation answered my question. "I hope so, Dean. I really do." She started for the door, waving her hand over my gun as she walked by it. Now I saw a small glowing ring on her hand. It hadn't been magic after all, just technology. I nudged the rifle with my toe and it moved freely.

"You're leaving?"

"Good luck. Don't share what you have here. It would be too hazardous," she said, and as silently as she had arrived, she was gone.

I sat on the edge of the bed and thought about using it right there and then. The old Dean would have done it. He was impulsive and straight to the point, but I'd put the others through so much, they had the right to know. If I attempted to use the Relocator now and it failed, they might think I was abducted from the hotel room and never know what had really befallen me. Plus, I didn't have my EVA here with me, and there was no way I was using this thing without it on.

I thought about waking the others up and making them leave for *Fortune* with me immediately, but they'd all been through a lot and deserved what brief rest and relaxation they could get. I held the Relocator and climbed into bed, positive I'd never sleep another ounce in my life. A few minutes later, my eyes closed, my breathing deepened, and everything ceased to exist.

TWENTY-FIVE

"Have you tested this thruster pack out before, Magnus?" I asked. It was strapped to my back and was of lighter weight than the old ones he and I had worn years ago, trying to stop a war with the Bhlat. He'd gone over the basic functions of it, and I was sure I'd figure it out if I was stranded in deep space with no other options.

"I've played around with them a few times, sure. As basic as you think. Now, do you need anything else?" Magnus asked. We were in the hangar, and the whole gang was huddled around awaiting my departure.

Slate set a hand on my shoulder and tapped on my helmet's face mask. "Are you sure you don't want me to test this? I don't mind, really. You have so much more to lose," he said quietly.

There wasn't going to be any more discussion about it. "I'm doing it."

"And Braylam thinks there could be a delay in returning? It has to charge?" Suma asked again.

"That's right. I don't know how long it'll take, so be patient. If I don't show up for a day or two, let's try not to freak out." I looked Slate in the eyes when I said that.

Karo came over to me and grabbed me in a hug, his long arms wrapping around my EVA suit and thruster pack. "Be well, my friend. We'll see you soon." His green eyes bore into mine, and I nodded.

"I'll be as well as I can be," I promised.

Natalia gave me a hug too, not meeting my gaze. "And you think it's going to have Volim saved into it?"

"Sergo made me think as much. There's no way for me to know, not without trying it." I gave her a slight smile, and stepped away from the group.

The entire assembly stood in a line now, between me and our ship. W was present too, beside Ableen, who seemed confused as to what we were doing here. I assumed Karo's translation had failed at some point.

"I'll see you all soon," I said before turning from them to face the exterior wall of *Fortune*. I didn't want anyone to behold the look of horror on my face as I pulled the device out and hovered my finger over the icon. "I'm coming home soon, Mary and Jules. We'll all be together. I have a few things to do first. Let's take everyone else home." I'd turned my earpiece off and whispered the words.

Then I closed my eyes and pressed the icon.

When I opened them, I was in total darkness. For a second, I began to panic, my breathing coming in shallow huffs, until I realized I wasn't floating in space. My feet were planted on the ground. I flicked my EVA lights on and found myself in a run-down room, a handful of bodies on the floor. I saw the familiar golden pollen on the ant-like Padlog and let out a shout of excitement.

I was in the underground hive of Volim's capital city, where I'd first met Sergo. This was the rear of the bar. I saw the same table we'd sat at with the sketchy character in the corner and let out another shout of joy.

"Where did you come from?" the chits and buzzes translated in my ear. I spun around to see two huge beetle-shaped Padlog stalking toward me. I reached for my rifle but figured something else might work with them.

"Sergo sent me."

"Is that so?" The greater of the two had huge black eyes; foot-long mandibles clicked open and shut as he spoke.

"Yes. He's setting up his penthouse on Haven and wanted me to gather a few of his things."

"Penthouse. He really pulled that job off? He was always bragging he was going to steal from those Inlor, but none of us thought he had the skills to pull it off," the chits translated.

"He did. I have to get going. If you guys help me reach the surface, I'll make sure to tell Sergo how well you should be rewarded for assisting me. He's throwing his new wealth around like a wild man," I lied, and they both perked up.

"This way. We'll bring you."

That was too easy. I still couldn't trust them, but I didn't have much of a choice. I kept my hand on the gun at my hip, and the other clasped over the Relocator. We stepped over the fallen drugged-out Padlog on the floor and wound our way through the hive's quiet inner corridors, eventually finding the elevator that would bring us aboveground.

They asked a few questions about Sergo's new place and made plans to go visit him. I took their names, not even bothering to remember them. I had other things on my mind.

It had worked! The Relocator worked!

I had to transport a message to Mary. There was too much to do, and the elevator was moving far too slowly for me.

It arrived up top, and I gave thanks to my new friends, who decided they couldn't leave my side until I made it to the embassy tower. Padlog of every variety were outside, walking and talking as they headed to and from their daily activities. Food trucks lined the open area between the sky-piercing towers, their roasting protein sending smoke into the sky. It was bustling and exciting as various insect-shaped humanoids talked and walked and lived their lives. I couldn't have been happier. My steps were light, and everyone I passed eyed me up and down as I bounded by in a full EVA with a rifle and thrust pack strapped to me. I must have seemed like a madman.

"Thank you. Sergo will be in touch," I said, and the two Padlog lumbered off into the crowds.

Once inside the building, I was greeted by the bright polished lobby, where possibly the same scholars from the last time we'd visited stood by a water feature, discussing topics only of interest to themselves.

I approached their small group and interrupted. "I need to speak to the Supreme."

In all the excitement, I'd forgotten to even check the charge on the Relocator. I opened my palm and saw three glowing bars. So it hadn't been fully drained. That was good to know.

"The Supreme is busy, I'm sure," one of the scholars said, his wasp head tilting upward as he tried to assess what I was.

"Tell them Dean Parker is here, and I need to urgently speak with the Supreme. He'll want to see me," I urged.

"Doubtful." The scholar left the group, who'd fallen silent at my arrival, and I waited at the side of the room. I couldn't believe it had worked. My cheeks were sore from smiling, and I couldn't stop.

Eventually, a tall green mantis-type Padlog meandered over to me and spoke. "The Supreme will see you now."

It wasn't long before I was in the same meeting room

on the third floor. The Supreme was waiting there, his short cricket form hoisted on a small chair.

"Dean Parker again. Why am I not surprised to see you?" he asked.

We'd been in discussion with the Supreme lately, though Terrance and the other Alliance of Worlds members were his contacts, not me.

"I hear you found your mate. How very lucky for you," he said.

"Yes. I am lucky. Look, I need your help," I said. I removed my helmet, setting it on the floor, and slung the thrusters beside it before sitting across from him.

"Very well. Speak your piece," the Supreme said, his small black eyes focusing on me with intensity.

I settled in to tell him my story, starting with Sergo at the Gatekeepers' celebration. He demanded every detail, and claimed he was going to kill the rogue Padlog if he ever got his tiny hands around his neck.

I kept talking, checking the Relocator halfway through, seeing it was up to four bars, and I felt some of the tension release from my shoulders. I told the Supreme about our chase after Magnus' missing ship, about the waylay on the robot world, about the failing portal stones, and about our experience with the Traders. He'd personally dealt with the same woman as I had on a few occasions and was impressed I'd made off so well.

He was surprised to hear about the crashed Keppe lifeboat and applauded our ingenuity at finding the location of *Fortune*. His arms wavered as I mentioned the Collector, making a buzzing sound like a cricket.

"And this Collector had Padlog?" he asked.

"Apparently. I didn't see it," I admitted. I kept talking until my mouth was dry and my tale was spent. "Then I arrived at Sergo's saved location inside the hive, far below the surface."

The Supreme opened and closed his small mouth a few times before saying anything. "And how can I help you now? Can you use that to transport your people here?"

I nodded. "I believe we can, though it will take a lot of time and work. The Relocator can carry multiple people with it, but I'm not sure how many or how far. We'll have to move in small groups, and judging by the charging time..." I pointed at the device, which was up to five bars now, an hour or so later. "This could take a few weeks to deliver the entire crew of *Fortune* back. I need a safe zone to bring them to, then we're going to require ships to transfer us all to Haven. Can you help us?"

"Of course. What good is being part of this Alliance if we don't assist others in need? I'm sure we'll be able to negotiate a fair price, after all." There it was: the crux of his motivation. There always was one.

"I'm sure we can. Thank you for the assistance, Supreme." I shook his little hand, and he settled into his seat. "Is there somewhere I can use to program the Relocator to arrive?"

"I have just the spot, Dean. Come with me."

The Relocator was at nine bars, and it felt like forever waiting for a full charge. I didn't bother with the EVA this time. It was bulky and hopefully unnecessary. The Supreme had given me full access to a huge landing pad in the middle of their ocean, a private location most of the Padlog weren't even aware existed.

It came complete with a dozen mid-sized Padlog

WASP vessels, which would give us enough space to transport everyone to Haven. From there, we'd have to use the portal stones to funnel the Keppe to Oliter, and us to New Spero.

The Supreme also sent a recording with a ship to Haven. Terrance would ensure Mary got the message. It wouldn't get there much faster than I would, but even a couple of days meant a lot when you were at home waiting for your husband to come home to you and your daughter.

I was alone on the floating island now, and as soon as the Relocator showed ten fully-charged bars, I set the location to return us here instead of below ground in a dingy bar full of unscrupulous characters. I didn't think they'd appreciate a full force of Keppe warriors arriving unannounced.

"Here goes nothing." I took a deep breath and tapped the icon.

A millisecond later, I was back inside the hangar beside our Kraski ship. Slate was spread out on a cot, snoring; Suma and Rulo were playing a game at a table, and the huge Keppe warrior almost knocked the table over when she saw me. She rushed over, picking me up and squeezing my ribs.

"Let me down!" I gasped between laughs.

Slate came to and was up in a blink, breaking into a smile. "Never doubted it for a moment."

"Where's Magnus?" I asked.

"Right here." He stepped off the Kraski ship and crossed his arms. "I can't believe you did it."

"You didn't think I'd pull it off, did you? I told you I owed you one rescue. Now we're even," I said with a laugh.

"What happened?" Suma asked. She was gripping my

arm tightly, as if she wasn't able to let me go.

I told them about arriving at Volim and the deal with the Supreme.

"We have a fleet to bring us home?" Magnus asked.

"We do. Once this charges, we can start transferring the crew. And us," I told them.

Everyone in the room cheered, pumping fists in the air and hugging each other. It felt great.

"Dean," Rulo said, breaking the excitement, "I'm not coming with you."

I was taken aback. "What? Why?"

She shrugged. "Kaspin asked if I'd like to stay with him, and I would. I've had enough of wars and adventure. My body's tired, Dean. I could use a place like this world to live out my days, and a man like Kaspin to spoil me."

"I can't make you come with, but it's your choice," I replied, and Slate pushed me out of the way, giving her a punch on one armored arm.

"We're going to miss you, Rulo. You're one of a kind," he told her, and I saw tears forming in her snake eyes. She wiped them away and cleared her throat.

"Okay, we have a lot to do to prepare. Are we sure we don't want to extend the offer to anyone else?" Magnus asked.

I thought about what Braylam had said in the hotel room, about the pandemonium it would cause. Still, leaving them all here with no choice was going to be a tough decision.

"It's not my choice to make. I can't do it, Magnus," I admitted.

"I know, Dean. I know."

TWENTY-SIX

It was only a week to travel by hyperdrive from Volim to Haven, and I'd completed the trek before, but it was going excruciatingly slowly. By the time I allowed myself to leave the Padlog world, over half of the Keppe ship *Fortune*'s population was on Volim, occupying the borrowed insectoid vessels.

Magnus assured me he was right behind, and I left Volim, ready to be back at Haven, and from there to New Spero. I had the device that J-NAK had made us to apply to the portal stones, and told Magnus and the others not to attempt using them without it.

We'd managed to use the Relocator to move ten people at a time to Volim, from the other dimension to which the Cloud had sent us. The only issue was the six or so hours it took to charge fully between jumps.

All in all, I was overcome with happiness at being on the final leg of the trip home.

The Volim ship was larger than the Kraski ship we'd had to leave behind, and we had twenty-five Keppe on board with us. Karo and Ableen were with Slate, Suma, and me in the dining room off the galley, and we were drinking the last of the coffee we'd brought with us.

"Quite the ride, boss," Slate said. He scratched at his thick blond beard. "Can you do me a favor?"

"Sure, what's that?" I asked.

"Stay home for a while. The last few years have been hectic with everything going on. The return to Earth, starting our colonies and cities there from scratch. The Alliance of Worlds, the Gatekeepers' Academy, and Haven's insane expansion. But at least that stuff lets us go home at the end of the night and rest our heads on our own pillows." Slate drained his cup.

"Deal. I think Mary would appreciate that too. We do have a serious problem to deal with," I said.

"What's that?" Suma asked.

"The portals. The Gatekeepers need to figure out what's happening to them. If the Theos" – I glanced at Ableen, who wouldn't understand me – "are disappearing from inside them, we're going to have a lot of missing Keepers out there. We're going to have to do a full count and find a way to bring them all home." I leaned back, wishing that was a problem for someone else.

"I'm sure my father is working on it," Suma assured me.

"But he won't have a way to traverse the portals safely. We left a message with him to spread the word, but what about those already on the other sides? They're going to be stuck." I swirled the dark coffee in my cup and finished off the bitter brew.

"There are a lot of Gatekeepers, and many of them have a lot more experience than we do," Slate said. "Maybe it's time to hang up the helmet, Dean."

He wasn't wrong. I could hand off the Modifier device from J-NAK and settle in on New Spero, or even my parents' old farmhouse in middle America. Thinking about the beautiful piece of land reminded me of the storm cellar beneath the home, the one only I could access, that led to the ship where I was storing the mini *Kalentrek* and time-travel tool I'd used to dispose of Lom of Pleva. When I got the Relocator back, I decided to hide it there too.

I changed the subject, unsure what I was going to do when I arrived. I'd have to speak with Mary first, then with Sarlun, to see how grim the situation with the stones was. "Karo, what about you two? What are your plans with Ableen?"

She'd stuck to him like glue since we'd found her, but she was coming out of her scared shell with each passing day. Under the right circumstances, I knew she would once again become that dynamic woman she used to be.

I couldn't imagine the rollercoaster of emotions she'd been going through, language barriers aside. We didn't have Theos in our databanks, so there was no translating it. Karo had always used English with us. She sat straighter than before now, her hands less fidgety, her eyes making contact with others. It was all quite positive so far.

Karo took a second to answer. "We're not sure. I want her to see what we have to offer for her, and she can choose."

"You're going to be by her side, though, right?" Suma asked.

"Only if that's what Ableen wants. She isn't my property, and just because she's a woman and I'm a man, that doesn't mean I'm going to assume anything further than what we have so far. I'm thrilled to have found another Theos. It's amazing," he said, smiling at Ableen. He translated to her, and she looked happier than I'd ever seen her. She said something, and he relayed it. "She's looking forward to seeing Haven. A world with dozens of races living in harmony, kind of like the planet we recently visited, she said."

We stayed there, chatting among ourselves for a few hours. The whole time, I was pressing away the desire to head home to my family faster.

Our arrival at Haven was expected. The messenger the Supreme had sent a few days prior to our departure was present, and I knew Terrance and Leslie would be at the landing pad outside the capital city, awaiting us.

W lowered us to the ground and landed with a soft touch while Slate opened the bottom of the WASP, letting warm air blow up and into the cargo hold. I ran, greeting my hybrid friends.

"Have you heard from Mary? Is everyone okay?" I asked.

"Yes, they're fine, Dean. Worried about you, but fine. We haven't been able to use the portals, but you knew that already. Where's Magnus? Did you really travel to another dimension and return?" Terrance's questions came out in a flurry.

"Magnus, Nat, and the kids are coming when the rest of the crew is safely on their way. Mag feels partially responsible for their predicament, and as their captain, there was no way he'd leave before making sure everyone got out," I told them. "And yes, we did end up being sucked through a dimensional rift, but we made it back."

Slate puffed out his chest a little. "Was there ever a doubt?" he asked with false bravado. The truth was, there was a time period that we didn't expect to ever leave. It had been like living a nightmare.

"As much as I want to fill you guys in, I have to make it home. Since I have the portal modifier from J-NAK, I'll bring you home first, Suma. Can you give us a ride to the portal?" I looked for a nearby lander.

"Dean, if you don't mind, I'll stay here until you return. I know my father, and he's going to want a meeting, and soon. I'll go home then," Suma said.

"Sure." I put an arm around her shoulders, pulling her in. "Thanks for being you, Suma. Once again, we couldn't have done it without you."

"I'm happy to help. Thanks for helping us home," she said.

"Slate? Keep an eye on her, if you don't mind staying." I turned and had nearly forgotten that Karo and Ableen were with us. I introduced her to Leslie and Terrance, and they promised to get the Theos woman settled into her own place for the night. Ableen agreed, as long as Karo was staying put. With everything settled, I hopped into the lander with Terrance, and we headed toward Haven's portal room.

"Terrance, I know I ask a lot of you guys, and you can always say no to anything, but is there any way you can make sure Suma, Slate, and Karo are ready to meet Mary and me here in twelve…make it twenty-four hours? We'll make the trip to Shimmal then."

Terrance didn't hesitate. "You never ask more than you need to. It'll be done. Also, what are we doing with Sergo? The messenger asked us to send him to Volim with them, under their control. I guess the Supreme isn't very happy with him."

I thought about this, wondering if I should cut the Padlog some slack. The Relocator did save our lives and take us home, but if he hadn't demanded it in the first place, it never would have been his for me to barter back.

"Send him to Volim. He was stealing from the Inlor, and they think he's dead. It wouldn't be good for our Alliance if they found out we were harboring a fugitive of theirs," I said.

Terrance nodded, and soon we were lowering to the grounds outside the portal.

"I'll see you in a day," Terrance said, smiling at me. "I'm glad to see you. Go visit your family, you deserve it."

"I will. Talk soon." I hopped out with nothing but my white jumpsuit on and my pack slung over my shoulder. The lander lifted away, leaving me alone on the arrival pad in the hot summer-like air.

At this point, I wasn't even sure how long I'd been gone from home. A couple of months at least, maybe three or four. The days were a blur as I thought of them, but I felt every second of the trip as I trod into the portal corridors, heading for the room.

I pulled out the device from the robot J-NAK as I entered the portal, the lights on the walls glowing brightly, and the stone activating as I approached. The table lit up, and I placed the tablet-sized unit on top of the symbols, turning it on. If I chose the icon for New Spero and didn't use the device, I might end up at any random portal stone in the universe.

I connected them and chose the icons on both the tablet and the table before pressing the symbol with a shaky hand.

The portal stone blinked before it shone white, and I'd never seen it do anything quite like that. I looked around, worried I'd been sent either nowhere or somewhere wrong, but found myself in the familiar portal room outside Terran Five on New Spero. Relief flooded me, and I couldn't stop my legs from running now.

Mary wouldn't know when I was coming, but I wasn't surprised to find a lander outside the mountain corridors, waiting for me. Two New Spero guards were stationed inside it, each of them surprised to find me in front of them.

"Mr. Parker. Welcome home!" a young dark-haired man with a wispy moustache said.

"We're honored to take you wherever you need to go," the woman said, her uniform crisp and so clean it appeared like she'd changed into it a minute ago.

"Home. Take me home."

The sun was setting as the lander lifted from my acreage. I heard Jules before I saw her or Mary's shadowy forms walking toward me from the porch. "Papa! Papa!" Jules was yelling, and I ran for them, arms outstretched.

I picked up my daughter, and my heart was pounding in my chest as I held her close, her small cheek pressed to my newly grown-in beard. "Jules, my angel. I'm home."

Mary's arm pulled me close, our daughter squished between us. "I knew you'd make it." She kissed me firmly, using her hand at my neck to make sure I couldn't break free.

"Papa, what bring me?" Jules asked, and I lifted her above my head and laughed.

"I brought you… me," I told her.

"Papa's silly," Jules said with confidence.

"I won't deny that." I turned my attention to Mary, who'd been watching Jules' and my interaction with interest. "Are you ever a sight for sore eyes."

"You've seen better days." Her eyes twinkled in the red dusk. "Come on in. I forgot to tell Maggie you were here."

The cocker spaniel was inside the front door, barking like she was about to explode. Mary opened the door and the cocker catapulted, jumping all over me, licking my face as I bent over to pet the girl.

"What happened out there?" Mary asked.

I thought about the crazy series of events and dropped my pack on the porch. "Let's go inside. You're going to want a glass of wine with this story." I scooped Jules up, and the whole family went into the house together. I glanced out at the front yard and smiled as I shut the door, sealing us in for the night.

THE END

ABOUT THE AUTHOR

Nathan Hystad is an author from Sherwood Park, Alberta, Canada. When he isn't writing novels, he's running a small publishing company, Woodbridge Press.

Keep up to date with his new releases by signing up for his newsletter at www.nathanhystad.com

CPSIA information can be obtained
at www.ICGtesting.com
Printed in the USA
BVHW032256010420
576655BV00001B/26